The Edinburgh Cuckoos

Wentworth M. Johnson

The startling adventures of William Reyner

Bill Reyner, the would-be detective, has one leading asset… a nose for gold. Stumbling through five dangerous adventures, William improves his gold to bullet hole ratio.

Fiend's Gold
William's first adventure. From university-dropout to millionaire.

Mania
An evil empire operated in the name of religion. William shakes the trees and bodies begin falling.

Edinburgh Cuckoos
Lookout rich people of the world the cuckoos may already be in your nest. William's nose for gold leads him into Scotland and lots of trouble.

Damp Graves
What price second hand bodies and parts thereof? Maintaining his Midas touch William remains one step behind the mastermind, but Newf is one step ahead.

Lions and Christians
A hunting lodge by a northern Canadian lake, but what do they hunt? William finds it easy to get in, but not so easy to get out.

Other books written by Wentworth M. Johnson available at www.e-booksonline.net

Bloodisland House
A madman with a time machine tries to defy the laws of God and nature.

The Dragon of Hope Island
An alien device left on earth and one child finds the secret of how to use it.

Matthew 5
The alluring and powerful story of ancient murders and unearthed skeletons.

EDINBURGH CUCKOOS

The butler's fired and a merry chase for evidence begins. In an attempt to discover if there really are dead bodies stored in the basement, William slips deeper and deeper into an unholy conspiracy of murder and misappropriation.

Published by e-booksonline (uk) ltd
Printed and bound by Antony Rowe Ltd, Eastbourne
If you have enjoyed this book, why not call again. This and other books can be found on www.e-booksonline.net where you are also able to browse through the millions of titles offered by AMAZON.co.uk by clicking on their logo at the bottom of our home page.

Born in March, Cambridgeshire, UK in 1939, **Wentworth M. Johnson** is a naturalized Canadian. He served for twelve years in the Royal Air Force - mostly on top secret sites - and was the last airman in Queen's Command (Maintenance) and also the last RAF man at RAF Kahawa in Kenya when he handed the station over to the Kenyan Air Force. He subsequently worked as a TV studio technician, and now works as a technical buyer for a local TV station, where he has now been for twenty-eight years. He has a passion for English history, from Julius Caesar to modern times, and writing has been a life-long hobby.

This book is dedicated to
Lynn Holly Johnson

1

Tales of the Occult

"I reckon she were witched, there ain't no other explanation, I tell yah. One minute we's all lovey-dovey, then she ups and fires me. Don't make no sense, not no how. All started when she come back from that holiday she took."

Gran put the tea tray on the table then addressed both men. "Would you like anything to eat?"

The grumbling man shook his head. "Nah!" Then he continued relaying his story to his companion. "I tell yah, it was this close." Describes distance with finger and thumb. "I felt like doing her in, for ten cents I would o'. All that pretence then the boot."

"Bloody cows, just typical of broads," smirked the second man.

Now there's at least two things that Gran doesn't like. One is people who cry in their beer, so-to-speak, and the other is descriptive terminology relating women with the oxen genus. She placed her hands on her hips, ready for verbal combat and glared at the offending individual.

"Sir, this is a respectable establishment. The management requires customers to adhere to the general rules of common decency. Poor language though widespread is not welcome here."

"You nuts, lady?" The offending gentleman looked around as though searching for something on the walls. "Where's the bloody sign, lady?"

Grumbler leaned over and placed his hand on his friend's shoulder. "Ease up, George. We don't wanna get chucked out o' here too. Sorry Missus, I guess it's all my fault. I complain a lot."

Gran smiled. "You look a nice gentleman. I'm most sorry you have been fired from your position, but please don't frighten my customers away with unacceptable language."

He smiled. "Certainly Missus. You don't need any help around here do you?"

"What do you do?"

"I'm a, well I was a butler come housekeeper at Donjon Towers. I can cook, serve, wash dishes, even sweep."

Gran softened. "Well, what sort of salary would you be looking at?"

Grumbly shrugged his shoulders. "Don't know. I was only fired today. I needs somewhere to stay. I was maybe gonna stay at George's place, till I gets sorted out."

"Well Mr. er-?"

"Beamish. Dagwood Beamish."

Gran grinned all over her face. I think she took a fancy to him. "As a matter of fact I do need help here. When could you start?"

"Anytime, Missus."

She slipped onto the chair at the side of the table. "Why were you fired?"

He coloured and fidgeted with his fingers. "We was getting married, but then she ups and fires me."

'Why?'

He shrugged. "D'know. She goes on holiday, comes back, all sick-like and fires me. No reason, no excuse. Tosses me out on the Street."

Gran eyed him up and down. He was a lot younger than her, around forty. Solid dark hair, more than I've got. A wise all knowing face, sort of reminded me of an undertaker. "And no papers, no reference given?"

"No. I was tellin' George. I reckon she were witched."

Gran smiled sweetly. "Was," she corrected. "Very well. Let's say start tomorrow, anytime in the morning. We can have a nice little talk and discuss your recompense."

Gran's a funny old girl; she started this sort of plush tearoom with Mr. Spadafora. Was all her money. See last year our house was burned to the ground, a really nice present for the new millennium. We made a profit on it though. There was almost a million in reward money for the killers of those girls, that's still in the hands of our lawyer.

North, Gran, and I live in the new house, same place as the old one. Mr. Spadafora's moving down permanent this summer. I guess he's got a lot of stuff to settle-up in Parry Sound. No more detective work for us. The last case was real dangerous. As usual I got shot, Newf, that's North, he almost died. No way, detective work is permanently off my list of things to do. This summer we're going to spend a leisurely time just fun-lovin' soaking up rays.

In case you didn't know, Gran's a wonderful cook. That's why she opened the tearoom. Doesn't need the money, just a hobby, something to keep her mind active. It was all Spadafora's idea. Anyhow I just got in with a vanload of supplies and was unloading them when this guy turns up.

"Excuse me son," he said. "I'm looking for the lady proprietor."

"Who, Gran?"

He shrugged. "The lady who runs this place."

"Just take a seat she's in the back putting supplies away." I walked round the back and told her this chap had arrived.

"Oh good, he can help you with the delivery, William. Then we'll all have a nice talk."

It was always a slack time in the mornings, evening time was when things hotted up. After we put away all the stuff, the three of us sat at one of the tables for a biscuit and a cup of tea.

"This is Dagwood Beamish, William. He's our new handyman."

"Hi," I said uninterestedly.

"Now, Mr. Beamish before I hand you this job and arrange your salary, I would like to know why you were fired from your last position. Then William can investigate it for us."

He sipped his tea and stared into the cup. "Well," he began slowly. "Cloey Macalister's her name. She inherited Donjon Towers from her dad. An only child, you see. I started work there five years ago, sort of general handyman and butler. There ain't no other servants. She was easy to care for, didn't ask much." He stopped and stared around the room, his eyes looking for inspiration. "Well, yah see. I got to know her quite well. She said it were unfair that I looks after her, and livin' in her house an' all. So we sets the date to get married. Even had the vicar to supper, an' everything."

"But, you quarrelled," hinted Gran.

9

"Nah! 'Twern't nothing like that. See she gets this letter in the mail. Sort of an advert for this place in Scotland. Some kind of holiday resort or something."

"And did you both go?" Gran asked.

"Nah! She decided it would be a good idea if I looked after the Towers for her and she would take a short vacation in this Scotch place. So I stays at the Towers and she goes off on this last jaunt afore we marries, see." He stopped; I think I could see a tear in his eye.

"Then what?" I encouraged.

He pouted his lips then chewed the bottom one. After a moment he began again. "Well she comes home, wearing a veil, all like a widow and everything. Ignores me as if I ain't there. Goes to her room and stays there. Gets written orders, 'couse she says she lost her voice, a cold up in the highlands. She smelled different too. Then she gives me written notice, see." He pulled out a fancy piece of letterhead paper and hands it to Gran.

She took out her glasses and balanced them on her nose. I could tell by the expression on her face something was amiss. She folded it gently and handed it back. "I am rather shocked," she said softly. "Is there any truth to the allegation?"

Dagwood shook his head. "I'm forty seven, Mrs. Hubert. I don't have any aspirations in that direction."

"I believe you, Mr. Beamish. Do you intend to prosecute the woman?"

"No. It's a closed book. I would rather not have anything to do with her. I thought I should show you the letter, so's we're fully open and honest."

Gran nodded her approval. "No more shall be mentioned. It is history. Welcome to your new position. My partner, Mr. Spadafora will be returning in a few days. You will be my right-hand man."

"I thought I was Gran?"

"William, you never work in the tea garden."

She was right; I'd given up detective work too. Dishes and guns just go against the grain. As soon as school ends I intend to go to England and find Priscilla. Since I got out of hospital I've bought me a new car, well one for the business.

10

She said a gentleman drives a sedate vehicle not a racing car. "A man's personality shows in his choice of women, horses and motor vehicles," she said, so good-by Jaguar and hello SUV. Besides making deliveries in a sports job just wasn't kosher.

Gran's a wonderful cook, I guess that's why she opened the tea garden on the old 99 highway a couple of kilometres out of Dundas, and it gives the old girl a chance to meet new people. My calendar was kinda full, school ends Friday so in order I have to teach Newf how to drive, clean up my room and visit England. Newf doesn't finish school for another week. Gran's having him educated, doesn't like the way he speaks.

It was Friday night supper, when Gran threw a screw into the works. We were all seated for the meal at the new house in Dundas. In her usual way she looked at me and smiled. "William, I have a little job for you."

I sighed to show my contempt for what I thought was coming. "Yes Gran."

"That new man, Dagwood Beamish." She poured the tea. "Did you hear his peculiar story?"

I shook my head and rolled my eyes at Newf.

"Well, he claims his employer, who was in a mood to marry him, took a holiday in Scotland."

"I know that, Gran."

"Did you hear the bit how she changed?"

"Sure."

"What do you think then, William?"

"I don't like him or trust him. I figure the tale was for your benefit. He probably had aspirations beyond his station and she fired the twit."

"Well!" she gasped. "I'm shocked at your attitude, young man."

"Sorry Gran. I'm only thinking of you. When does Mr. Spadafora get back?"

"Next week."

"Good. Until then I'll stay close, just to make sure you are safe."

She smiled sweetly. "Anyhow, to cut to the chase. I would like you to investigate Mrs. Macalister."

"That's a Scottish name isn't it, Gran?"

"Quite possibly so. I would like you to meet the lady."

"And what exactly should I ask her?"

"We could freten 'er," Newf added gleefully.

"I don't think that would serve any purpose," Gran growled. "And I thought you were learning English. That's threaten, with a TH not 'F'."

"Yes Missus H."

"Then will you do as I ask, William?"

"Sure, Gran. I'll do it when Mr. Spadafora gets back and North has finished school for the summer. I would like to know exactly what I'm looking for. I've quit on the detective stuff. I don't want any more dangerous cases. I don't want any cases."

"I completely agree, William. This is just a simple little inquiry. No guns, no one dies, not even any fighting."

"Is that a promise?"

"Certainly. I think all I really want to know is why she fired Dagwood. You could pretend to be a prospective employer and ask her for references. That should be simple enough."

The following day Newf went to school and I took a trip out to the tearoom. I wanted to interview this Mr. Dagwood Beamish myself, and preferably without Gran's interference. It wasn't difficult. I think Gran knew what I was doing. He was cleaning in the kitchen; she left to tidy up in the seating area.

"Mr. Beamish," I said authoritatively. "I would like to ask you a few questions."

"Of course," he said softly. "Anything you like."

"Okay. Stop with the cleaning and tell me why you were fired from your last job."

He smiled. "You don't believe my story."

I nodded.

"Well, Mr. Reyner, I'm not in the habit of lying. I started work for Cloey Macalister almost ten years ago. You see I answered and advertisement in the local newspaper. Miss Cloey was a young and energetic woman at that time. She has a tendency to... to be very private and so had only one servant, namely myself."

"So who did the laundry?"

"Farmed out to a professional company. They called twice weekly. Groceries, bread, and milk too were delivered. Mr. Edwards the grocer would spend time with Cloey and arrange to deliver the week's supplies."

"So what did you do?"

"I, sir, made Miss Cloey comfortable, anything she required. It was because of this she suggested we marry. I think her reasoning was that she could gain tax deductions for a dependent."

"So there was no sex or anything?"

"Good heavens, sir. No, absolutely not, madam is not that kind of person."

"Alright, I'll buy all this; how come you got fired then?"

His expression changed, you could see the distance in his eyes. "One day she read this advertisement in a magazine or something. She told me the idea had come to her, to take a vacation. I was not invited." A tear trickled down his face as he recalled the incident. "I was against it right from the start, but, well, what could I do. My post was to care for the house while Miss Cloey visited the old country. "I rue the day. I knew something was terribly wrong when I met her on the homecoming. Faithfully I awaited Cloey in the airport, she wore black."

"That's significant?"

"Madam never wore black. Black is the colour of death. Miss Cloey always wore sombre colours, never black. Besides she wore a veil; madam never wore any form of head covering. When I spoke to her she did not react as though she knew me, and replied only in writing."

"Writing?"

"Yes, she used a notepad, explaining that due to a severe cold she had lost her voice."

"If what you say is true, it sounds obvious that the lady who came back to Canada is an impostor. Someone impersonating Cloey Macalister."

"I had considered that possibility."

"And?"

"I think not."

"Why?"

"Madam had knowledge that only madam would know."

I sighed. "Like what?"

"She knew her social insurance number, she knew the correct number to open the safe combination. In fact there was nothing she did not know. It was when I complained about the lack of ability to speak, she fired me. I am certain witchcraft comes into it. Somehow they have stolen her soul."

I shrugged and walked away, poor guy was a simpleton. I told Gran I thought Dagwood to stupid to be harmful. At that moment a crowd of old ladies came in for their morning tea I had to let Gran and company do their thing. Convinced that Dagwood was harmless I drove back to the house in Dundas. I had a couple of important things to do. Somehow I missed Newf's company, since Gran sent him to school we just didn't seem to have any time together.

The house was also a disappointment. Loving craftsmen had built Gran's old house, which stood on this same spot, the new one had been thrown together. Lath-and-plaster walls replaced with wallboard, two-inch thick solid wood floors replaced with plywood. The new windows are okay, but it's a definite step down. Lying on my bed staring at the ceiling just wasn't the same.

I picked Newf up from Mohawk College at noon on Friday; end of term. Why I like that goof I can't really think. Watching him approach the car made thoughts scuttle through my head. A tall, skinny, silly looking bean post with bright ginger hair. Poor Newf was a couple inches taller than me and about half the weight.

"Hi! Bill. Fanks for picking me up."

"Get in."

"I bin lookin' forward to this summer, Bill. Do you fink I should get a job?"

"No. We're going to England. I'm going to find Priscilla."

"Coor, neat!"

I drove downtown, parked the car in the parkade then we walked. There was a couple of toys I thought we may need. First we went to the Bell Centre I bought both of us a new cell phone. The girl promised me they were the most worldwide. She said they'd work all over Britain, US, and Canada. Next we went to a chandlers, I figured they'd have what I wanted. I bought a hand held GPS.

The weekend passed lazily and slowly. I may add the last worry free weekend for a while. Gran said I had to teach Newf how to drive before I left for England. She wanted him independent for the next school term. As I had nothing better to do I figured we could put six or seven hours a day into it. Monday we began the hair-raising experience of teaching an idiot to drive in Gran's car.

McMaster University has a giant parking lot in the backwoods of Westdale. There being no school I figured this would be a place where Newf was least likely to run over anybody, or thing. I put him in the control seat and explained the workings of a car. With eyes wild and excited he put the thing into gear and shot off like a rocket.

"Stop," I yelled.

Jesus. He slammed on the brakes and almost sent me through the windshield. "'Ow's 'at, Bill?"

"Yeah, great. Now can we try it very slowly, and don't forget to turn left before we reach the end. Okay?"

"Sure."

The second experience was little better than the first. After half an hour, my nerves were shot. I could see this was leading to a nervous breakdown, mine. Even if the car could take the punishment, I couldn't. Facing Fiend's ghost or even the mass murderers at the TOD were a mere breeze compared to teaching Newf to drive. It had to stop before I became incapacitated. I sure as hell hope he never wants to learn to fly an airplane.

A brilliant idea flashed through my mind, rather like the proverbial straw passing a drowning man. With an ironic smile I told Newf to stop and turn the engine off. Poor kid the sweat was pouring off his face in little rivers. "'Ow'm I doin' Bill?"

"Not to worry, Newf. Here let me drive, we'll have a little fun."

We swapped positions. I figured manual gearshift was just too much for him; he needed something easier to drive.

As I drove off I explained how I did it and why you change gear at certain times.

"Where' we goin', Bill?"

"You need something easier to drive, I've got the very thing." In a few minutes we were downtown. I drove down Barton Street, easterly, then crossed to Cannon Street and headed back toward town centre. After a few seconds I found what I had been looking for. Pulling into the British Car Importers, I parked in the front lot.

"Come on, Newf. Let's go get a car you can drive."

His eyes lit up like a navigation beacon. "Get a car? You gonna buy a car?"

"Sure. We need something new around the house."

I walked boldly into the posh showroom and stood staring around. I figured it wouldn't take too long before someone either threw us out or tried to sell us a car.

"Can I help sir?" Said this overweight pompous git in a light blue suit.

"Sure, I'm looking for a car."

He eyed me up a down with suspicion. "Where did sir leave it?"

"Very funny. How about that one over there?"

The tub-o'-lard coughed as though something stuck in his throat. "That, sir is a Rolls Royce."

"Well, if you've nothing better, I'll take a look at it."

"I'm sorry, sir, I think you'll find something more to your standing at Rent-a-wreck, across town."

I pulled out my wallet. "Looks like a well used demo. What yah want for it?"

He raised one hand above his head and snapped his fingers. One of his minions came running over. "I think this gentleman and is companion are leaving, Mr. Osgood. Would you kindly show them where the exit is?"

"If you throw me out, I'll buy this place and fire you. Now show me that car."

He turned a neat shade of scarlet. I thought something was about to explode. I tore off a check and walked over to his desk on the sales floor. Both Tub-o'-lard and Osgood followed me. "If you do not leave peaceable, sir I shall have to call the police and have you removed."

"I made the check out for $250,000, and signed it, then handed it to Tub-o'-lard. He stopped quacking and read it. Before he could say anything I snatched it back and wrote VOID across it, then I handed it to him again. "The name of my bank is on the check. I think it would be in your interest to give them a call."

Indignantly he snatched the check and walked to his office. Osgood stood and glared at me. "Please don't start any trouble," he said softly. "I'm in bad books with the boss as it is."

"Don't worry, Mr. Osgood, you're in good hands. Come on, Newf let's take a look at our new car."

After a while, Tub-o'-lard came waddling back. With his size and speed, he reminded me of Stephenson's Puffing-Billy. Talk about grovel, it's enough to make a skunk sick. He fair bubbled over with obsequiousness. "I do apologize for our earlier misunderstanding Mr. Reyner," he said bowing and scrapping. "Which car would sir like to see?"

"The blue one." I'd taken a fancy to the steel blue Rolls. It spoke to me, and just looked like it needed a new owner.

Tub-o'-lard hovered around and bubbled on about the merits of a real car. I sat there in the height of luxury; this car had more widgets than a tinker's bench. Suddenly some real pointed words drifted into my ear-hole. "Would sir like to have a nice little test drive?"

"Yes."

"Excellent. Mr. Osgood will give you all the help you need."

Moments later we purred into the courtyard, Osgood stepped out leaving the engine running. "It's all yours, sir."

Eagerly I eased into the captain's seat and slid everything into a comfortable position. Newf's eyes remained like saucers as he climbed in beside me. The only sound I could hear as I drove off was Newf's breathing and my heart beating.

"You just pinched the most expensive car in Canada," Newf hissed softly.

"Not quite. Just sit back and relax. When we get out into the country I'll let you drive. This one's easy, all you gotta do is steer it."

After Gran's old rattle trap, man! This one felt like a dream. I just had to show Gran, I knew she'd love it. She was busy with customers when we entered the tearoom. The very time I needed to show off, she was busy. Newf remained in the car admiring the luxury and smelling the upholstery. After a few minutes I saw my opportunity.

"Gran, Gran, come and see what I've got."

She glared at me. "William this is a place of business. You can show me your new car after hours."

"Gees, Gran. Come take a quick look at it."

"Where's my car?"

"It's safe. Come on Gran, humour me."

With a shrug she walked to the front door. "It's very pretty, how much?"

"Don't know, I just got it on a test drive. Come on, Gran, you'll love it. There's an automatic everything."

"I really would rather see it after work."

Talk about disappointing. I leaned against the mechanical marvel as she walked back to the tearoom. Suddenly she turned. "William, there is one thing you could do for me."

I could see the glint in her eyes. "What is it, Gran?"

"Why don't you let North drive our new vehicle and you can kill two birds with one stone."

"Like what?"

"A simple little bit of detective work."

"We agreed, Gran. I've given up PI'ing, it's too dangerous."

"This is not dangerous, or even difficult. Drive over to Donjon Towers and interview Miss Macalister."

2

The Towers

The Rolls quickly adapted to Newf's style of driving. They got on very well together. I recognized the characteristics, he drove just like Priscilla. Firstly we went downtown Dundas to the Army-Navy store where I bought Newf a captain's hat. "Okay, James, drive us to Donjon Towers."

"Which way, Bill?"

"Up the number eight, head for Cambridge." He was doing well, even with all that power, no squealing of tires and a nice smooth pull off. I figured he drove better if I kept my mouth shut, though I kept an eagle eye on things. The GPS kept me amused, albeit I hadn't fully figured it out yet. Gran's navigation left a little to be desired. Though she had given us the address, a rural route wasn't much to go on.

Pulling my new cell-phone out I dialled Gran's establishment. After a few seconds the very person I needed answered. "Hallow, Dundas Tea Gardens"

"Hi, Dagwood. This is William Reyner. What did you say the grocer's name was who serviced Mrs. McAllister."

"Edie's Corner Store. Mr. Edwards runs it. Is there a problem?"

"No, not at all. What street is it on?"

He thought for a moment. "Well, it's the other side of the river, north. I think it's called Doon Road."

"Great, thanks Daggy, see you later." I folded the phone and put it in the holster. "We'll have to go right downtown Galt. Okay?"

"Sure." Newf looked at ease, he was a real quick learner.

After getting lost once, well not lost, I had the GPS. We weren't sure where the rest of the town was, we knew where we were. We found the store. Not exactly what I had expected. I thought it would be a grocery store, or a supermarket. Instead it turned out to be a junk shop. "I think this is the wrong one, Newf. Still, stop over there and we'll have a look inside."

An old fashioned open bell on a spring announced us opening the front door. The place smelled musty, the floors were wood and uncovered. A tall dark brown counter lined one wall and on the other side, piles of boxes. A man in a dirty pinafore came running from a back curtained-off area.

"Yes, sirs. What can I do for you today." He was short and bald with a friendly smile and voice.

"Hi, I'm Bill Reyner. I wonder if you know Cloey Macalister?"

His eyes lit up. "Certainly. Does she need anything?"

"No. I'd just like to ask you a couple of questions."

He shrugged. "What's the problem?"

"No problem. I thought you ran a grocer's."

"Oh, no. I do general deliveries, anything, anywhere, anytime. If it's broke, I'll fix it, if it ain't fixable, I'll replace it."

"You sound like the man my Gran should meet. You knew Mr. Beamish then."

"Dagwood, sure! Though I haven't done any business lately. Since she's bin abroad she don't call me no more."

"So how does she get her food and stuff now?"

He shrugged. "D' know."

He gave me a quick description of how to get to the towers and we left. "What do you think, Newf?" I asked as we walked back to the car.

"I fink the Rolls is the best car in the world."

"Not that, you nit-wit. Miss Macalister?"

"D' know."

Before allowing Newf to drive us on the last leg of our journey I fiddled with the GPS. Eventually I figured it out and managed to mark our location, I called it EDS, short for Edwards. Next time the GPS will be able to tell me how to get here. "Okay, James drive."

"James?"

"You, Newf."

"I ain't James."

"Drive, for heaven's sake, drive."

While he concentrated on controlling the car, I pointed the way. Eventually we entered an area I sort of recognized, we were vicinity of Beverley Swamp. Narrow roads, wooded and wetlands. "Stop," I yelled as we sailed past a mailbox with the name Macalister painted on its side.

Newf backed slowly down the road until we could make a turn into the driveway. A tree lined one lane road curved round to the left. On the right was swamp with tree stumps poking through the green water. Just over the next rise the house came into view. I don't think I've ever seen such an ugly house. It had been constructed from red brick and where visible, the roof looked like blue slate.

The house sat on a grassy manmade rise, giving the appearance of a castle on an elephant's back. Three stories high with a square tower on every corner of the box-like design. In the centre of the roof stood this really ugly circular tower, taller than all the others. Whoever designed this place; if it was designed; must have had a thing about mosques. At a quick glance it looked like a really cheap imitation of a genuine Middle East religious structure.

There didn't seem to be anywhere to park. The driveway ran up along side the house with a small footpath to the front door. We stopped opposite the path and got out. The front door was huge, talk about Alice in Wonderland. The knocker reminded me of something used on a demolition site. After using it I expected some monster of seven foot, with a bolt through its neck to open the door.

After a very short interval the huge door rattled and creaked. A matronly middle-aged woman in a black dress sporting a long pointed nose growled; "What is it?"

"I'd like to see Miss Macalister, please."

"The mistress isn't receiving guests today. Good-by."

Easing my foot into the doorway I said: "I've come a long way to see her and I'm not leaving till I do."

"You can't park that car there. Put it in the compound round back. And servants cannot come in this way."

"I'm not a servant."

"That one is," she said pointing to Newf.

"Put the car in the compound," I said turning to my newly elected chauffeur.

"Me? All by myself?"

"Yes."

He smiled and ran back to the car. The lady hustled me in and pointing to a room and said: "Wait in there."

Nothing seemed to be as I had expected. The room had a plain wooden floor with one single carpet in the centre. Everything looked austere; the table that stood in the centre of the carpet had no paint or polish. The sideboard looked like an antique from Mennonite country. The chairs, all six were comb-back plain knotty pine. I sat and looked out the curtainless window. The view inspired me less than the room.

A short shrew-like woman in her early forties marched into the room. Her black hair though short and straight, shone like coal. "What?" She snapped.

"What!" I echoed and stood up. "I'm William Reyner, Miss Macalister."

"And what would you want here?" She said with a slight Scottish lilt.

Somehow she made me feel uncomfortable. Her gaze penetrated me like a pair of fifty-watt lasers. "Do you know Dagwood Beamish?"

She turned away from me and stood with her hands behind her back like a sergeant major inspecting troops. Concentrating on her imaginary soldiers in the field beside the house she said: "And what would Mr. Beamish want with me?"

"I... er... well, that is, he came to me for a job. He has no references."

She turned and smiled, her pointy little nose twitched like a cat smelling the mouse. "Are you a personage of substance?" Her eyes flashed as she anticipated the answer.

"Yes."

"Please come into the parlour, Mr. Reyner." She led the way back into the hall and then into a room across the way. Opening the door Miss Macalister smiled kindly. One cannot be too careful, a woman alone. Please take a seat, I'll call for tea, unless you would like a wee dram."

"Tea's great, thanks." The room was a completely different world. Very heavy velvet drapes, thick carpet, wall-to-wall. Weighty Victorian, French polished furniture. The

instant I walked into the room it reminded me of a
fortuneteller, you'd even expect to see a crystal ball on the
table. Lots of pictures on the walls, yet none of people.

"Please make yourself comfortable," she said
indicating a leather divan near the fireplace.

I sat. "Thanks."

After pulling a rope near the very tall mantelpiece, she
sat opposite me and pulled an ornate coffee table in front of
us. "What, is it that you wish to know?"

"Well. Did you actually employ Mr. Beamish?"

The doorwoman came into the room. "What?" She
growled.

"Tea, Gladys, tea for two."

Macalister coyly smiled at me again. "Yes, Mr.
Beamish worked for me. He's lazy and has desires above his
natural position. I sacked him for that reason. If you employ
him I would recommend you watch him, especially if there's
lose change about."

"Are you saying he's dishonest?"

She smiled and didn't answer. "I suppose you are here
for your parents?"

"No. I'm independent, except for Gran."

"Just the two of you in a wee little house?"

"No, just three of us. Gran, North, he's my driver, and
myself in a very big house."

"I suppose your wealth comes from your father?"

"No, my uncle. I'm the last of the Reyners."

"Very interesting." She walked over to the sideboard
and extracted a pamphlet. "I'm sure you'll find this very
interesting."

I took it and had a quick read. "A holiday lodge?"

"Yes. I went there. It made a new woman of me.
Magnificent scenery, I strongly recommend it."

"How did you hear of this place?"

She smiled. "I have a friend who recommended it.
Now are you here to interrogate me or learn about Mr.
Beamish?"

"Yeah. So you don't think I should employ Beamish?"

"No, He's a nasty little man."

"What about Edwards?"

"Edwards?"

"Yeah, the guy who used to deliver your groceries."

She scowled for a few moments, then brightened up. "Oh, you mean that fool with the van. I have a real grocer now."

Gladys burst into the room with a tray in her hands. Noisily she slammed it on the small table. "Yah, tea." She turned and marched out.

"It's very difficult to get good servants these days," Miss Macalister said and began preparing our drinks. "Milk or cream?"

"Yeah, I know what you mean."

"I think you and your Grandmother would really enjoy a nice holiday in Scotland. It's very peaceful and beautiful. Cromlet castle is amazing."

I nodded. There was nothing suspicious about this woman or her strange house. Dagwood Beamish was obviously the bad guy, a liar and possibly a cheat. I should get to Gran and get her to fire this guy before we regretted it. "Can I keep this pamphlet?"

"Oh, certainly. You should seriously consider going. Think of the adventure, the excitement, the lovely lassies."

"I'm going to England this summer."

"Then you should make it a special point to go up into the highlands and see Cromlet. I could give you a letter of introduction, if you like."

"Nah, that's okay. I really think I should be going now." I downed the lukewarm tea.

"Very well. We'll leave via the compound. Your servant's in the scullery." She led the way back into the hall then toward the back of the house, and into a drab room with plain wood furniture. Newf was sitting at the table looking bored, Gladys was bending his ear. They both jumped to their feet as we walked in.

"We're going now, North," I said authoritatively.

The car had been parked in a walled off compound, sort of a back yard with a three meter brick wall on two sides. The house on one side and a slew of sheds or garages at the back. Newf had difficulty turning the car round. It was the first time he had to do close manoeuvring. Eventually we made it and headed back to Dundas.

"So what do you think of the Macalister's, Newf?"

With his eyes glued to the road ahead he said: "She's an impostor. The real Mrs. Macalister's dead and gone."

I laughed. "Where'd you get a notion like that?"

"'Cause, Gladys said so. She said Beamish is all part of the plan. There's a room in the basement filled with dead people."

How he could drive and spout such amusing stuff mystified me. "You daft, sod," I said. "If there was a room full of dead folk, who killed them, why, and how? And if Cloey Macalister's an impostor, what would be the reason? You just don't use your brain, Newf. It'll give Gran a good laugh."

"You fink so. Well I don't. Mrs. Macalister fools rich people into finking she's their friend then she bumps them off and takes their money. That's why the basement's full of corpses."

"Alright, how's Beamish involved?"

"Gees, Bill, sometimes you're real fick. Beamish is already wheedling 'is way into your Gran's life. At the right moment, 'e bumps 'er off and takes 'er money."

I shook my head in disgust. Poor Newf just didn't have the brainpower to see how stupid the whole idea was. I pulled the pamphlet of Cromlet Castle out and gave it a good read. It sounded good; a beautiful sixteenth century feudal castle nestled in the hills by a small loch. The picture was great too. The place offered challenging experience and excitement, something new, adventure. "What about her visit to Scotland then?"

Newf snickered. "All fake, she ain't never bin nowhere. Beamish is the one we gotta wheedle out. 'E is the one. 'E is going to knock off your Gran."

"Doesn't make sense, Newf. I'm there. If anything happens to Gran, I inherit."

"'Ave you seen 'er will?"

"No."

"Then 'ow do you know. I bet she'll leave it all to Beamish. That's 'ow they gets all their money."

"Well this time they've bit off more than they can chew. Gran would never fall for that kind o' crap. She's smart."

"She's old, and gullible. Beamish is a sweet talker."

"I can't swallow that crap, Newf, but I'll see to it that Mr. Beamish finds himself other employment. What did you think of the house, Donjon Towers?"

"It's a ugly pile of rocks. I fink it needs a bulldozer froo it."

"Pull over, Newf. Let me drive. I'll have to take this car back. What d' yah think of it?"

Carefully he brought the car to a halt at the roadside. He certainly learned fast, and felt comfortable in a Rolls. "You want the 'at?"

"No, you can keep the hat." We swapped sides. I pressed the comfort set button. The seat, steering-wheel, and peddles all aligned themselves to my position. "You want me to buy it?"

"Coor! Yeah, sure. I 'd love it. I'll do all the drivin' if you like."

"When's your driving test?"

"I ain't applied for it yet."

"Let's get back to the dealers, and then we'll think about it."

I drove the Rolls back and parked it beside Gran's old wreck. Tub-o'-Lard came running with a sickly grin on his puss.

"Ah! Mr. Reyner, sir. How was your drive?"

"Okay." I didn't want to sound too enthusiastic. "What extras are there?"

"Extras?" He looked puzzled.

"You know, fancy shit to bump up the price."

"Oh! Sir. There are no extras on Rolls Royce."

"You telling me it's got everything?"

"Every car is custom built for its owner, there are no extras, unless you count fuel."

"Mercedes have a duel braking system," I said as if complaining.

"For what purpose, sir?"

"Well, if the main system fails you still got brakes."

"There, sir. You said it yourself. The word fail does not enter into it. A Rolls Royce needs no backup system." He coughed surreptitiously into his hand. "One has heard the term, 'Jerry-built,' sir?"

"Alright, when can I take it?"

"Take it, sir?"

"The car. When can I have it?"

"As soon as it's built, sir."

"Built? Don't you have any in stock?"

His eyes opened like two Adis lamps. "Stock, sir. A Rolls is not a stock car sir."

"Well I want one now."

"Oh, of course, sir. We can't let you ride away from here in, that," he said pointing to Gran's heap. "It would not be fitting. If sir would go with Mr. Osgood and sign the contract we will assure your complete satisfaction."

"Contract. I don't want any contract, I'll pay cash."

"We prefer to call it a contract, sir. The term sale is rather demeaning."

"Oh!"

A bunch of gutless turds, I always believe in calling a spade a spade. Osgood asked me a thousand questions and made careful note of the answers. No one ever mentioned money. When at last it was all over, Mr. Osgood was pleased and said I could take the vehicle we'd been using all day. They would bring our new car to the house as soon as it arrived, about six weeks.

"What about the price?" I asked.

"Oh, It's generally impolite to mention earthly things like that. Mr. Evandale will send you the bill and you can make arrangements with your bank to settle it at you leisure, sir."

I figured, Evendale must be Tub-o'-Lard. "What about insurance and vehicle license?"

"We'll take care of everything, sir. Even the number. You said you would prefer PI-1 if available."

"Sure." It felt kinda funny buying a car without haggling the price, and they're going to personally deliver it. We climbed in and I drove back to Dundas. I would have been happy to keep the demo model, and Newf was ecstatic either way.

"What about, Mrs. H's old car?" Asked Newf.

"They said they'd find a good home for it."

"Won't she kinda get upset?"

"She's got the SUV, and I'll let her use our new car anytime she wants."

"What we gonna do about Mr. Beamish, then?"

Newf had hit the tack right on the head. What indeed was I going to do about Mr. Beamish? I had to think for a moment. Gran's new business had its disadvantages, like no lovely smell of cooking in the house, and no meals ready when you get home. Then there was this Beamish twit. Somehow I had to get Gran to fire this man as soon as possible. At that moment I heard the front door close. Moments later ex-inspector Spadafora walked in as bold as brass.

"Hi," I said standing to greet him. "You're back then?"

He smiled his usual 'I suspect you of something,' smile. "Zelda will be home soon, she's bringing supper."

"Oh." I sat down. "Have you met Beamish?"

"Sure."

"What d' yah think of him?"

Spadafora sat leaned back and crossed his legs. "A crumb, creep, nefarious underdog. Apart from that, I don't like him."

"I think we should fire him. I've been to Donjon Towers. Can't figure it out. The woman, Mrs. Macalister has a Scotch accent, and her house servant is real rude. There's no reason I can find for her to fire Beamish, unless Newf's right."

"What's your theory, North?"

"They gets into over peoples lives, then knock 'em off."

"For what purpose?"

"Gladys says, they does it for the money. See Beamish will get Mrs. H to change 'er will in 'is favour, then they'll knock 'er off, see."

Spadafora chuckled. "I wouldn't worry about that lads. Zelda is the smartest woman I know. If Beamish and company intended that she would have read his mind the day she met him. No, don't worry about Zelda. I understand your going to England William?"

"Yeah, I gotta teach Newf to drive first. Then I'm going to find Priscilla."

"Good. Your grandmother wants to investigate this Macalister woman. I think she has plans for you and North."

"No detective work, I told her, no detective work. Every time I look into something it turns out to be a real rat's nest. No way. I don't want to get shot again."

Spadafora chuckled. "This one's a simple bit of snouting around. No guns no dead people."

"So what's the object?"

"Zelda says her nose tells her there's skulduggery afoot."

"Gladys said there were 'undreds of dead bodies in the basement. All the poor suckers they'd bilked."

Shaking his head Spadafora said: "Then we'll have to find out who all these dead people are."

"He's nuts," I snapped. "There's no dead bodies in the basement. That Gladys is just winding you up, Newf."

"Just to be safe, I'll check the missing persons reports over the last few years."

"I thought you were retired, no longer a cop?"

"True, but I do have friends."

Gran dropped a bombshell when she came home. Oh, there was nothing wrong with the meal. Can't complain on that front. Just as we finished eating, and with her eyes sparkling that special Gran sparkle she said: "William, you'll be working in the Tea-Room next week. I would like time off to investigate our Mrs. Macalister."

3

Cromlet

I figure the thing, is not to shout your mouth off without giving it some thought first. I told Gran there was no way she could get me detecting again. Bad move. What I should have said is: "I won't get shot again." Now instead of being out there enjoying the excitement and freedom, I had to wear a pinafore and help that twit Beamish in Gran's Teagarden. Newf's lessons would be evenings only.

Only an hour into the first day, and fourteen seconds short of punching Beamish out, Gran turns up. Like a customer she sits at one of the seats with Spadafora and snaps her fingers. Beamish does the serving. "Two teas, if you please," Gran said with a huge grin. "I would like to speak with William,' she added.

I felt indignant, I mean, with my education, and the owner of a Rolls Royce, I should be doing work closer to my station in life. "What?" I snapped.

"Sit, William."

I sat. "Now what?"

"What happened to my car, William?"

"Your car? It… er… I left it at the car dealers."

"You did indeed, William. What makes you think you can give my property away?"

I shrugged. There was no answer I could think of.

Gran shook her head in a show of mock disgust. "Mr. Spadafora and I will be using your Rolls today. Do I have any argument?"

"No, Gran. Where you going?"

"We are taking a day off to do some research and investigating. Someone I know would rather serve tea than do a little detective-work."

"I never said that. Why's Newf not here helping me?"

"You have Mr. Beamish. Sidney and I have to do your work."

"Sidney? My work?" Gran sure knew how to hurt a person when she wanted to. I felt demeaned, used, and foolish. As usual there would be no point arguing. I would have to serve my sentence and hope for early parole. Sidney Spadafora sat there with a silly grin on his face, just absorbing the ambiance with carefree abandon.

"Now you be a good boy and we'll discuss it tonight at supper. Sidney and I will be back at work tomorrow, dear."

Fortunately we had a light day, the old ladies guild turned up at two in the afternoon. I think it was sort of a weekly special. They only stayed an hour then Beamish and I were alone. Let's talk in the kitchen," I suggested.

He seemed such a nice person, quiet, helpful and hardworking. We had a small staff table in the kitchen where we could sit without the customers seeing us. "I can tell," Beamish said, "that you don't like me."

"Oh it's not that. I just don't know you."

"Mr. Reyner, sir. I never asked for this job, Mrs. Hubert offered. I was fired by Cloey Macalister. If you knew her like I knew her, you'd know she was an impostor."

"That's what Newf said. But why? What's the purpose?"

"Money, just money."

"I can't see that. By my way of thinking it's ridiculous. How could someone just turn up and pretend to be someone else? People would notice."

"I noticed."

"So why didn't you go to the police?"

"I would have, but. Well." He stopped to think. "Alright I'll tell you. I was so sure she's a fake I went into her room and searched her documents. I wanted to see her passport. That would be proof."

"And?"

"I found it alright. I don't understand how, but it had her picture alright. Not a picture of Cloey, it was the impostor. That's when she caught me and I got fired."

Now that made me feel a lot better. The story just began to make sense, except for the substitution of Miss

Macalister. How and why? At that moment customers began turning up. Silly old biddies just looking for someone to talk to. The garden began to fill; I guess a tour bus must have stopped. From then on it was hard slogging until closing time.

At long and difficult length the working day came to a close. Although it was hard work, I can assure you it's a lot easier than pumping gas. Gran had made me responsible for shutting down the equipment and locking up. The drive home takes only a few minutes. I parked the SUV near the garage and walked in the house. Disappointment, man! No glorious smell of food. Instead an odorous pong of grease wafted from the kitchen.

Newf sat at the table eating fish and chips from a plastic tub. "What are you doing?" I demanded.

"Eatin' supper."

"So where's Gran?"

He shrugged and continued stuffing his face.

"Where's my supper?"

Newf shook his head.

"What is this, a revolution? Where'd you get the fries?"

"I went out and bought them."

"What'd you use for money?"

"Mrs. H left me some. She said she'd be 'ome late."

I'm not a difficult person to please, but this I call abandonment. Even Newf helped himself without thought for those of us who work for a living. In anger I turned and marched out again. A quick check of my wallet then drove to the Royal Hotel. At least there I'd get a welcome, or my wallet would.

Somehow it's not the same. Oh, the food was okay, though just not the same as eating at home. Gran is a far better cook than the chef at the hotel. At the end of the day you just want to talk to someone, eat in good company and reflect the day's events. I was the only unaccompanied person in the dining room. It's funny, you can't think seriously on your own. I had to keep checking to see who was watching me, as if I had become the exhibit at some awful zoo.

With a deep sigh I paid the check and drove slowly home. I should have taken Newf with me. Maybe I should have called home. I guess I must have been suffering a bout of depression. Gran still had not returned home. Newf was curled up in the sitting room eating tacos and drinking milk.

"You don't want you supper then?" He said.

"Supper, what'd mean?"

"I got fish and chips for yah. You want I should nuke 'em?"

"No, I'll go without. Where's Gran?"

"D'know."

I settled in and watched the box with Newf. There didn't even seem to be anything worth talking about. I began daydreaming about Priscilla and mentally planning my trip to England. Eventually Gran and her boyfriend turned up. Mr. Spadafora fair sparkled with delight and unwarranted enjoyment. Gran seemed gracious and happy. How could I ruin her day by complaining? Even Newf was happy. It felt like I'd missed something, missed the point of life maybe.

"How was your day, William?" Gran asked.

"Okay, I guess."

"Any one for tea?"

That sounded better, more like the Gran I remember from yesterday. Spadafora sat close by, a sickly grin on his face. "Sorry you had to take over, William. Zelda really needed some time off."

"I don't see why she bothers with that place. She's got enough money to buy the town and then live comfortably for the rest of her life. What's the point?"

"Zelda needs to be needed. It's an escape from reality. I just didn't want it to turn into a drudge."

"I need Gran, if she wants to be needed, I need her."

Spadafora smiled. "You're going to England, Zelda's staying here."

At that moment the lady in question returned. "William," she began and sat down. "I have exciting news."

"Oh! What?"

She grinned that all-knowing, I'm a smarty, smile. "Among other things, Sidney and I have been doing something you don't like."

"Oh, what?"

"You said you do not want to do any more detective work."

"So?"

"Well, Sidney and I have been doing some. You brought this pamphlet home. The one concerning Cromlet castle."

"Any tea, Gran?"

Without another word she got up and walked to the kitchen. Spadafora said: "She wants you to stay here, while we go to England to explore this castle."

"No way. I'm not nursing your tea garden while you lot gallivant around the world. No way."

Gran returned with the tea makings on a tray. "Well, dear, you said you didn't want to do any detecting. What alternative is there?"

"I'm not working in that shop of yours."

"Tea-garden, dear."

"Exactly. I won't do it."

She smiled, it was that, I told you so, smile. Pouring the tea and still smiling. "When I took you in young man you were a lazy lay-about. I do believe you worked in a doughnut store, and with a university education. Our dream was to become a famous detective, but alas we seem to be too lazy. Buying a Rolls Royce does not make you any better a man."

"I don't want to get shot again. It hurts, Gran."

"My darling William. I would give anything to protect you from such things. Are you going to spend your life hiding, in case someone has a gun?"

"No?"

"Then perhaps you should take training. Go to a school that will help you overcome your fear."

"I'm not afraid."

"Fear is something we all have to overcome. You must face it, William."

"Why you picking on me, Gran. What've I done?"

"Since you failed at university you have showed promise, but now you are slipping back into your slovenly, cowardly, and uncouth ways. You are turning back into the lay-about failure you were three years ago."

I didn't see it that way. "Sorry, Gran. How can I change your opinion of me? Should I take the car back?"

Gran looked sad. "I want you to enjoy your life, William. I want you to be more than a point of monetary distribution. Make something of yourself, be someone, not just the man with a bottomless wallet. I thought we were getting along well, though now I see the failing in our relationship."

I didn't know what to say, she had never said such things to me before. "Gran, Gran, I." Words failed me.

She came over to me and kissed me on the cheek. "You know I love you, William and want nothing but the best for you. Today was a day without me. Did you enjoy it?"

"No."

"You will have to learn to do without me. I won't live for ever."

I felt she was going to tell me something terrible. Something final, like when mom and dad died. She had me on the verge of tears. "I love you, Gran. I'll take care of you."

"I know you will, William. I want you to have the ability to be independent. Will you learn that for me."

"Sure, Gran."

"What about work to occupy your intellect?"

"Like what?"

"I think the idea of being a detective, a good and independent detective. Someone who will go down in history."

I nodded in agreement.

"Good, then we'll hear no more silly moaning."

"Sure, Gran."

She sighed and sat to enjoy her tea, my lecture for the day was at an end. She, as always was absolutely right. I had had the worst day of my life without her. No proper meals, at least nothing I enjoyed. "Do you want me to go back to Donjon Towers and do a real investigation of that woman?"

Gran smiled. "Maybe. Sidney and I will run the tea garden without your assistance, if you can find something constructive to occupy your mind."

"Okay. Me and Newf'll go and do some digging."

"Newf and I."

"Well if you go, Gran, what'll I do?"

She pulled an expression of exasperation. "I was correcting your English, William, not making a statement of fact."

I couldn't help giggle; sometimes she was so easy to wind up. "I know, Gran, just teasing."

Mr. Spadafora coughed, a sort of signal to Gran. She brightened up, and placed her cup on the table. "Now, I have to tell you what Sidney and I have been doing all day."

At least this would mean she had stopped insulting me. "Okay what have you been up-to?"

"Well," she said enthusiastically. "Cromlet Castle has had quite an exciting past. After the defeat of the Jacobites at Culloden Moore in 1746 the English passed some very nasty legislation. Scotland was all but defeated. They stole the land from under the Scott's feet. In 1749 Cromlet Castle was taken from the Laird and the family tried for treason. Some were exported to the new world, some were executed."

"So what's all this got to do with anything, Gran?"

"The castle, no longer occupied by a Jacobite sympathizer had to be kept in good order. A castilian was appointed. Alistair McLoud. His purpose was simply to hold the castle for Lord Grosvner. The Grosvner family declined, and the McLouds continued to hold Cromlet. 70 years later, in 1819 the castle was stormed by the McLeans. The strange thing is, they claimed to have taken the place in the name of the only remaining Grosvner, who had the unfortunate name of Adolph."

"That's all very interesting, Gran. But what does it have to do with anything?"

Still ignoring me, she continued. "Lord Adolph Grosvner moved into Cromlet and there he died several years later. He left his entire fortune to the McLeans. Where they seem to have stayed, even though the family own Drumvanich Island. Now Cromlet is a private hotel for elite and selected guests only. According to my studies, the house is exactly as it was two hundred years ago."

"And the point of this, Gran?"

"I would like you to investigate Cromlet. Go there and take a good look around."

"What would I be looking for?"

"Will you go?"

I nodded and shrugged at the same time. "Guess-so."

"Excellent. You are going to see Priscilla, you can take a nice Highland tour while you are there."

"Okay, what am I looking for? I mean, is this supposed to be more detective work?"

"Exactly. Nothing dangerous, no guns, no fisticuffs, just a pleasant drive and few questions."

"Why?"

"Miss Cloey Macalister went there before she changed. See if you can find out why she changed."

"Wouldn't it just be better to go to Donjon Towers and poke around there a bit?"

"Maybe. Yes that's a good idea, William. You can do a little poking around there if you like."

"There's no mystery. Macalister is an impostor. The real Cloey's probably been murdered."

"Excellent, William. I see you are at last thinking."

"Oh! I get it. You believe that geezer Beamish. We have a case. So who's going to pay for this one, I don't come cheap, Gran."

She smiled and her eyes twinkled. "Sidney and I will confine our efforts to running the tea garden and leave you two boys to solve this simple case."

"Okay. Newf and I will start first thing in the morning. We'll visit Donjon again. Daft name that. I guess it was designed or built by two dim-wits, Don and John."

Gran shook her head. "Donjon is a word, William. It means the central tower of a castle keep."

"Well, I still think it's a daft name for a house. It's an ugly house too. So when do you want me to attack Cromlet castle?"

Gran sighed audibly. "William, we are not at war. I would like you to surreptitiously take a look at the castle."

"And what would I be looking for?"

"Here," she took a small booklet from her purse and opened it to a specific page. "Here's a picture of Cromlet."

I took it and looked at the painting. A very beautiful looking castle nestling in the trees at the edge of a lake. The towers were a brownish grey with little pepper pot-looking smaller towers on the corners. "Wow. Looks great."

"That's a painting, not a photograph. I want you to get me real photographs. I would rather the occupants did not know you are taking pictures."

"Sure, Gran. When?"

"She thought for a few moments. "Do you have a valid passport?"

"Sure."

"And North?"

Newf shook his head. "I don't fink I ever 'ad one."

"Very well," Gran said. "As soon as North has a passport you may book the flight to London. I suppose that's where Priscilla is?"

"No, it's Gatwick."

"That is London, William. You'd better start planning how this trip will proceed. You'll need a car, accommodation should be alright you can use B & B."

A feeling of excitement swept over me. "Great. What about this Demijohn Castle?"

"That's Donjon,"

"Oh! Yeah, sure. What do you want me to do?"

Gran's a funny old girl, always likes to have everything just so. She soon produced a large book of British maps and pointed out where Cromlet castle supposedly nestled in some trees by a loch. Gran said that's Scottish for a lake. England seemed small and Scotland even smaller. On a map it was only a meter or so from London to Glasgow. Cromlet's about sixty kilometres north of there, just a few centimetres on the map.

While I studied the British Road Atlas Gran refreshed the teapot with hot water and rustled up some more biscuits. "You know," she said placing the tray beside me. "They never found Lord Grosvner."

"What d' yah mean, Gran?"

"I mean they never found him. His death was reported by a local doctor, and that was it. No funeral, nothing."

"So?"

"Well what do you think happened to him?"

"I guess they shoved him in the dirt in the castle grounds. He's bound to be dead now, that was hundreds of years ago."

"That'll be your reasoning for visiting the area."

"Like what, Gran?"

"You'll be a student of Celtic history, investigating the stories of the Jacobites. That would lead you to Cromlet, a natural progression. While your there investigating the present owners you can pretend to be digging up history on Lord Grosvner."

After a bad day, I guess I was feeling better again. Gran had that thing, that ability to turn me around. I suppose that's why I stay with her. She sort of keeps me on the rails. I don't think at the time I really wanted to look into this Donjon place, or that Miss Cloey Macalister, still, what can I say? Gran thought it worthwhile. I really did want to go to England and see Priscilla.

"What to you think, Newf?" I said out of the blue.

He looked at Gran, then me. "About what?"

"DJ towers and Macalister."

He shrugged. "D'know. I fink we should take a look in the basement. If we finds dead people, call the cops."

I shook my head in disgust, then breathed out as loud as possible. "There aren't any dead people in the basement. I think you've got Toditis."

"Well," he said scrunching up his eyes and scratching the end of his nose. "It wouldn't do no 'arm to take a butchers."

"To do what?"

"We should maybe break-in in the middle of the night, see just what is in the basement."

"Hm, get arrested and spend the summer in jail instead of England," I said.

"Nah. There's only one broad livin' in the 'ouse. We can do a nice quiet enter, an' take a look-see. If we finds' anyfing leave and call the cops. It's easy, nofin' to it."

I looked at Gran in the hope she would say something sensible to the contrary. "I have thought about it," she said. "North speaks a lot of truth."

"A lot o' twaddle," I growled.

"No, I think he's quite right. If there is a crime being committed here, we should get to the bottom of it. Is there any links to Cromlet? If so what? And of course, how? North's suggestion would probably yield more information than asking the woman. She probably lies through her teeth."

"Gees!" I exclaimed. "You want me to break the law to see if anyone else is breaking the law. "What do you think, Mr. Spadafora?"

He glared at me. "I have heard nothing." He got up and left the room.

Gran smiled. "So, what's it to be, William?"

I sighed in desperation. "I don't know. If you want. When?"

"I'll leave that to you and North." She left the room.

"What do you think, Newf?"

"I fink it's great. We could go now."

I looked at my watch. "No, it's too early. I figure if this thing's to happen we should get there around two in the morning, that's the time most people are sound asleep."

His eyes lit up. "This is great, hey, Bill. We're back in business again. You an' me, great detectives."

"Well if there is a crime here, I suppose we'll find it. Better get out your blacks again, don't want to be too visible."

Newf smiled, he was as pleased as Punch to be doing something illegal.

4

The Waxworks

The Rolls Royce is absolutely the best car for a burglar. Who would expect a car of such class and stature could be on a mission of low character. The quietness of its operation lends to the natural stealth of the sortie. I let Newf drive in order that I could navigate with my GPS. Surprisingly we encountered a fair amount of traffic on the main highway to Cambridge.

"Turn right here Newf." For a scatterbrain nitwit he really took to driving, handling the Rolls like a pro. Though I didn't recognize the scenery the GPS led us directly to our target. On our previous visit I marked the house and allowed the device to map our route. We simply retraced our earlier route. "Okay Newf, we'll park on the highway and walk from here."

We found a spot where we could pull off and park without lights. For safety I marked the spot on the GPS. In dark or light the device would navigate me to within six meters of the parked car. "Put your blacks on, Newf. We'll walk up the driveway."

Moments later we were on our way. It really wasn't all that dark. In the moonlight I could see the tree stumps sticking up out of the bog on our right. They looked even uglier by night. At the house there was a single light over the front door, everywhere else looked dark and dismal.

"I fink we should go in by the back door. Stay to the edge of the road so's we don't stick out."

"Okay Newf. Can you open the back door without using brute force?"

"Sure. It's real old fashioned. Nah, keep your voice down."

There's always a certain degree of excitement at such moments. The absolute quiet, the pounding of my heart droning out other sounds. I almost fainted as we walked into the back courtyard; a brilliant light automatically came on. We ducked into the shadow. "Now what?" I growled.

"No problem Bill, I'll go unscrew the bulbs."

"What if they have an alarm system as well?"

"Nah! I looked. They ain't got no alarm. I'll go get them bulbs, as soon as the light goes out meet me at the back door, alright?"

"Sure."

He's good, even though that light lit up the area like the resurrection, he slithered round the edges and then into the shadow near the house wall. Moments later I saw this tall gawky figure at the light. He unscrewed one casting half the courtyard into darkness. I started walking. The second light went out and the darkness was complete.

"You alright, Bill," Newf whispered from his position of invisibility.

"Sure. Now what?"

"I'll jigger the lock in 'alf a mo."

He knelt down and poked something into the keyhole. "What if there's a bolt on the inside?" I whispered in his ear.

"There ain't no bolt. Shut up."

After a few moments the hinges of the old door creaked as it swung inward. Newf grabbed my arm, "Stay close, don't use no light."

We entered a long room, more of a wide corridor, it stretched the full width of the house. An intersection in the middle led to the front of the house. Newf stopped; he listened for a moment then flicked on his flashlight. A quick sweep showed us that we were close to the stairs that led to the basement. Descending the steps gave me a feeling of trepidation, like walking into a sleeping bear's den.

At bottom a lengthy corridor led all the way to the front of the house, with two doors either side. "There's four rooms," I whispered.

"You look that side, Bill, an' I'll look this side."

I didn't like the idea of letting Newf wander off on his own though I agreed. The first door led into a large empty room. Concrete floor and a wooded partition to my right. Nothing interesting beyond the division wall. The next room turned out to be even less interesting. Again a concrete floor, washtub, sump pump, and an oil-fired central heating furnace. Newf met me at the door.

"There's nothing down here," I said.

"We'll 'ave to look 'igher up."

"Higher up. What do you mean?"

"The ground floor."

"There's nothing there. We saw it for ourselves."

"Keep your voice down, Bill. I fink maybe we should search everyfing while we're 'ere."

With tongue in cheek I agreed. Newf had this uncanny ability to navigate in strange places almost as if he could see in the dark. We crept back to the ground floor. Nothing in the Kitchen, living room, an empty room, a room full of antiques, a storeroom, and sort of pantry.

"Well I whispered. I haven't found anything."

"'Ush, Bill. We'll take a butcher's up the stairs."

"No we won't. I'm leaving."

"Come-on, Bill. Even if she catches us, she's only a little broad. We'll just make a run for it. We won't 'urt 'er."

I sighed. "Alright, nice and quiet like, okay?" The thought struck me this could be another good occasion to get shot. Little Miss Macalister could be waiting for us with a very large and loaded shotgun. Newf led the way. In the front hall, well it wasn't a hall, more of a passage that led from the front door to the back. There were two staircases, one on the right wall, leading from the front and one on the left leading from the rear.

Typical of an old house, the stairs creaked under our weight. Every step sent a shriek of lumber in pain that could be heard three counties away. I just knew it had to be a bad idea. My poor heart pounded like a Harley Davidson on a steep hill. By the time we reached the top, I was drenched in sweat. The landing seemed to stretch forever in the dim light we carried.

A huge room presented itself to us. Both staircases emerged in the centre of the floor separated by a hole. At the very end were two more sets of stairs one leading right the other left. At least half a dozen doors, around the landing and all closed offering us a midnight game of Russian roulette.

Cloey Macalister probably lay listening to every night sound behind one of the many doors. Newf indicated to turn our lights out.

For a moment or two we stood in the dark, then Newf put his light on and signalled me to walk with him. We moved to the end of the upper hall. "Let's go up these stairs," he whispered.

I nodded and began the ascent. Again the old wooden steps creaked under our weight. At the top the way was barred by a locked door. I began to feel like a trapped rat, as Newf did his thing with the lock. After what felt like several hours the door creaked noisily as it swung open. We moved in and Newf closed the door.

"This is one of the towers," he said.

"How do you know?"

"I used my brain."

Not the recommendation I really wanted. "So what now?"

He searched the room with his light. "There's only one uver door. I'll open that one."

While he worked on the lock I took a look around. The room had no windows and one rickety little staircase leading to an upper floor. I walked up carefully. At the top was a junk room, again no window. What a dump! Sacks and bags neatly folded in piles, a few seed trays and boxes, and a dozen baskets.

"Bill," came a hoarse whisper. "I done it."

Quickly I descended the narrow stairs and joined Newf. The door he'd opened led out onto the roof. "Well that's bloody brilliant." I growled.

"Nah! Look, there's the uver towers."

"Christ Newf I don't want to spend the rest of the night searching bloody towers. Let's get the hell out of here. There's no dead folk in the basement, and I can't see how we're going to learn anything up here."

He ignored me and walked to the centre tower, incidentally the only circular one. Even before I reached him, Newf began working on the lock. "What are we looking for?"

"Anyfing to prove she's a fake."

I shook my head in disgust. This was a complete waste of time. "I thought we were supposed to find bodies in the basement, not the roof."

The door opened, we entered and Newf closed the door. Somehow he found a light switch and flicked it. No bodies not even any murder weapons, but nonetheless a very strange place. Two wooden butcher's tables, a hoist, a large butcher's refrigerator and a bathtub with a gas heater under it. The tub was half filled with a milky white solid stuff.

Newf scraped the stuff with his fingers. "It's candle wax."

"Candle wax?" I walked over and tested the substance for myself. It was definitely candle wax. That's what the gas heater was for. Why would anyone want twenty gallons of wax? "What do you think, Newf?"

"She makes money producing fancy candles."

It's always the same, when you only know half the story, it doesn't make any sense. I continued to search the room. At the back were shelves and cupboards almost the full size of the wall. One part looked like a desk, with a pull-down work surface and a chair. I sat, and with flashlight in one hand I dug into the paperwork with the other.

Newf let out a shriek that almost caused me to fall off the chair. I leapt up expecting to see at least half-a-dozen hideous monsters. "Quiet, you idiot," I growled.

"Look, Bill."

Walking over I illuminated what had caused the alarm. In a bucket the other side of the bathtub lay two hands and a foot. No blood. Close examination made me smile, they were made of wax. "Dummy," I snarled. "She makes people out of wax. That's why you got that daft story about dead people in the basement. We better get out of here, you've probably woken up the whole county."

"Wax people?" Newf said slowly. "I ain't never 'eard o' such a fing."

"Believe me it's more common than you think. There's a place in Niagara Falls, I'll have to take you there sometime."

"What she do wiv 'em?"

"Put them on display, like shop dummies. Come on we're wasting time. I sure hope you haven't complicated our escape. Can you re-lock these doors?"

"I ain't never tried that."

"Well now's your time to try."

We left the waxworks and Newf tried to lock the door. "I can't do it," he said after awhile. "We'll 'ave to leave 'em unlocked."

"Come on then, let's get out of here."

I walked back to the down-staircase. When I opened the door, strong white light gleamed out. "Oh shit," I hissed and closed it again.

"We 'ave to go that way, unless you wanna jump off the roof."

"There's another fine mess you've gotten me into. I'm not jumping off any roof. Keep quiet and follow me." With extreme caution I eased into the tower room and began descending the stairs. Every step creaked loud enough to stop my heart. At last we reached the bedroom level without being detected.

As we tried to stealthily creep to the exit stairs a key rattled in a door opposite us. Panic ensued. I flew down the stairs as if the devil himself was on my heels.

"Is there anyone there?" Came a female voice. "I am armed. Show yourself."

I dashed through the first door at the bottom and closed it behind me. My heart pounded. Desperately I tried to think, which way led to the outside world. Newf, the dimwit, was lost. What if that woman calls the cops? I figured it would take about fifteen minutes for them to respond, so I had that long to get out and make a run for it.

In my panic to open the next door I dropped my flashlight, it rolled across the dark floor. After a few hair-raising seconds I crashed noisily into the front door, it was locked. From there I knew the whereabouts of the exit. Breathlessly I fled through the corridor and out into the courtyard. Heart pounding and sweating profusely I leaned against the wall to think.

Slowly I began walking back to the car, I figured if the cops came I'd see the lights and just hide till they pass.

Toward the entrance of the driveway I entered the copse of trees. Sitting at the base of a tall pine I waited and listened. The night was as silent as the grave. Time dragged on by, no cops and no Newf. It felt as though the world had ceased to exist.

It's easy to be disoriented in the dark, especially when you're in unknown territory. Quickly I switched on the GPS and let it find a few satellites, then I recalled the 'mark' where I left the car. The backlit screen made everything easy. There turned out be only one serious problem. When the GPS said I had reached the 'mark', there was nothing there. The car had vanished.

"Oh shit!" I exclaimed aloud. That stupid moron, Newf had driven off without me. How in hell was I going to get home?

I needed to find a phone, like a moron I'd left the cell in the car. The sky glowed where the city lights of Cambridge illuminated the clouds. I gave the GPS a 'goto' Cambridge. Six kilometres, it said and reported the exact bearing. Feeling rather foolish I began walking in the direction the instrument indicated.

Almost an hour later I saw my first street light. Unfortunately the GPS couldn't guide me to a telephone. I trudged on hoping to find a plaza or corner phone. A half hour later I found what I needed. A bus stop with a pay phone beside it. Quickly I grabbed a handful of coins from my pocket and stuffed a couple in the phone.

"Hallo," Gran said in a sleepy voice.

"Hi Gran! It's me William. I got problems."

"Oh dear, William. What has happened?"

"I've lost Newf, North. Worst of all I've lost the car. Well not worst of all."

"Then what is the worst, William?"

"Well... I... er... you see. Well, I think Newf's been captured by the enemy."

"Where are you now, William?"

"I don't know."

"Brilliant. If I should come for you in the car, how will I know where you are? Perhaps I should drive every street until I see you."

I quickly checked my change. "Okay, Gran. I'll run to the end of the street and read the sign. I'll call you back with the street name. Okay?"

"Very well, William. I'll await your second call."

At least I felt encouraged. Gran would come and pick me up, but what about Newf? Minutes later I found a street corner where a sign proudly proclaimed the name of both streets. Quickly I ran back to the phone and called Gran again.

"Hallo."

"Hi, Gran. Me again. I'll be at the corner of Willow and Denmark. Be quick I Don't want to get arrested for loitering."

""Where's your car, William?"

"I'll explain all that when I see you."

I hung up and walked to the corner. Two thoughts worried me. What happened to Newf? And what happened to my car? It seemed a quiet night, no police patrols. If I see one I'd just pretend to be walking. An all-night doughnut store would have been ideal. No such luck.

Time past slowly, at any minute I expected some good Samaritan to phone the cops about loiterers. Eventually I heard the sound of a car, and turning I figured it must me Gran. The car stopped, the driver was Sidney Spadafora. "Hi!" I said weakly.

Surprise of the century. The passenger in the front seat was Newf. "Where the 'ell did you get to Bill?"

"Never mind me," I said climbing in the back. "How the heck did you get here?"

"Easy, I phoned Mrs. H, and told 'er where I were. I tried to call you, but your cell phone weren't on."

"Smart-ass I lost it along with my new car. So where did you get to I waited ages for you at the Towers?"

"I ducked into anover room, when she chased you. She didn't know I were there."

Spadafora said nothing. Calmly and with a silly grin on his face he drove us home to Dundas. Gran waited up for us, she had the kettle on and all the makings standing-by. I felt kind o' stupid. Some detective, I felt like the burglar who went on a job and someone stole his ladder.

"I've told you before, William, always carry your cell phone. It's of little value in the glove box of a stolen car."

I sighed. "Yes, Gran."

"Did you learn anything?"

I shrugged. "No, well maybe. She makes wax figures."

Gran's eyebrows raised. "Wax figures?"

"Yeah, like in the wax works. I think that's where the story of bodies in the basement came from."

"Were there any bodies in the basement?"

"No, Gran. And the wax stuff was up in one of the towers on the roof."

"So at the approximate cost of a quarter of a million dollars, we have learned nothing?"

"I did," Newf said softly.

"You did what, young man?"

"I learned somefing."

"What?"

"Well, when she chased Bill, I ducked into anover room. The light were on. I fink it were 'er office or somefing. Anyway I was looking for somewhere to 'ide when I sees this desk, an it's open. What do you fink I found?"

"I don't know," I said. "Do tell us."

"Sittin' on the top of a pile of papers were two fings, a passport, an' a letter."

"Is this going to take long Newf, I'd like to go to bed and cry over the loss of my car."

"Nah! The passport were in the name of Miss Cloey Macalister."

"So?"

"The picture weren't the lady we saw."

"You didn't see her, how the hell would you know?"

"Cuz when we left she came wiv you to the back door. I saw 'er. An' it weren't the woman in the photo. Look. He handed me the passport.

"Christ, Newf. You nicked it." I opened it and looked. It was out of date by several years and the picture was definitely not the Cloey Macalister I saw. I handed it to Gran. "That's not the woman I spoke to."

Gran took it and stared at it with a thoughtful expression. "Very interesting."

"So what's the letter then?" I said.

Newf smiled from ear to ear. He reminded me of the Cheshire cat. "You read it."

The letter turned out to be a love letter from Cloey Macalister to Dagwood Beamish. "I don't believe it," I snapped. Why would she write to Beamish, and even if she did, what's it doing in her own writing-desk?"

The question did nothing to diminish Newf's grin. "Why not ask, Dagwood Beamish?"

"I will, first thing in the morning."

Gran scrutinized the communication for several moments then said. "From what I gather, this letter was dispatched from Scotland. I would suggest it was written the moment she arrived. Notice the notepaper is from the Regal Hotel Glasgow. The date would indicate it to be the beginning of her holiday."

"I fail to see any significance, Gran."

"We'll see, William. Tomorrow we must find your car."

Mr. Spadafora came into the room at that moment. "I've already reported it stolen. You can collect it tomorrow."

"Collect it," I said jumping to my feet. "What do you mean, collect it?"

"It wasn't stolen. The OPP found it abandoned on a country road, parked under a 'no parking' sign. They thought it may get stolen or broken into. It's been towed."

"Oh, crikey," I said trying to hold down my language. "If Macalister reports a break-in, they'll put two and two together. This is not working out very well. How did you escape, Newf? Did you kill her or something?"

"No. She came back into the 'all an' went upstairs. As soon as I 'eard the floor creek above me, I lit out. You'd gone, so 'ad the car. But I brung the evidence wiv me."

You did, fine, North," Gran said encouragingly. "You are a smart boy."

With a sigh of resignation I left the room and went upstairs. Gran was in one of those funny moods. She was punishing me for being stupid by praising everyone else. She's a very hard lady to please. Tomorrow I would start again, get the car and plan my trip to England.

5

On the Move

Getting my car back turned out to be simple, it just required money. Miss Macalister, or whatever her real name is, never reported the break-in. That in itself was suspicious. It was August before we were ready to visit England. Newf failed his driving test, the dummy drove through a stop sign. His next test would be in December.

It's always stinking hot in August. Having never been to Britain, I really didn't know what to expect. Newf was as excited as a young puppy. Everything came as a surprise and something new to him. I let him have the window seat. First class seemed very nice. The attendant fussed over us all the time. When at last the plane lifted off the ground, Newf fell silent and glared out the window.

No matter what, it's a boring trip, the movies old and nothing else to do. I played with my GPS, I could read the plane's heading, altitude, and speed. At long and leg-aching last the captain announced, we would be descending for a landing at Gatwick. At eight in the morning Britain looked a bleak and dismal place. A certain look of cleanliness shrouded in miserable grey.

With three hundred passengers, the disembarking and customs was mayhem. Though I think they were more efficient than Pearson Airport, back home. Eventually we reached the free side of the establishment. The sun had risen higher in the sky, and there seemed a slight chill in the air. Although it is the most expensive way to do it, I took a rental car at the airport. Now driving on the wrong side of the road is hair raising. Man! The car fortunately had all the controls on the wrong side too. I figured I'd maybe let Newf drive once we reached the country.

When you look at the map, England is a tiny place, but when you get there, it's big and complicated. I marked the airport on the GPS, though it didn't help me find Priscilla. I'd forgotten to download British towns and cities. She lived at a place called Cottenham Hall in the village of West Lavington. Locating the place on a map was fairly easy, finding the real place became a nightmare.

I had no idea England could be so complicated. The signposts were of little use. You had to stop and read them. I guess if you were driving a horse and cart they would present no problem. Man! We got on the main super highway, and whizzed right passed the place. Coming back we used back roads, that was a mistake. As soon as you ask someone the way they started talking some incomprehensible local dialect.

Around two in the afternoon I found West Lavington. Not exactly what I'd expected. One church, two public houses and maybe five or six residential homes, no stores. Eventually I found a pedestrian and asked the way to Cottenham Hall. Newf seemed to have a better understanding of the people than me.

Man! Cottenham Hall turned out to be a mind blower. I hadn't seen any house that size ever before. There must be around two hundred rooms. The mansion sat in a lightly treed valley next to an artificial lake, with black and white swans. Peacocks walked around free making a terrible sound. I parked near the house on the huge gravel area.

Priscilla's father had to be some kind of lord or at least a millionaire. A French maid opened the door and curtsied. In a thick accent she asked what we wanted. "I've come to see Miss Priscilla," I said.

"I am sorry Monsieur, Mademoiselle Priscilla is not 'ere. She will be 'ome at seize, ar-, six of the clock."

My French being nonexistent; I nodded and smiled, then walked back to the car. "Nice 'ouse," Newf said, trying to break the ice.

"Sure. She's not at home. We'll come back at six." I pulled out my GPS and marked the spot. No matter where we went returning would be easy. "I figure we'd better find a place to stay the night."

"What about the village, there's an inn there?"

"So are you thirsty?"

"Thirsty, what's that got to do wiv anyfin'?"

"An inn is where you drink, it's a pub, you dolt."

Newf laughed. "I fort I were the fick one. A inn is like a 'otel. Didn't you ever read the Bible? Jesus was born in the stable cuz there weren't no room at the inn."

I started the engine and drove back to the village. Smart-ass was right. We booked a room with two beds then went for a drive. The traffic was total insanity. We found all the things we needed, maps, tourist guides, flashlight, which they call a torch, and batteries for my GPS.

At dead on the dot of six, I pulled the bell chain at the mansion door. This time a geezer in a monkey suit opened the door. "Good evening, sir."

"I'd like to see Miss Priscilla."

"Would sir please step inside?"

The entrance hall can only be described as magnificent. A large almost octagonal room with chandelier and grandfather clock. The floor area was big enough to use as a skating rink, and a huge curved staircase up to the second floor. Monkey suite walked off, through a large oak door, and after a few moments returned. "Mistress Priscilla will receive you in the drawing-room, sir." He led the way.

The drawing room turned out to be some kind of middle-ages museum. I was too nervous to sit on any of the pieces so I stood and waited. Only a few moments later Priscilla came in hanging on the arm of this tall blond athletic-looking guy. "Hello, dear William," she said and pecked me on the cheek.

"I've come for you," I said like a goof.

"That's just too sweet, William. This is Godfrey Whiteshore, my fiancée."

After all I'd been through, the stupid broad hung onto this geek. I was dumfounded, and must have looked the right nitwit with mouth open as I tried to think. The obvious thing would be to bash his brains out; I don't know why I didn't. Somehow I mumbled something about, 'good to see yah,' then left feeling totally embarrassed.

Newf sat in the car with his feet on the dashboard just enjoying life. "Did you see 'er?"

"Shut-up and get your feet off the dash." I jumped in and roared off down the drive toward the gatehouse.

"You met the new boyfriend, eh?"

"Shut up. Get the map out we're going to Cromlet." I sure felt like I needed to thump someone, and Newf was the nearest.

"What about our room at the inn?"

"Alright tomorrow, then."

Early next day we were speeding through the countryside on a road they call the A1. A little less than two hours and, feeling tired I pulled into the fairly large town of Peterborough. Managed to get lost and eventually found this very pretty park by a large river and a huge cathedral. I just needed to stretch my legs. Newf wanted to explore the cathedral.

We found somewhere to eat, and then got directions back to the A1. The idiot that told me Britain was only a small place should be made to drive this road. After two stops and five hours driving we arrived in Edinburgh. Man what a fantastic place, almost beyond description. The huge castle dominates the town, and the buildings looked older than anything I've ever seen.

Finding an inn for the night was simple. On Princes Street there was dozens to choose from. We stayed at a very archaic establishment called the Bonny Prince. Terrific food, and excellent accommodation. I fell into that Scottish bed and remained unconscious until almost ten the next day. After thoroughly stuffing myself at breakfast, we set out on the last leg of the journey.

The village of Pitcalver is so small it's not marked on the map, yet the Loch Aaron showed clearly, about one hundred miles from Edinburgh. Even though I was not on the way to Gretna Green with Priscilla, the Scottish air felt invigorating and exciting. As I drove northeast the road got smaller and smaller, and the hills steeper and steeper.

Eventually we got lost and found a small lakeside village, again not marked on the map. I parked outside the local pub and entered. Talk about old world, man! All the ancient geezers stopped talking and looked around as we entered. You'd think we were naked the way they ogled us. I ordered a pint and asked directions to Pitcalver.

The barman pulled two pints, narrowed his eyes, and put his hand out for the cash. I gave him a five-pound note. Without speaking he pointed in a single direction. "That way?" I said softly.

He said nothing, but by the expression and silence of all the patrons I figured it wasn't a good place to stay. Nodding and backing up like a Chinese peasant I left. It wasn't till I reached the car that I realized I'd left Newf in the pub. Feeling totally stupid I sat in the car and waited for him to return. Ten minutes later he turned up with a broad smile on his face.

"They don't get many visitors 'ere," he said and climbed into the car.

"Looked to me more like they eat most of them."

"Nah! They's real friendly. Said stay away from Cromlet, reckon the Garstons are dangerous. Them's bin dangerous since they turned up."

"So who are they?"

Newf shrugged and I drove off in the indicated direction. Wasn't really difficult, there being only one road. Eventually we reached a crossroads with a sign pointing to Pitcalver. Unbelievably the road was just wide enough to take one vehicle. The road wound round a hill and descended into a beautiful valley by a small lake. A huge ancient house stood in well-manicured grounds.

I stopped the car. "I think that's Cromlet. Somehow we've missed the turn."

"I didn't see no turn."

Gran said not to let them know we were here. Slowly and carefully I turned the car round and headed out again. Back at the crossroads Newf discovered the problem, some smart-ass had rotated the sign. He turned it until one arm pointed to Cromlet then we travelled the road to Pitcalver. You wouldn't believe the scenery, man! A beautiful little hamlet nestling in a valley between a couple of mountains.

The church looked more like a mosque, even had a gold roof. Strange as it may seem, there's only one pub, the Cuckoo inn. Parking out front we walked into the establishment. An attractive house with low doors and ceiling

Beams ran across holding the ornate ceiling up. It felt like a warm and friendly place.

The lady at the bar smiled sweetly. "Good evening gentlemen."

"Hi, do you have board guests?"

"Noo," she said in that lovely Scottish accent. "All o' our guest are interested, enthralled, even."

"No I mean do you have rooms?"

Aye that we doo, nine of them, if you doon't count bathrooms and cupboards."

"Can I rent a room?"

"Auch! I thought you'd get around to it eventually. Around here we tend to say what we mean. And we doo have a room for rent. Will you be staying long?"

"No, well I don't know. It's a touring holiday. I'm from Canada."

"Aye, it shows. Will you be wantin' food."

"Yes, no. I'm not sure."

"Then let me know when you get hungry, then we'll see if there's anything we can do for you."

"Yeah, sure. How much?"

"We'll figure that oot when you describe how long. Please come this way."

"Thank you."

She led the way to a very nice little room with a canopied bed and a window that overlooked the street. "What about my friend?"

"Auch! We do have other rooms. You can have one each."

"What do I call you? Landlady?"

She laughed. "Auch! Noo. Call me Ellen. We doon't take plastic. You'll have to pay cash, there is a wee bank in town."

She was sweet and trusting. A good-looking woman in her thirties, in one way she reminded me of mom. First things first. "Do you do meals?"

Smiling sweetly she nodded. "Aye, that I doo. Get yee'sel organized and come doon to the dining-room an' I'll see what I can doo."

"Thanks."

We moved some of our stuff from the car into our rooms then went for a walk into the village. There was a small bank, but being a hick area it only opened from ten to three and only three days a week. I checked my calendar watch, good, it'll be open tomorrow. The largest establishment seemed to be the village lawyer Edward Cameron.

"Notice anything strange, Newf?"

He turned a complete circle, then shrugged. "I fink it's all very strange."

"No I mean one thing in particular."

"Nah!"

"This is a village, and look at Edward Cameron's place. It would take a dozen clients daily to keep that place in business."

"So?"

"So do they bring them in by the coach load?"

Newf shrugged. "D'know."

As the bank was closed and there didn't seem to be anything else in the village, we walked back to the pub. Another strange thing; I didn't see any other inhabitants. A half hour had passed and we'd only seen Ellen at the inn. At the far end of the village stood a gas station; the sign said open, yet it was quieter than a grave.

Ellen appeared like as if she had radar or something. With a wave of her hand she conducted us into the dinning-room. Only one fairly large table with eight chairs parked around it. No other furniture except a sort of sideboard with no doors. The window looked out onto the street, which is more than people sitting in the room could do. The glass allowed light in, but it was so distorted you couldn't make anything out.

"What would you like for tea?" She asked.

"Tea?"

"Are you not hungry?"

"Yeah, sure."

"Then what'll you eat?"

I shrugged. "Don't know, what have you got?"

"If you're no in a hurry, I'll get yee a nice hot meal. Suet dumplings, beef and greens, be alright?"

"Sure."

She disappeared through a door at the back. "I think we've landed in loony land," I said.

"I fink it's great. I wana take a look at that church. What about Priscilla?"

"What about her?"

"What are you going to do?"

"You're as daft as this village, Newf. I'm not doing anything about Priscilla. We'll take a quick look at Cromlet and go home on the next plane."

"Next plane? Ain't we gonna 'ave a 'oliday?"

"We'll see. I just feel that all this is a big waste of time. This place is deserted. It's not going to be much of a holiday, Particularly without Priscilla."

Next morning, even before the early bird got his worm, Newf and I were up. Ellen made us a fantastic breakfast, sausage, beans, toast, and English coffee. Didn't like the coffee, tasted like road tar. Ellen said that by road, Cromlet was about four miles, but by back trail only a mile. The trail started right beside the fascinating looking church.

I switched on the GPS, clipped it to my belt and sallied forth. A magnificent day, butterflies and birds, the like of which I'd never seen before, flying all over the place. For a place where there didn't seem to be any inhabitants, the path looked very well worn. Twenty or so pleasant minutes into the walk we reached the end of the forest. Man what a view.

For several moments I just stood there, mouth open and absorbed the sight. A beautiful-fairy castle with pepper-pot turrets, whitewashed walls and dark-slate roofs. Immaculate laws and gardens made the place look like a model, a toy sitting beside a picturesque lake.

"Wow!" Exclaimed Newf. "I ain't seen no place like that afore."

"Me neither." For the first time we saw people. There was a garden party or something going on to the east side of the castle. Tents, and things, with lots of people milling around. I looked at my watch, only 8:15 am.

"Should we go take a butcher's?" Newf said.

"No. We'll take a few photographs and leave it for today. Gran will be amazed. I don't think she has any idea what this place looks like."

"I fort you 'ad a pamphlet wiv a pitcher."

"Yeah. But it sure as hell didn't look like that. It's so big, clean, and just fantastic. Let's get back to the village." I marked the spot on the GPS. If need-be we could find it in the dark.

"So what, we gonna do?"

"Well we could come back at night, maybe take a poke around."

"What for?"

"I don't know."

"What if they got dogs?"

"I'll get a pepper spray."

The walk back to the village seemed just as pleasant. I think I was beginning to like the Scottish air. Back at the village I saw a car, other than ours, and three people walking. The lawyer's office remained closed and the bank wouldn't be open till later. Ellen smiled and greeted us from our walk.

"We walked over to Cromlet," I said.

"Come into the lounge, and I'll tell a little of it," she said in the beautiful Scottish accent.

We sat. "I had no idea the highlands were so beautiful," I remarked.

She smiled. "Would you like a wee drink?"

"Sure."

She ran off; I couldn't help notice the way she was dressed. For an older woman she sure looked attractive, with a sort of open top tight bodice showing a lot of flesh. A kilt instead of a skirt accentuated the roundness of her hips. In moments she returned with three glasses in one hand and three cans of coke in the other. With expertise Ellen filled the glasses and shared them out.

I took one and said. "When the bank opens I'll go get you, your money."

Ellen smiled. "I trust you, but I have to give you a warning."

"A warning? What warning?"

"I know you have been looking at Cromlet." Again she smiled sweetly and sat opposite. "Cromlet is filled with, well with- McLeans." She chewed her bottom lip for a second. "Well, actually, Garstons."

"So?"

"They are very bad people. The family live on the isle of Drumvanich, but the cuckoos live at Cromlet."

"Cuckoos, who are the cuckoos?" I was baffled, completely puzzled.

Ellen frowned as if what she wanted to say came with great difficulty. "You're a very nice laddie, and I would'nay want you to vanish. Please stay away from Cromlet."

"Vanish? What do you mean vanish?"

She smiled sweetly, leaned over and stroked my hair. "You're a bonny wee laddie. 'Twood be a terrible shame to loose you so soon." With that she rose and walked away.

I felt stunned. Gran would understand, I sure as hell didn't. "What do you think, Newf?"

"I fink Cromlet is the place where they 'ave dead people in the basement. The place is big enough."

"You've got dead people on the brain. Come-on let's go visit the local banking establishment."

The bank lay just beyond the huge lawyer's office. 'Edward Cameron attorney at law,' the sign proudly proclaimed. The bank was straight out of Dickens. Enormous dark-oak counters, almost shoulder high. A huge-strong iron grill all the way along with polished-brass fittings. The place echoed like a tomb. I could see only one person behind the counter.

I walked up and placed a handful of traveller's checks on the tall counter. "I'd like to cash these, please."

Scrooge picked them up and examined them over his half-glasses. "They're of no value here," he said and thrust them back at me.

"No value, no value. What do you mean no value?"

"We canna take sassenach paper here."

"I need the money to pay some bills. They're worth cash."

"Not here. Now goo awa afore I call the bobby."

Stunned, mind-boggled, and incensed, I wandered out onto the street with Newf in tow. A quick glance at my watch told me the time was just after 10:00 am and 5:00 am in Dundas. "Well now's the time to find out if this thing really works internationally." I pulled my cell phone and pressed the buttons. It rang and rang and rang.

"Halo," came a familiar and tired sounding voice.

"Hi, Gran. I need help."

"Oh dear. Now what trouble have you got into?"

"I'm stuck up here in the Highlands, Gran. They won't take traveller's checks. I got a hotel bill to pay, what'll I do?"

"Firstly, William, we will calm down. Traveller's checks are legal tender. Someone should take them. Try a larger town. Have you learned anything about Cromlet Castle?"

"No I haven't had time."

"Very well, William, they are tourist wise. Perhaps they will change your checks."

6

Cromlet

With great difficulty I explained my dilemma to Ellen. With a sly smile she said. "I'll take your passport, when you pay me you can have it back."

"That's fair."

Passportless, we jumped into the car and drove off. I didn't tell her we were going to Cromlet castle; I thought maybe she wouldn't agree. I guess it was around three in the afternoon when we decided to make the drive. The place we thought to be Cromlet on the day before was only the gatehouse, which looked like a castle compared to where Gran lives.

Farther along the drive we came to the genuine article. Everything, and I do mean the whole shebang stood in immaculate condition, perfectly cared for and clean. Not a single blade of grass out of place. We saw at least half a dozen people working on the gardens and grounds. It had the air of a nunnery, with its tranquil serenity.

Unlike a regular tourist place, Cromlet had no signs, no written rules or explanations. Ours was the only car in the enormous parking lot. The fair, or whatever looked deserted. There was an open entrance in a front-central tower. Up the half-dozen steps and through the open door. The foyer would blow your mind. All wood panelling two stories high. A balcony with no obvious stair access ran across the back wall above which, on the wall stretched a circle of old guns. Looking like a giant daisy, each weapon being a petal.

A fireplace on the left had a fire burning brightly, and in the centre floor stood a round table with ten chairs encircling it. Weapons and animal heads festooned the huge walls. On the right an arch led into another large room. Newf and I stood with mouth open trying to absorb the opulent surrounds. I mean, like, Gran's rich, but this place made the house on Fiend's Rock look like a beggar's shack. A dark haired man with staring eyes walked over to us. His hair looked far too black for a man of his years.

What do yah want?" He asked rudely.

"We're lost," Newf said.

I don't think I have ever met anyone as rude as this geezer. He lifted up one leg, strained and let rip with the biggest fart, you ever heard. For a moment I stood stunned, just wide-eyed with shock.

"Have yee never heard anyone break wind afore?" He said.

I nodded; he'd blown all the thoughts out of my mind. For a moment I went totally blank.

"Dinna mind father," came a sweet female voice.

Looking round I saw this tall handsome woman in her forties standing behind us. She wore a simple one-piece dress with a gold crucifix dangling on a gold chain. Her hands were together, like a bishop or pope. "Hi!' I said weakly. "We're lost."

"Where is that you would like to be?" She asked approaching.

"I... er... we... er-."

Newf interrupted me. "We're not lost goin' anywhere. We's just drivin' abart. Come from Glasgow and can't figure art 'ow to get back."

"Your car was'nay hired in Glasgow. You're touring no doubt."

"Yeah," I said, getting the gist of the conversation. "We're from Canada, just having a look around."

"Will you be staying the night, then?"

"Yes, no. Well, yes, but not here. We haven't booked, you see."

She smiled very sweetly; her mannerisms were kind of religious, almost like a nun. "Allow me to show you our humble abode."

Father let rip with another thunderous bum-clap, mumbled something and walked away. "Who's that?" I asked.

"Oh, dinna pay-heed, that's Father. He's the chief of our wee clan, and a famous lawyer."

"Oh!"

"I see by the cut of your cloth you're no a peasant."

"Peasant? I'm from Canada."

"Aye. An who is this gentleman?" She said, sort of curtsying at Newf.

"I'm 'is driver. 'E's my boss."

"Yes," I agreed. "North is my chauffeur."

"Come then, you'll enjoy our little house." She pointed up the short-wide staircase. "The dining room is up there, maybe we'll have a look there later."

Walking directly opposite to the entrance, we followed the woman. Considering the huge crowd seen here earlier, the place seemed empty. "How many guests do you have?" I asked.

She giggled. "About twelve permanent, all the others left late yesterday."

"Oh! I saw the tents and things."

"Ooo, that. Noo. It's not a thing for the guests. It's archaeological. The tents are to protect the valuable ruins. This is the tapestry-room for obvious reasons."

A huge room of unbelievable antiquity with enormous carpet-like things hanging on all the walls. Each carpet was a huge picture, some of battle scenes some just animals. One in particular displayed the wedding of some ancient person. Everyone dressed in armour and stuff like that.

"The house is filled with history," she said holding her cross in both hands. "Please follow me."

I began to feel a little nervous at being led deeper and deeper into the spider's lair. We walked a long corridor with porthole-like windows on one side and two huge doors on the other. "What's in there?" I asked.

"That's the wardrobe. A museum of clothes. Come at the end here. You'll find it most interesting."

"Well I really should be going. We... er... we-. Well we are expected somewhere."

She opened a door at the end of the passage, curtsied and smiled. Man! A room the size of a large house. Wooden floor and windows painted, or stained glass. The entire room was filled with furniture laid out like four smaller rooms. The mind-boggling effect capped by dozens of people sitting, standing, and otherwise doing things. A frozen moment in time.

"What, the?"

"It's been a family custom for well over a hundred years to make wax replicas of our ancestors. This is the wax-gallery."

"The dead people," Newf said under his breath.

I laughed and began to explore the wondrous displays. This room is the centre of the silly stories of dead people in the basement. Unbelievable! The dummies were exceptionally lifelike. The eyes almost followed you around. Each person was dressed in the appropriate period and doing work as they would have in their own time. Newf looked dumbfounded; I guess I should have taken him to Niagara Falls to see stuff like this.

Our guide really knew her history. At every display she told us the historical facts. I'm not sure how long the tour lasted, the time sheer flew by. As we finally completed a circle, arriving back at the entrance, she said. "Well, what do your think of our humble museum?"

"Amazing. How come you don't charge people for the tour?"

"Oo, well! 'Tis the good Lord that gives us our history, why should we profit from it? The museum is a wee family thing, ever since Madame Tussaud invented the idea. It's free, for no one would come here just to see it. Would you like to stay a few days?"

"No, No thanks. We've settled. How much does it cost, say for a week?"

"Depends on the season, the guest, the requirements. People make application, then we work out how much the time will cost them."

"Oh, I see."

"Would you like to see the accommodation?"

"Umm! Sure. Okay."

"Guest accommodation is in the east towers, come." She led the way back to the room with the staircase. Up the stairs cross the landing and into another stairwell.

I could easily get lost in a house this size. One floor up another corridor had four doors and another staircase. She opened a door and we all entered. "Wow!" I exclaimed in shock.

"This area of the house is called the comings. It's where all the comings and goings occur."

The room was twice the size of my bedroom with it's own fireplace, a four-poster bed and furniture straight out of the Middle Ages. Although it was a huge room, it felt close, comfortable. The carpet was so thick you could sleep in it. The sort of place that made you feel embarrassed because you're wearing shoes. The antique value must have been in the millions.

"Are all the rooms like this?"

"Oo, yes, with wee differences."

"We're from Canada."

"Aye, I know, that."

"Yeah, well we're sort of booked, see. Although we'd love to stay here we aren't able to change our plans. Maybe we could come another year."

"Could you afford it?"

Newf's eyes lit up, he felt insulted. "Bill's a multimillionaire. He could buy this place."

He's wrong on that account. I couldn't think of anyone in the world who had that kind of cash."

"Then a thousand pounds a night wouldnay frighten you?"

"No," I said with a smile."

"Good, we don't charge anything like that. If you are accepted as a guest the fee is very small. We had a visitor earlier this year from Canada. A lovely lady from, I think it was Cambridge."

I felt my face turning red and my temperature rising. "I... er... I'm. That is we're from that area."

She smiled a sweet smile and her eyes flashed. "A Miss Cloey Macalister. Lovely woman. Got the right heritage too."

"Oh, yeah. No I don't know her well. She actually gave me a pamphlet. As we were passing this way, well, we thought we'd take a look."

"Quite commendable. Will you stay for tea?"

"No, no, thanks. Could you change a few travellers checks?"

She gently gestured with her head. "Well, we'll have to ask Flora, she's our accountant and cashier."

Moments later we found Flora and asked the critical question. You'd think we'd asked for a pint of blood. I thought she was going to burst into tears. "How much would you want?" She asked extracting her hanky.

"Five hundred pounds. Just pocket money."

She immediately flew into a panic. "Oh, my God, I can't doo that until the time lock goes. Oh dear."

"When's that?" I asked stupidly.

She looked at her watch, and with a few gasps of surprise and embarrassment, she said: "Oh dear, oh dear. It' won't open until six. I can't do anything until six."

"Oh don't worry," I said. "We'll come back."

"Nonsense," Miss Stephanie said. "You'll both be staying to tea. That's at five. In the meantime why don't we complete the tour of our humble home?"

Again the feeling of being winched in came over me. She had the power to do just as she pleased. If it wasn't for the stupid suspicions I had about this place, I would have been able to enjoy myself. Cromlet was the most fascinating location I had ever seen. "Your house looks much better in real life than it does on your pamphlet."

"That's deliberate."

'Why?"

"A wee bit of psychology. If the picture were as beautiful as the house, there would be no shock. As it is people are very pleased at the look of the house. Would you like to see our dungeon?"

"Dungeon? No."

She laughed. "I promise not to take you prisoner."

"Oh!"

"I'd like to see it," Newf said.

"Come along gentlemen I'll show you our dungeon and tell the story of Alistair McLoud."

"Who's Alistair McLoud?"

"Come this way." She led us back to the entrance hall and through a door at the back. A dark and dismal passed leading to a set of stone steps descending into the bowels of the earth. She flicked a switch and the way became lighted.

At the bottom of the stairs we found a dismal place with a flagstone floor. Dim electric lights glowed behind iron grills. The area was divided into three zones. Two cages, surrounded by rusty iron bars, and the main area. Talk about give you the creeps. The cages each had an old wooden bed with straw for a mattress. The main area looked a bit like a blacksmith's shop. A forge and several benches.

Stephanie waved her hand at the cages. "Alistair McLoud died in one of these prisons."

"Who was he?"

"Well when the sassenachs defeated the Jacobites at Culloden Moor, Alistair McLoud was given Cromlet. He was a very bad man and ran the fife as if it were his own. The villagers became his personal slaves. His son took over after him. His name was also Alistair McLoud."

"Ah! So it wasn't the original who died in your jail?"

"Noo. The family got sorely upset one day when the second Alistair McLoud's son raped a girl called Rachel."

"Who was she?"

"Rachel was a McLean and protected by our family creed. It was 1819 when we took the castle and gave it back to the Grosvner family. That's why they call us the cuckoos."

Oh! Do they. Why's that?"

She lifted her crucifix and kissed it. There was'nay a fight. Our people came to supper one night, and stayed. At the appropriate moment Alistair was jailed here."

"So what happened to the son?"

She smiled sweetly. "I could'nay imagine. As I recall, he was never found. Of course there's been no trouble in this area since."

"Wow, since 1819?"

"Aye. Now we look after the village and its inhabitants."

"How do you make money? I mean, how do you all live?

"Generosity. Like yourself, if you take a liking to us and believe in our cause, maybe you'll make a donation as many others do. Or maybe leave something for the estate in your will."

"Oh!" She was a good-looking woman and obviously intelligent, though somehow she came across as a bit of a ghoul. Just the way she spoke sent shivers down my spine.

"Come gentlemen, let us go up for air. The gardens are very pretty this time of year. Do you have a camera with you?"

"No."

"Not to worry."

"Actually I only came to Britain to see my girl, but she's hitched up with a useless dude from somewhere. So we decided to drive north. I'd seen your pamphlet, seemed like a good idea."

"Very sensible. You'll have to speak with Bonny, she has a knack with the lovelorn."

"Oh!"

The grounds of the house were even more beautiful when you understand the wonders. Stephanie was the perfect guide with knowledge of everything. The woman seemed to be a walking encyclopaedia. History, botany, even geology, she knew it all. Apparently even grass has several names, and types. The fishpond had huge goldfish that came to the surface when she whistled. Like magic, and they took food directly from her hands.

I don't think I've ever seen any human so in tune with nature. Even the birds were not afraid of her. I have to admire that woman, although she acted a little pious she had it, she really had it. After a long walk around the beautiful grounds, she led us into the house.

"Come, let us retire to the dining-room." She said.

When we walked into the foyer the table had been set for all ten places. "I thought the dining-room was up those stairs."

She smiled, kissed her crucifix then said: "That's only for the guests, there are reasons why the family eat here." She walked slowly to the table and after quick examination said: "This seat is for Mr. Reyner, and this one is for your friend.

I felt rather out of place and uncomfortable. We all sat, with her to our left. Then Father made a thunderous entrance. At first I thought someone had started a lawn mower.

That's why we doon't eat with the guests," Stephanie said. "This room's well ventilated and the fire keeps a nice draught."

Four identical men walked in, they all looked to be about 45, clean shaven upright and muscular. Father was already sitting, and like Roman guards the four sons stood two either side of him. I didn't know whether to stand or sit.

"These are our muscles," Stephanie remarked in a sarcastic tone of voice. David, he works in the village occasionally."

I tried to rise and shake hands.

"No laddie, sit." Steph said.

"So what's this? Two new ars-holes in the clan?" David said and took his seat.

Stephanie continued the introduction. "This is Alistair, he also occasionally works in the village."

A broad smile spread across the man's face, he leaned on the table and beamed at me. "Glad to see you laddie. Here's my card. If you drop dead, give me a call. I'd love to be pootin' you away. We do a lovely spread."

"Yes thanks," I said taking his card. 'Alistair MaLean, Garston Undertakers Ltd.' Again I nodded and smiled.

"This is Ian, he's our head gardener."

Ian said nothing, just took his seat and selected one of the sandwiches. "Hi," I said softly.

"Finally we have Aulay, he is our head of internal affairs. Looks after our wonderful house."

He looked at me as if I'd just raped his grandmother. "If you're after one of our girls, you'd better be changin' your mind."

"Oh, right!"

Moments later the rest of the family arrived. Two of the women wheeled in a couple of dinner trolleys loaded with an array of wonderful looking food.

"This is my sister Flora, you've already met."

"Hi," I said politely.

She clapped her hands to her face and ran from the room. She seemed very upset about something.

"And this is my favourite sister Bonny."

Bonny curtsied. "Very pleased to meet you sirs."

For an older woman she had the sexiest smile. "Hi!" I managed to gasp.

'Pharrrrrrt'

"Father I do wish you would control your bodily functions at mealtime."

"Shut your gate, Stephanie."

Weepy Flora came rushing back into the room with a large bowl of jelly. If it didn't know better I would say she was simple minded. No one bursts into tears because they left the jelly in another room.

Stephanie stood up, kissed her cross and took command of the household. "Before we eat, we will bow our heads in thanks to the Lord for his generosity."

'Phaaaaaaaarrrrt-phart-ph'

"I am sure the Lord would rather we speak through our mouths Father. Dear Lord, we thank thee for this bountiful fare and pray thy forgiveness for Father's occasional eruptions. Amen."

"Auch, lassie you're a reet dilly," Father said. "The Good Lord made ars holes, he must know what they're for."

"That's enough of that talk. Thank you Father. We have guests."

Stephanie remained amazingly calm under fire, and came back with an answer every time. She ruled the family, even though Father was theoretically the boss. I still couldn't get over the four clones. After we'd started eating I asked Stephie: "Are they quads?"

"Quars? You mean quadruplets?

"Yes. Are they?"

"Ooo- noo, they're all different ages."

"So why don't you girls look alike?"

She gently patted her lips with a serviette, smiled and kissed her cross. "We believe when the boys were born, there was only one brain to go round, so they shared it. This gave them the exact same diet and consequently the same silly look. But as everything has its four sides so are they, 'tis the same coin, though it has four faces."

I don't know if she really believed that, or she was jerking my chain. Nobody argued. The meal had to be one of the best I'd ever had. The fire gave a friendly glow and crackle of burning logs. An amazing scene of peace, beauty and tranquillity, punctuated by the occasional Spitfire flying under the table.

The meal ended with a toast of home brewed wine, again by Stephie. She poured her wine and passed the bottle round the table. All eyes were on her awaiting the signal. Gracefully she stood up and raised her glass. "I would to toast our honoured free guests, and the long standing of Cromlet."

"Aye, our guests and Cromlet," the boys barked and downed the elixir.

It was the perfect ending to the perfect evening. Flora drank half her wine, slammed the glass down and rushed off weeping. It seemed all so romantic, unreal, out of this world. I could see why rich people came here. The McLeans were a perfect-living example of the Mad Hatter's tea party. They were so fascinatingly insane that even Newf was totally overshadowed, just Stephie stood out like a fairy princess. Sort of Snow-white and the seven dawks.

Stephie led us to the cellar of the clock tower. There the time vault opened exactly at six. The only way to the vault was through a maze of tunnels and doors, all locked. When at last we reached our destination, I was beginning to get a little hot under the collar. Only one door need be locked and we'd never get out. The money-room looked like Flora, poor woman. I just knew it was her room the moment we entered.

She had the only Bonsai Weeping Willow I've ever seen. The walls had sad Victorian drapes all over them in sweeping U patterns. A statue of a naked weeping woman. Three imitation frightened children huddled in a corner. Like some dreadful chasm controlled by the gods, the clock struck, a machine started and as if resisting temptation the huge unseen bolt withdrew slowly, squeaking and graunching in its metal housing.

I half-expected something from Mothra or Godzilla to walk out, but it was only a vault. Weepy Flora took my checks, rushed into the vault, and after a few moments rushed out with the cash. She gave it to me, pressed a button and burst into tears. A claxton sounded, and the huge door very slowly began closing.

The entire experience at Cromlet has become a major leaf in my life's diary. As I left I kissed Stephie's hand. I think she appreciated the gesture.

"So what yah think Newf?"

"I fink yous soft on 'er. I reckon we auta do Eddie's place."

I pulled the car to a halt outside the inn. "Sometimes, I think there's nothing between your ears Newf. Haven't you learned anything at all, today? And who the hell's Eddie?"

"We ain't gonna learn anyfing at Cromlet. I fink we should do Edward Cameron's place. It's nice and close."

7

Edward Cameron

Ellen beamed from ear to ear when I handed her the wad of
cash. "I knew I could trust a beautiful city man like yeh-sel.
Will you be stayin' on a wee?"

"Sure, well at least for today."

"Do you mean tonight?"

"Yes, I guess so?"

We did, we stayed another night. Newf wanted to 'do'
the lawyer's place, as he put it. I couldn't see risking a jail
sentence for nothing. The McLeans had to be squeaky clean.
No one could run a big house like that, a waxworks an' all, a
whole village, and get away with it for two hundred years.
Only an idiot like Newf would still believe in those dead guys
in the basement thing.

"I got an idea," I said as we sat at breakfast. "What if I
get Gran to fax a picture of Cloey Macalister, and we take it to
Cromlet and put a fright into the McLeans? What'd say?"

Newf smiled. "Now yous finkin' like a Sherlock.
While we's waitin' for the picture we'll do the lawyers. I fink
there's evidence, and loads of clues there."

"I remember Dagwood has a picture, and the one in
the passport. I'll get to it." I pulled out my cell and dialled. It
rang and rang. "I guess maybe Gran's out, it's around 1pm
there."

"Hallo!" Came a sleepy voice.

"Hi, Gran. Been having an afternoon siesta?"

"Oh, it's you, William. Have you any idea what time
it is?"

"Time you were up and at-em, Gran."

"I'll up-and-that-them, you when I lay my hands on
you. It' a little past three in the morning. Have you no sense of
decorum?"

"Oh! Gees! Well, sorry, Gran."

"Well what is you want?"

"I need a photo of Cloey Macalister."

"Oh very well, I'll just pop round with one."

"Ah, Gran. I'm sorry if I upset you. I added five hours, when I should have subtracted."

"Yes dear, I would suppose something that complicated would have been a little easier if you'd finished university. Now how do you expect I should get you this picture?"

"You've already got the picture in the passport, North borrowed, and Dagwood has one."

"Should I use Concord? Perhaps you have a landing field in mind?"

"Please don't be upset, Gran. We've been to Cromlet, met everybody, just need a little visual help, that's all."

"Very well, William. What number?"

"Oh, hang on a second." I Ran off looking for Ellen. She was in the bar. "Do you have a fax-machine?"

"Noo."

"Is there a fax machine in the village anywhere?"

She thought for a second. "Why?"

"I need to get a picture sent to me."

She exhaled deeply. "You could use the one at the church."

"Oh good. What's the number?" As she dictated the number from a small card kept behind the till I relayed it to Gran.

"Very well, William. I will send it within the hour." She hung up.

Great, at last I'd accomplished something. "How do I get into the church to get my picture?"

Ellen sucked her bottom lip for a few moments. "It's normally not open till Saturday, but I could maybe get the key today."

Man! What a civilization, only one fax machine, and that's locked up. She agreed to do whatever was possible while Newf and I explored the sights. There was only one sight we intended to explore, and that was the interior of the law office, just down the street.

"So when?" Newf nudged.

I looked at my watch, a mere half of eight. "Nothing moves in this town until ten. I figure we'll walk in, look around and walk out again."

"When?"

"Oh, come on, let's get started."

Trying to be as inconspicuous as possible, we sauntered down the street in the general direction of Edward Cameron's law office. The village streets were deserted, but who could be looking behind lace or net curtains. I leaned against the door and scanned the street as if enjoying the sight. "Can you open it, Newf, or should we try the back-door?"

"Nah, these people fink the back's where the break-ins always take place, it'll be too 'ard. The front door'll do nice." He pulled out his little book of tricks and began tickling the lock.

"What if' there's an alarm?" I whispered.

"I'll crack, push it in, an we'll walk away. If the alarm goes off, scarper."

Suddenly I didn't feel so good. My heart began to pound. What on earth were we doing, breaking in on a main street in broad daylight? And what for?

"I's open, le's walk."

With a sigh and feeling of being as prominent as an octopus in a teacup, I walked and whistled a Scottish tune. After a few seconds we crossed the street, took our time looking around, walked up the street, crossed again and meandered to the offices. Nothing, not a single person, dog or even squirrel appeared to notice us; we sure as hell didn't see any of them.

Inside I closed the door quietly. "Can you lock it Newf?"

"From the inside, sure. No sweat."

"Then lock it." Somehow I felt much better being trapped in an unlighted building. The windows had dark-heavy drapes, except the front windows, which were rooms unto themselves. "Now what?" I asked, as if Newf really knew.

"I fink we should start looking at some files and fings."

"What are we looking for? Signed confession of murder, maybe?"

"I don't fink you're in the spirit of it, Bill. Aint'cha got no interest left, no curiosity. Or are you moonin' after that Priscilla still?"

"No. I just don't see how this place has anything to do with Cromlet, and even if it did, we wouldn't know what was useful if we found it."

The main room we found ourselves in was huge, and filled with your typical office layout. Shoulder high removable barriers, desks, chairs and stuff. It had a look similar to any government office, except here there were no people, no coffee, or clicking line printers.

"You don't believe that anyfing is wrong, do you? You fink Dagwood is just an old git wiv no brain, don't yah?"

"Yes."

"Well, who cares? We's 'ere lets be snouty."

"Alright. What would be interesting?"

"Well, 'ow about 'oo owns Cromlet? Maybe the info's 'ere."

"Alright, let's start looking." I had no idea what I might be looking for, or where, in such a large room there would be any chance of finding it. I walked the aisles between the cordoned off office areas. There should have been fifty or more employees in a place like that. These were just subordinate offices, where the slogging occurs, the secrets, the real stuff would be in a hard walled room, that would be lockable.

Newf did his thing, slipped off somewhere while I reasoned things out like a real detective. I was on my second meandering, still having not made up my mind what to vandalize, when the door rattled. I looked over to see if it was Newf, but he was across the room looking at me. Instant panic; we both dived to our respectively nearest cover.

I crawled into one of the office areas and huddled under the desk. At least two people came into the building. "That bloody lock," one said to the other.

"It was-nay a problem when I locked up."

"Come on, let's get this over with, and gan alang hame."

They parked in a cubical just over from me. One of them picked up the phone. I heard him hammer a few buttons. "Hallo," he said in a deep voice. "This is John Edward Cameron."

Then unmistakably, phaaaarrrrtt!!! No one on Earth could zip a bum-rumble like father McLean

"Yes," he said. "Well, I've been up into the highlands. No. No." Pause. "I've arranged it. No, I went where the mobiles don't work. Very-well, I'll inform you next time." The phone slammed down. Another lengthy shirttail breeze and he said in a soft voice. "We'll have to do something aboot tha' man. I am-nay gooin to stay here and work, when there's nay a thing ta doo. Come."

The two eased up, footsteps paced the distance to the door. "This time make sure it's locked." The door slammed.

Gingerly I crept from my hiding place. Had it been night, we'd have been caught for sure. Neither of us could have gotten to the lights quick enough. "Newf, are you there," I half whispered.

He stood up and walked over to me. "You know oo that was?"

"Sure as hell do. It was the brown bugler. What was that call all about?"

"D' know. Let's find what we want and get out."

I would if I'd known what it was. At the far end of the large room seemed to be the only real door. I ambled down the aisles to it and tried the handle. Very encouraging. "Hay! Newf. Come open this one."

In moments he had the thing open. This looked far more promising. An office with a safe and filing cabinets. On the wall hung the law diploma, it too presented a bit of a mystery. Close examination revealed it was issued in 1919, making Father well over a hundred years old. "Did you hear the farter on the phone?" I asked.

Newf laughed. "Same guy from tea, eh?"

"Exactly. He said he was John Edward Cameron."

"Yeah, so?"

Did he look a hundred years old to you?"

"Narh." He looked where I pointed on the certificate. "Oh, wow."

"You see what I mean?"

'Maybe, they're vampires. You know, vampires live for ever."

"Yeah sure, and Gran's got fairies at the bottom of her garden."

"Really?"

"No, you dawk."

We set about the serious task of finding some incriminating evidence. I didn't think they were body snatchers, nevertheless something peculiar was happening at that beautiful castle. Newf sat on the floor and worked on the safe as I searched the records files. Some of the cases from the Glasgow assizes went back into the 1920's, mostly land claims and perimeter disputes.

"I don't understand all this," I said softly. "Father couldn't be that old."

"Quiet, I've almost got it." 'KLUNK'

"Is that it?"

The door squeaked on it old rusty hinges. "Yeah. We's in."

I kneeled down beside Newf and we began rifling through the contents. A box with a brand new diamond necklace, a bunch of old photographs, and a few old useless papers. Then I spotted it, almost a book in size. I took it out. "This is it."

"What?"

"It's the deeds to Cromlet castle." I took it over to the desk and sat down to study it. It was written in old-fashioned law language, "The party of the first part," sort of crap. "Well," I said looking up in surprise.

"What?"

"I think we've landed in wonderland."

"Oh come-on, Bill. What's it say?"

It says that the castle and grounds are the property of one, John Edward Cameron."

"So?"

"It also carries J. E. Cameron's signature and the date 1897. All this stuff about Alistair Mc'whatever. It's crap. Stephanie's been spinning us a load of old cod's wallop.

They're called cuckoos because they are. They don't own Cromlet, they stole it from John Edward Cameron."

"Well even Stephie's not that old."

"You're right Newf. Maybe she doesn't know. I would guess it's the farters father or grandfather who stole the place."

"So 'ow do they pay for it. The taxes must come to millions a year, and repairs?"

I shook my head. "Now I think we really have found a mystery to investigate. Poor Stephanie, I rather liked her. Let's do a little more looking there may be a clue or two as to how they obtain the money."

"Maybe they steal people's identity and drain their bank account. Just like Dagwood said. This is real exciting, ain't it, Bill?"

I sat down at the desk and stroked my chin in thought. Gran said, always think things through and try not to jump to conclusions. The obvious is not always as obvious as it seems. Gees, how I wished she was there, we could talk over the facts and come to some conclusion. "What d' you think, Newf?" I said softly.

"D' know. Why?"

"Well how could John Edward Cameron, be still alive? It was Father from Cromlet. Why such a big office place and no workers?"

Newf shrugged. "I fink they must be up to no good."

"Like dead people in the basement?"

Newf walked over and sat on the edge of the desk. "Dagwood said Mrs. Cloey Macalister was 'ere, 'e said she changed. I fink 'e should know."

"Dagwood's a nit-wit. Nothing around here makes any sense. Wax people, ancient jails, lawyers that don't exist, offices that do nothing. People just don't do these things unless there's money, drugs, or women involved. I mean Stephanie makes her own wine, the boys do the gardens and the girls do the housework. If they have so much money, why don't they hire staff?"

"I don't know," Newf said and unthinkingly slid a desk drawer open. "I fink, we 'ave to find 'ow they pays for everyfing. Maybe Ellen knows."

I pulled the folder from the desk drawer, that Newf just exposed. The file heading read, 'The Others.' Typical of everything in this area of Scotland it made less sense than the Mad Hatter's tea party. There were six names, each dated in chronological order, with address. 1975, Rhoda Holmes, London. 1983, James E. Burton, Peterborough. 1987, Christopher McWittie Glasgow. 1998, Ester J. Annison, Liverpool. 2000, Marion Brindle, Bristol. Then the one that just blew my mind when I read it. 2001, Cloey Macalister, Cambridge.

For several moments I just sat there holding the paper and stared at it. "We need a photocopy off these addresses," I said.

"There ain't nofin' 'ere that modern. What's it say?"

"They are the addresses of six people, including Cloey Macalister. I figure we should investigate these people and see for ourselves what the similarities are."

"Then what?"

"I think this is the first evidence we've found."

"Evidence of what, Bill?"

"Whatever crime they might have committed I feel sure these people will know the answer."

"We already know Cloey Macalister vanished. Maybe all the others did too."

"We don't know anything of the sort. We'll know more when Gran sends that photo. Come on, let's make some notes and get out of here."

As carefully as possible, we made our copies and exited the law offices. The sun made the world seem clean and worry free. A refreshing change from the dismal offices. Still the streets were deserted, not a single human or dog. Ellen sang merrily as she worked in the inn's kitchen. "Hallo," I yelled. "Anyone home?"

Newf and I slipped into the barroom and sat at a table. Ellen entered gaily, a magnificent smile on her face. "I have your picture," she announced and handed it to me.

It was a fairly low-resolution picture straight off the passport. It would do, you could easily recognize the woman. "Thank's," I said at long last.

"Are you the police?" Ellen asked.

"No, why?"

"Then why do you have that picture?"

"I'm looking for her."

"Then you are police."

"No. Actually we're private investigators."

Ellen pouted her lips for a few seconds. "Then why are you looking here for her?"

"This was the last place she was seen."

She shook her head slowly. "I dinna think so."

"Oh! Why?"

"She was here earlier. I remember her, though I dinna remember her name. She stayed at Cromlet, then caught the plane for home."

"How do you know she caught the plane?"

"Well, after her stay at the castle, she came here to the village, she had a Glasgow taxi. Said she was going to the airport and back to Canada. Wanted some memento to give to her butler."

"So why didn't she go to a store?"

"I have the only place in toon that sells genuine island whisky."

"What do you know about John Edward Cameron?"

Ellen smiled and said: "There isnay such a person. Cromlet owns this place, and they own the law office too. Cameron died many years ago."

"Why is it such a large place and no one works there?"

"Ooch! Yah do ask peculiar questions. Cameron used to operate the Pools Office."

"What?"

"Oo, man d'yeah no ken the pools?"

"No."

"People buy tickets and win lots of money."

"Oh, you mean the lottery?"

"Sort of like. Anyhow the pools office was the only work in the village. 135 people used to work there, checking and making the payout slips. Then they took the work to Glasgow. The village all but died, most of the houses are empty and Cromlet pays to keep them looking good."

"So the village really does belong to the castle?"

"The whole village is built on Cromlet land, 'tis all part of the estate."

"So how do they make the money to keep this place going?"

"You should have asked the old wind-bag questions when you were there."

"Don't you know?"

"Ooo, yeas. When Eleanor McDuff died she left something like ten million trust for the estate. Her husband John Garston, is the executor, runs it from the law office."

"Who's John Garston?"

"The old fart from Cromlet, they call him father."

"Is he the father?"

"Ooo yes. The children are all from Eleanor McDuff."

"I had the impression you were either afraid or nervous of the Cromlet people when I first came here."

She sighed a deep sigh. "Meall, the youngest of the eight children. She's a, well she's a man-eater. I was afraid she'd try to take you away from me."

"What? How do you mean?"

"It's difficult to get a nice young guest, with her in the county."

"I don't think I saw her. There were three others."

"Ooo, they're of no account. Meall is the man-eater."

Newf was shocked. I could tell he'd taken what she said literally. "Newf," I said. "A man-eater doesn't really eat men."

"Oh! Fank goodness. I fort she was a Tod'er. Don't want to brush wiv any Tod'er again."

"What's he mean?"

"Oh don't worry about it Ellen. It was our last case, they actually did eat people."

I borrowed a pair of scissors and trimmed the picture of Cloey Macalister then put it in my wallet. My intention was simply to ask Stephanie if she recognized the woman. I paid my bill and we set out on the last leg of our holiday. First stop Cromlet, then Glasgow airport and home. Priscilla's a waste of space, and I don't know anyone else.

Clouds rolled over the hills and scurried across the lake, the sky and ground a great contrast. The inclement conditions gave Cromlet Castle an even more dramatic and beautiful look. The stark white walls, and blue roof against the deep velvet thunderclouds. A rainbow would have completed the picture. Parking the car I noticed the tents and stuff from the archaeologist people had been removed.

Just my luck, weepy Flora came running to greet us. She bowed and scraped for a few seconds. "Are you here to stay?" she asked.

"No." I put my hand in my pocket and removed the picture of Cloey. "Do you recognize this lady?"

Flora clapped her hands to her face, shrieked and fled back into the house. Moments later serene and ever composed Stephanie glided from a door and into the foyer. "Good-day gentlemen?"

"Hi. We are on our way back to Canada. I just wanted to stop and say good-by. I love your castle."

She smiled sweetly and kissed her cross. "Mr. Reyner, you are forever welcome."

"I wondered if you recognize this picture," I said and showed her the print.

She is either the finest actress, or honestly had nothing to hide. Taking the photocopy, she smiled and said. "Not a very complimentary reproduction. I don't remember her last name, it's Miss Cloey. Why do you have this picture of her?"

"Just wanted to make sure I had the right lady."

"Right lady?"

"Yeah, she came here for a holiday, then vanished. No one's seen her since."

Stephanie smiled, kissed her cross then looked me directly in the eyes. "Then how did she show you a pamphlet of Cromlet?"

My blood froze for a moment, caught in my own net. My brain went into fast forward looking for an explanation. Steph glared at me awaiting the jewel of all knowledge. "I lied," I said slowly and turned my face away.

"Aye. I ken."

"She didn't actually show me-."

Newf interrupted. "'E nicked it. Before she came. Saw it on 'er table and nicked it."

Stephanie laughed a hearty laugh, grabbed my hands and pulled me toward the stair room. "Come," she said giggling. "Let's see if Father remembers her."

8

The Big City

I'm sure Newf felt that we were about to be eaten or otherwise destroyed. However Father seemed helpful and as impolite as usual. "I showed the picture of Cloey Macalister to Flora," I said. "She fled like a frightened rabbit."

Father scowled, let rip with a thunderous rearguard, attack and said: "The girl's a loony. Has a thing aboot crying. Leave her alone."

Somehow I felt bad about the McLeans of Cromlet, sorry for them. They all worked hard, and under difficult circumstances. As we drove toward Glasgow I said: "You-know, Newf. I feel sorry for them. I think I'll send Miss Stephanie a check for a couple of thousand, what yah think?"

"I fink yous soft in the 'ead. If yous gonna give them money, why don't we stay there a while."

"So you're not afraid of them any more?"

"Nah. I fink they's just unlucky, loosing the pools fing an' all. You should 'ave their bank accounts investigated, see if they's really broke."

"Alright, I tell you what. Let's not go home just yet. We'll get an hotel in Glasgow and do a little digging."

"In what?"

"One of the people on that list we found in the law office comes from Glasgow, why not look them up? Ask a few questions, and then decide what to do from there."

"What about your Gran?"

"What about her?"

"She'll be expecting you."

"Nah. I'll phone and explain the delay. She won't mind."

It was settled, a stay in the hustling-bustling city of Glasgow. I figured it would be different and exciting, something new for the pair of us. The city turned out to be larger than I had anticipated. We got thoroughly lost, good job we weren't taking a plane, couldn't find the airport either. Eventually we found a respectable hotel on Bruce Street.

The Bannach Hotel, a very nice Victorian place with a lobby like a railway station. The receptionist was snoring, hiding just below the tall counter. I banged the bell several times. The snoring stopped and a middle-aged undertaker with an enormous nose peered over the countertop. "Yes," he said very nasally.

"Have any rooms?"

He smiled. "Would sir like to sign the register?" He spun the book round and pointed. "Single or double, sir?"

"One room, two beds. Do you have a suite with two bedrooms?"

"No sir."

"Then one room with two bed's will be fine."

"How long, sir?"

"I don't know one or two days. I'll let you know."

He barked an order into the office behind him and another man arrived. "1234," he growled and handed me the key. "I'll need your credit card sir."

"Sure."

When all arrangements were finally complete the other undertaker carried my only suitcase to the elevator. We all entered and crawled to the twelfth floor. The room was really nice, thick carpets, two double beds, a TV, a view of the dockyards. "Thanks," I said and gave the man a pound coin.

He grunted and walked to the door. "Dining-room opens between. 10am and 10pm. Room service till midnight."

"Thanks."

Newf's eyes sparkled with joy. "I like this 'otel. I like this town. What'll we do nah?"

"Well," I said dropping down onto one of the beds. "I think we'll take a look at the city, then try find this Christopher McWittie." I pulled out the slip of paper and read it aloud. "Mr. Christopher McWittie, the Ferns, Glen Roy Heights."

"'Ow will we find the place, then?"

"Easy, we'll take a taxi and I'll run the GPS. That way we'll know where we are at all times."

"When?"

I thought about it for a minute. "Well, today we'll visit the museum, tomorrow first thing we'll hit the trail."

I marked the position of the hotel, called a taxi and we were off on our first adventure in Glasgow. I didn't want to drive, the English are mad, but the Scotts are crazy. Cars whizzing all over the place, and a million signs, you just don't have time to read them all.

The museum turned out to be a lot bigger than I had expected. A huge Georgian edifice with giant Doric pillars. It looked like a king sized version of Grant's tomb. The amazing thing, especially for Scotland, the entrance was free. Unlike Gran, I'm not really into museums. I enjoyed it, and at least will have something to tell her when I get home.

Back at the hotel I phoned Gran and gave her the news. This time I got the timing right. It was only just gone five in the evening in Canada. Gran seemed pleased that I at last was using my brain. She always said my brain was in my muscles. I can't think why.

Bright and early, and after a fine Scottish breakfast, we called a cab and set out to find Mr. C. McWittie. Man Glasgow is a big city. The Glen Roy Heights turned out to be several miles out of the city toward the town of Greenock. I can see why they called it the heights, great cliffs and stuff. At last the taxi stopped outside the gates to a large estate. They were firmly closed.

"Yah, wantin' in?" The taxi driver asked.

"No, I just wanted to see the place. You can take us back to the hotel, please. Have you any idea who lives at this place?"

"No. Back to the hotel it is?"

I marked the spot on the GPS. We arrived back at the hotel around noon. I had no idea how far away Glen Roy Heights was. The taxi-man made enough out of me to retire. After an excellent lunch I showed Newf how to navigate with the GPS. I set the range to two kilometres. We gassed-up and set out. You have no idea how frightening it is to drive in the mad city of Glasgow with a dim-witted navigator.

With sweat soaked collar we found the road to Greenock, and left the hustle and bustle of the big city behind.

Once Newf got the idea of how to use the GPS we got along fine, and soon found the gates to the estate. I jumped out and pressed the intercom.

"Hallo," came a thin metallic voice.

"Hi! I'm William Reyner, I would like to speak with Mr. Christopher McWittie."

"Are you joking, came the male-metallic voice?"

"No. I just want to speak with him."

"Why?"

"I... er... I-. Could I come to the house please?"

"Clunk," an electric motor started, the gate swung open. Quickly I jumped back in the car and drove through the gateway, it closed behind us. A long-winding drive led to a castle-like house. I parked near the huge front door where a man in a dark suit awaited me. Even before the car stopped the man came over. "Hi!" I said weakly, and climbed from the vehicle.

"Good day, sir. Lord Bennington will receive you in the drawing-room." The doorman walked us to a large room. For a rich man's house it was rather barren, not a bit like Cromlet. A youngish guy in his thirties, tall and with ample dark hair marched into the room. He wore riding breaches and carried a crop.

"Good afternoon, sir," I said.

He smiled, and in a very English accent said: "What's all this about?"

"Sir, I just wanted to speak with Mr. McWittie."

"Yes, that much I know. Why?"

"Why? Well I've just come from Cromlet. I wanted to know if Mr. McWittie enjoyed his stay."

The tall gentleman smiled and slapped his leg with the riding crop. "This is a joke isn't it? Who put you up to it?"

"No sir."

"I purchased this house at the dissolution of Mr. McWitties estate, when he died in 1988. Thirteen years ago. Since then I've lived here."

"I had no idea," I said. "I'm sorry to have troubled you. What happened to him?"

"I'm sorry you came on a wild goose chase, Mr. er-."

"Reyner."

"Yes. Mr. Reyner. Very sorry." He pulled out his wallet and extracted a card. These people may be able to help you."

I looked at the business card. "Justin, and Justin attorneys at law." I grinned weakly. "Thank you sir."

Moments later Newf and I were on our way back to Glasgow. "So what do you think, Newf?"

"I fink they's all dead. The whole list of 'em."

"I'm beginning to think your right. I just find it hard to believe that Stephanie is one of the bad guys."

"So we' gonna see these lawyers?"

"Sure, tomorrow. Let's just relax for now. This driving's reducing me to a sweaty dishrag. I should let you drive."

"Sure, great."

"Yeah, in a pigs eye."

The food at the Banoch hotel tasted original, and I do mean original. Like the same stuff they served when the place opened. It sure made me miss Gran's cooking. After a well-cooked breakfast we set out on our second adventure in the big city of Glasgow. I called the number on the card and made an appointment with one or other of the lawyers. They managed to squeeze us in at noon.

I can tell you, I don't like Glasgow. The local residents drive like they're on the speedway, pedestrians are a free-for-all target. Twice I almost lost Newf to ambitious drivers. And parking, man! Parking is a form of Russian roulette. I think they have one-meter maid per parking meter. If you don't leap out and put the money in within five seconds, you'll be presented with a ticket.

Surprisingly the law office turned out to be an old Georgian tenement block. Very clean and spacious, but old. Our footsteps echoed in the hollow edifice as we walked to the lady at the desk. "Good morning, sirs," she said brightly and looking like a well-dressed store dummy.

"Hi. We have an appointment for noon."

"Mr. Reyner?"

"That's right."

"Mr. Justin's just in. Come this way please." She led us through a door tall enough for Andre' the Giant.

Another hollow room. I got the impression the decor had been deliberately designed to make you feel small. The big man sat at his desk way over in the distance.

"Mr. Reyner and friend," she announced and left, closing the huge door with a boom that resounded through the building.

The small squinty-eyed little man remained seated and beckoned us over. "You have five minutes, then it's my lunch."

I pulled the card from my pocket. "Lord Bennington said you'd be able to help me."

"And your question is?" He adjusted his wire frame spectacles.

"What happened to Mr. Christopher McWittie?"

He took his glasses off, carefully wiped them with his fresh-white handkerchief. "What happened? He died."

"No I mean, well, could you elaborate?"

"Elaborate! He died, they buried him, end of story."

I had the urge to walk round his rosewood desk and smash him one in the face. "McWittie was rich, what happened to his estate? Where is it now?"

He replaced his spectacles and glared at me. "Is there a problem with the will?"

"I need to know."

"The full answer could be very expensive."

"Money is no object." I think I must have pushed the right button.

Justin sat up, smiled, readjusted his glasses and put out his hand for a shake. "Sorry I can't rise to greet you. Motorcar accident, you see. My fee is fifty pounds per hour for consultation."

"No problem."

"Please sit Mr. Reyner. What exactly do you need to know?"

"I'm investigating the disappearance of a woman. I need to know what happened to McWittie and all his money, there could be a connection."

"I handled the estate for Lord Bennington, the purchase and land transfer. I actually know nothing of this Mr. McWittie, though I could look up the probate records."

"Great. When?"

"Speed is expensive, Mr. Reyner."

I leaned forward and placed two hundred pounds cash on his desk. "Will this do for a start?"

Cash money had exactly the power I thought it may have. His eyes watered as he glared at the love of his life, then picked it up. "I'll count it later. What exactly do you want to know?"

"We want all the details of McWittie's death, and what happened to his estate."

"Yes, yes." He grinned a gleeful grin. "I'll have what you require, next week. Come see me in one week."

"Tomorrow or no deal?"

His expression changed to one of sadness and distress. "I canno' do it that quick."

"Sorry. I'll have to find someone who can."

"Very well. I'll try, but it'll cost you."

It was my turn to smile. "We'll be back tomorrow."

On the way out we made an appointment with his secretary. I felt good, at last we may be getting somewhere. I just wished Gran was there. I needed someone intelligent to talk to. Newf usually had stupid ideas, way out on the left field. I guess Glasgow is okay if you know the place, I continually got lost and the people seemed too busy to help a stranded stranger.

Fighting one-way streets, insane traffic and pedestrians who didn't understand the use of sidewalks, we eventually found our way back to the hotel. I gave Newf fifty pounds and he skipped out to have a look at the town. I felt exhausted and didn't want any part of it. I phoned Gran at around three in the afternoon.

"Hi! Gran. Just thought I'd better make a report."

"Did you get the picture alright?"

'Sure, Gran. We went to McWittie's place, he vanished too."

"You'll have to explain, William. I do not know who he is."

"Oh! Well we found a list of names, and Cloey Macalister was the last on the list. McWittie was another. He

looks to have been very rich, died. I'm checking into his estate
to see where the money went."

"Excellent thinking, William. How's Priscilla?"

"Don't want to talk about it."

"Oh! I see. How's young North?"

"He's okay, out on the town at the moment. I'll let
you know when we get some information. I think the
McLean's of Cromlet are innocent, but old man Edward
Cameron may have a lot to answer for. It was in his office we
found the list."

"Well you be careful, William. Stay away from fast
women and loaded guns."

"Sure, Gran. Can you look up the family Garston?
They live on an island somewhere. I think they own it."

"What is the connection?"

"They're supposed to be the people who actually took
Cromlet in the 1800's. I think they may be the bad seed, but I
can't prove anything at the moment."

Gran's a real smart old girl, I figure she'd go see some
of her library cronies and come up trumps. She usually did. I
felt a lot better just talking to her. It's sort of reassuring
knowing that someone else with a brain is looking into the
same things. She shouldn't have mentioned Priscilla, though.

Our appointment had been set for four o'clock. Not
wishing to endanger anyone's life, we took a taxi from the
hotel and arrived several minutes early. The secretary-
receptionist said nothing, she pointed to the door. Newf and I
entered together. Justin sat at his desk a broad smile on his
silly face.

"Good afternoon, gentlemen. Please to take a seat."

We sat. "Did you get anything?" I said trying to be
authoritative.

"Aye, I certainly did. Your bill will be five hundred
pounds. I had to grease a few palms."

"Well?"

"Could I be seeing the colour of your money, sir?"

I pulled out my pocketbook, and peeled off two
traveller's checks. "I only have Thomas Cook on me."

He leaned forward and gloated over the two checks, then grasped them firmly and read for a few seconds. "Please sign them."

I did and sighed.

"Thank you, now for your details." He pulled a buff envelope out of his drawer and pushed it across the desk to me. "Evidence," he said. There seems to be no problem with the estate. I checked with the findings of the probate court and with the executor. All seem to be well within the law. I'm thinking that maybe there would be a little, jiggery-pokery. None was evident."

I took the envelope and peered inside. There were several pieces of paper, one with legal-verbal diarrhoea. "So in short, what happened?"

"It would seem that Mr. Christopher McWittie died of natural causes in 1987. The funeral was a private affair, there being no living relatives."

"So what happened to the estate?"

"All property was to be sold off, the taxes paid, and the remaining millions bequeathed to the castle of Cromlet estate."

I suppose it was no shock, after all we found the name in the law office owned by the Cromlet estate. "How much was it?"

"Well, it's difficult to say. As you'll see it's listed in sale value item by item. The executor Mr. Edward Cameron, never totalled them up. At a quick guess I'd say ten or twelve million pounds, in cash money."

"John Edward Cameron, was the executor?"

"Aye, indeed he was. You know the gentleman?"

"Yeah. I would have thought there'd be some conflict of interest. He owns Cromlet."

"Noo. As you will see in the documentation, Cromlet is owned by the Garston family, and they live on Drumvanich Isle. Edward Cameron lives at a place called Pitcolver. 'Tis a wee village."

"Yeah thanks."

Newf and I left with no further conversation. I could see by the expression on Newf's face he had come to the same conclusion as myself. Not to give too much information to Justin, we left with the envelope and a thank you.

"I fink we's in trouble," Newf said as we climbed in a taxi for home.

"Why?"

"Didn't you 'ear what that twit Justin said?"

"Go on tell me."

"'E said 'e checked wiv the executor of the estate."

"Well of course he did."

"An' oo's the executor?"

"What are you getting at Newf?"

"Blimey Bill, ain't you got no brain? Cameron's the executor. An' 'e knows us."

I knew that, Newf's an old woman. "So?"

"Well, won't 'e sort of get upset cuz we's checking up on 'im?"

"Nah. He might blow a few extra farts, but why should it bother him? I think we're wasting our time. There's nothing shady about Cromlet."

"I fink if you walked on broken glass, you'd spend four days wondering why you's got sore feet. They done McWittie just like they done Cloey Macalister. Uverwize why would she be on the same list?"

"We'll go home tomorrow, Newf. There's no mystery here that needs solving. I'll call Gran tonight, and let her know we're coming home."

"So why did this geezer leave all 'is money to a bunch of weirdoes?"

"On the same thinking, Newf, why hasn't Cloey given all her money away? I think you're just trying to make a mystery out of nothing. I like Cromlet. We'll take a holiday there next year. I reckon that'd be great fun. Now shut up, you cost me too much money solving non-mysteries."

Poor Newf sulked for the rest of the evening. I'm not sure whether it was because we were going home, or because there was no mystery to solve. I set my alarm watch for 3am and settled in for a serene and refreshing sleep. Newf had the awful habit of striking a true chord. Although she may be a lot older than me, I really did like Stephanie. She seemed sweet, clean and honest. An exciting and deeply religious woman.

The alarm went off; at first I thought it was a passing fire engine. As my consciousness returned I realized what had happened. The cell phone was close, though at first my head was fuzzy and my eyes blurred. I put the bedside lamp on and sat up. Gees, I dialled and the phone rang and rang, eventually a familiar voice answered.

"Hello?"

"Hi, Gran, I'm just calling to let you know we'll be coming home today."

"You do pick the most inopportune times to phone, William."

"Sorry, Gran. We investigated the McWittie thing, no problem there at all. Looks like we're barking up the wrong tree."

"What about the picture, was it useful?"

"Oh, that. Sure. Cloey was at the castle, the real Cloey that is."

"Then the woman at Donjon is an impostor?"

"Err! Well, I guess so."

"Oh, dear, William. I do wish you would use your intellect. At what point in time do you think this impostor could have become Miss Cloey?"

"I don't know, Gran. What do you want me to do?"

"Firstly, look into her journey, start at the Castle and try to determine where the swap took place. If she took a taxi, find the driver. Use your head, William."

"So you think there is a mystery, Gran?"

She sighed. "I checked into this family Garston, they're a bad lot. Two have been hanged for murder, the last in 1945. Since then they have had three jailed for various crimes, including fraud and attempted murder."

9

A Brush with Death

As always Gran had it right to order. While in Scotland we should check what happened to Cloey Macalister. Newf woke up cheerful and full of vigour, I felt a little under the weather. "We're not going home," I said to his delight.

"Great, why?"

"I phoned Gran in the night. She said we should find out what happened to Cloey. Follow her trail from Cromlet until she vanished."

"Bart-time we did some detectiving. What's first?"

"Breakfast, then we'll drive back to... to-, erm. I think we'll see Ellen first at the inn."

"Great." His eyes sparkled like a child's.

After another stodgy all Scottish breakfast, we paid up, fuelled up and set out on the adventure. Finding the way back to Pitcolver was a breeze using the GPS. We both looked forward to some palatable food, salted watery oats should only be given to cattle. Rapidly the scenery changed from the hurly-burly of the concrete jungle to rolling hills and trees.

No one could have shown greater surprise, when we walked into the inn, Ellen fair exploded with excitement and enthusiasm. "Have yeh come back to stay a wee?"

I shook my head. "No, well just a very short stay."

"Is it you've forgotten something?"

"No, we just couldn't leave Scotland without one more fine meal. Are we in time for lunch?"

She brushed her hair excitedly with one hand. "It'll take time. What would you be liking?"

"I'll leave it up to you. You're the finest cook in the Highlands."

She blushed. "I'll be honoured. Will you be staying the night?"

"No," I said with a sigh. "We have to leave as soon a possible."

"No we don't" Newf said and poked me in the ribs. "We could stay one night, couldn't we, Bill?"

"Sure, we are on holiday after all." I didn't really want to stop, because I felt uneasy at being close to Edward Cameron. I suddenly remembered someone telling me that his real name was Garston.

We had a pint of fine English beer each then went for a stroll in the village. I figured I'd question Ellen at the lunch table. I guess it was around three when we finally sat for the meal. She had done us proud with some strange doodad like bag of cooked various meats and stuff. Vegetables and a soup. "What's the stuff in the bag?" I asked.

"Ooh, its a store-bought mini haggis. Something quick."

"It's great, wonderful. Did I tell you we drove all the way here from Glasgow just to get some real food?"

"I think you're buttering me up," she fluttered her eyelashes. "Is there anything else you'll be wanting?"

"I... er. Well, remember that woman, Cloey Macalister, the one in the picture on the fax?"

"Aye."

"How did she leave here?"

"I told you last time, she left in a taxi."

"You're a wonderful cook. I just love the meals here. Did she go back to Cromlet, or to Glasgow?"

"Neither, she went directly to Prestwick, for the flight home. Why are you asking all these questions?"

"Oh, I just need to know. I'm still looking for her. You don't happen to remember what taxi she used?"

"Of course I do. She had a Blue, from Glasgow."

"You're wonderful, Ellen. Thanks."

We'd booked out of our hotel in Glasgow, so we figured we'd may as well stay the night in Pitcolver. Ellen was delighted, and immediately brightened up. You could see the change in her face when I told her.

Breakfast was bright and early. Ellen hummed some Scottish tune. "I haven't seen any other guests." I said.

She smiled, flashing those beautiful white teeth. "You will'nay."

"Why?"

"There aren't any except you."

"So how do you live?"

"The inn belongs to Cromlet, I only look after it. We get enough visitors to pay a living."

I felt really sorry for her. What an awful way to live. "Where's Prestwick?"

"Ooo, Prestwick is the international airport. About twenty to thirty miles the other side o' Glasgow."

It's funny how things change, like I didn't think much of Pitcolver when we first arrived, yet now, it seemed like home. I could easily enjoy living there. As we approached the city of Glasgow the traffic became heavier. We stopped at a small plaza and examined a phone book. It quickly revealed the number of the Blue Cabs. I called one; it arrived only a few moments later. As I climbed in, Newf said: "I fink I'll 'ang around 'ere, till you gets back."

"Why?"

"I'd like to check some of the shops out. You don't need me."

"Alright."

"Where to?" the taxi driver asked.

"I'd like you to take me to your headquarters please."

I thought he was going to give me an argument, but, no. He drove off with out another question. I've no idea where headquarters was. We arrived in a large courtyard with a garage at one end. Several cabs were parked around and some in various states of dismemberment.

"Office is over there," the driver said pointing.

"Wait for me, keep the meter running."

"Alright, sir."

The office was a lean-to addition on the garage. Inside seemed very business-like. The radio dispatch had two girls and another two girls writing at desks. I walked up to one of the writers. "Excuse me, I wonder if you can help me?"

"What?"

"I... er... I would like to know if one of your men picked up a lady at Cromlet."

She stopped doing whatever, and looked me straight in the face. "We run 150 taxis, and do thousands of pickups every day, and you want to know if we picked up someone at Cromlet?"

"Yeah, please."

She shook her head. "I don't have time to play silly games, Mr. We're running a business, not a library."

"I'll pay well for the answer." I pulled out my wallet and peeled off a couple of ten pound notes.

Her attitude changed. "Well, sir. I'd love to help you, but it would take days going through the records. Each cab reports its call, so it would be in the file. I don't have time to find it, now."

"I don't have days, though I do have money."

She smiled. "Alright, come back after lunch, I'll see what can be done on my break."

"Thanks a lot. I'll pay well for the information."

The cab still awaited my return. The driver stood beside his vehicle smoking. As soon as he saw me he tossed the cigarette and climbed in. "Where to?"

"Back to the shopping plaza where you picked me up."

I paid the guy, tipped him and walked back to my car. Newf was nowhere to be seen. The car had heated up in the sunlight; I started the engine and turned on the air-conditioning. The city didn't seem so hurly-burly from the quiet and comfort of my vehicle. After a few minutes a cop came and knocked on the window.

I opened it: "Hi, what can I do for you?" I said politely.

"Please step out of the car sir."

I did. A second cop leaned in and turned off the engine. "Mr. Reyner?" Said the first.

"Yeah."

"Please come with us." It wasn't really a request. A third cop stood behind me.

"What's going on?" I asked feeling like I was trapped.

"You'll come to the station and answer a few questions. Won't you sir?"

"About what?"

"This way Mr. Reyner."

A police van suddenly pulled up, you'd think I was number one on the most wanted list. They put me in the back and locked the door. At the station, three of them escorted me into the interview room. A plainclothes cop and two uniformed remained in the room.

"Sit," said plainclothes.

I sat, and the uniform turned on the tape. "Ten thirty-five. DI McIntyre and constable Moodie interviewing Mr. Reyner."

Every one except the cop at the door sat. Detective Inspector McIntyre glared at me and said nothing. If he was trying to make me feel uncomfortable, he was succeeding "So what d' you want?" I asked.

He licked his lips slowly and deliberately, his eyes searching me. Still he said nothing.

The uncomfortable feeling slowly spread throughout my body as if there were bugs crawling through me. "Do I need a lawyer?" I asked.

He smiled. "What have you done?"

"I haven't done anything. Why am I here?"

"Where were you last night?"

A sudden rush of cold swept over me. "Not Ellen?" I gasped.

"Where were you?"

"I was at Pitcolver."

He smiled and nodded approval. "Pitcolver's almost a hundred kilometres from here. What time did you arrive in Glasgow?"

"Early. I didn't look at my watch. I went to the Blue cab office straight away. You can ask the girl there. So what have I supposed to have done?"

"When did you last see Meall McLean?"

"Who?"

"Come now. We know you were at Cromlet looking for a woman. We think you found her."

I began to feel a little hot under the collar. "Meall's not at Cromlet she's away somewhere. Ask Stephanie, she knows."

The inspector leaned forward. "I know, you know, now why don't you just tell us so that the tape will know."

"You're, nuts. I've been looking for Cloey Macalister, she disappeared on her way to Canada."

"We have a report that you and your buddy, were looking for Meall McLean. Our sources say you found her. We want to know where you put the body. And where's the friend of yours?"

I looked at my watch. "You're barking up the wrong tree. I'm investigating a missing woman alright. Cloey Macalister. I figure your Meall person is the woman that replaced her. She's not missing; she lives at Donjon towers in Cambridge, Canada. I'm trying to find out how the swap occurred, and where."

"Where were you last night?"

"Pitcolver. We stayed at the Cuckoo inn. Just check. Ellen will tell you."

How did you come to be in Glasgow this morning?"

"We drove."

"It's a hundred kilometres."

"So we started early, is there a law against that?"

What were you doing at Glen Roy Heights?"

"I went to see Lord Bennington. He cleared up a couple of small questions for me. Here," I pulled out my wallet and removed the card. "This is the lawyer I went to see, Justin and Justin. If you don't believe me call him."

At that moment another cop came into the room, he beckoned Inspector McIntyre with his finger. For a moment the two conferred in whispers. The inspector walked back to the table and raising his voice said: "Interview with Mr. Reyner terminated at 12:55am." He turned to me and smiled. "You can go. I would suggest you don't leave Glasgow without informing us first. Is that clear?"

I shrugged. "Got it wrong again, eh?"

Calling a taxi, I realized there was a problem or two. Newf was lost, and I had to go to the Blue Cab offices to get the information. I wondered if the cops would be following me about. Sure wish Gran was here. She always knew what to do. The cab arrived and took me to the Blue Cab offices. The same young woman smiled when she saw me.

"Did you get anything?" I asked.

"It's going to cost you."

"Sure, everything costs somebody."

"The driver was William Allen." She handed me a piece of paper. "That's his address. Now about my fifty pounds."

I peeled off a few notes and handed them to her. "It's nice doing business with an honest person. When's this guy on duty?"

"He's on his two off. You're lucky. Do you know there has only been one ride to Cromlet this year?"

Now I had a double problem. Should I find Newf, or should I see this William Allen? On top of that I was tired and hungry. I made the decision to go to the Banoch Hotel on Bruce Street. I figured that may solve several problems in one shot. First I had to get my car.

They recognized me at the hotel and gave me the same room. As soon as I got settled in I phoned Newf's cell with mine. After three rings it was answered by a grunt.

"Hi Newf, where are you?"

'Click,' the phone went dead as the receiver was switched off. It didn't make any sense. I resolved to go see this taxi driver. Again not wanting to become a traffic statistic I took a cab. Oh how I wished I could taste Gran's tea and listen to her solve the quandary I was getting deeper and deeper into. I'd lost Newf and had a strange brush with cops; all in all I'd learned nothing.

William Allen's house looked like an old Victorian tenement, a block of three-story houses as long as the street. Number six Benton Row. I knocked. After a few moments a woman opened the door. She was wearing an apron and had her hair in curlers, a cigarette hanging from her lips. "Yeah?"

"I'm looking for William Allen."

"Who ain't?" She slammed the door.

I knocked again, this time using the brass knocker. Eventually she opened the door again, just standing there glaring at me. "I need some information," I said.

"Bill ain't here. Go away."

"I owe him some money," I said knowing that cash seemed to have a serious effect on people in this town.

"That's different," she said then screamed at the top of her voice. "Bill, there's a geezer here to see you."

She walked inside and a elderly man came to the door. He was tall thin and almost toothless. "What?" he snapped.

"I just want to ask you a couple of questions," I said pulling out my wallet. He watched with interest as I removed a five-pound note. "I wondered if you were the driver who picked up a woman at Cromlet castle, earlier this year."

"Can't remember."

"Have you ever been to Cromlet?"

"Can't remember."

I put the money back in my wallet. "I know it was you, I just need to ask a question."

"Fer, five I can't remember."

"So how much does it take for you regain your memory?"

He smiled. "Well, how much is it worth to you?"

"Twenty-five."

"Alright, I think I remember. Yes I do remember. I did go to Cromlet."

I gave him the twenty-five pounds. "Where did you take the woman you picked up?"

"Can't remember."

"I thought you said twenty-five would give you recollection."

"Some; you know, the old brain goes numb real quick."

I sighed aloud. "Alright. Ten more."

"Nah, twenty five a question."

"I'll tell you what. If I like the answers I'll pay you thirty more pounds, if I don't like the answers I'll beat the living shit out of you. How does that sound?" He tried to slam the door, but I jammed my foot into it and grabbed his collar. "Is every Scotsman a bloody thief?" I growled.

"Nah, but you bleedin' yanks think you own the bleedin' world. Flashin' all that money. Piss off back to America."

"Listen porridge breath, tell me where you took that woman or I'll do you an injury."

"I took the old bag to the Ferns, Glen Roy Heights."

At that moment the lights went out all over the world. The darkness slowly turned to a miserable grey wet mist. My ears ringing like a peal of church bells and a headache beyond belief. Disoriented, cold, wet, and confused, I sat up. There were streetlights in the distance. At first I couldn't stand, every time I tried the world seemed to spin and I fell over again. It's funny how important it is to stand up. With everything hurting to the nth degree I still had to stand up. My collar and right shoulder were caked in blood, though I couldn't tell where it came from. My first thoughts were for Newf. Where could he be? I should never have left him. My wallet had gone, all my papers including my passport and two thousand pounds in traveller's checks, and more than five hundred in cash.

The light of the street in the distance acted like a candle to a moth. I don't know how long it took me to stagger there. At last I leaned against a street lamp, exhausted and pained from head to toe. "Where the hell am I?"

It was night, not even a light in any of the houses. Gran once told me that the numbers on the houses always got lower as you approach town centre. Using that maxim I began staggering in a direction that diminished the address numbers. The street ended at a 'T' junction. I did the same thing, after a while I fell down and could not get up. I think I must have fainted.

A kindly Scottish voice said: "You'll be alright the-noo, laddie. You relax and breathe deeply."

I looked into his eyes. I could see he was a good person. They loaded me into the ambulance and rushed off with the sirens blearing. It was daylight, the comforting blanket felt good. I think they must have given me a shot of something. I felt totally at peace with the world. The ringing in my ears had ceased. I could smell Gran's cooking.

When I next opened my eyes, the world looked clean, sterile and regimented. Newf sat on a chair beside me. "Well, welcome back," he said.

"Back, where have I been?" I tried to sit up, but I couldn't.

"You just lay there, Bill everyfing's gonna be alright now. I told Mrs. H. She weren't none too 'appy, eiver."

"What happened?"

"You cloff-'ed, you got mugged."

It all came flooding back to me. "Where's the car?"

"It's at the 'otel where you left it."

"Where were you?"

"Some geezer scoffed me cell phone. I was in the knick makin' a report. I fort you'd go back to the same 'otel. I 'ad the fuzz lookin' for you."

"We've found a right crowd of bad-guys," I whispered. "There's one in particular I'm going to sort out."

Newf's eyes lit up. "You're gonna bash 'im?"

"Pulverize him."

"Oright!"

They let me out of the hospital the following morning. Newf was a Godsend, he had called Gran and sorted out the money problems with the bank. When I walked out the door, just everything had been taken care of.

"No, Blue cabs." I snarled.

"It ain't far, we can walk if you're up to it."

I was up to it. The mugger or muggers had actually done me very little damage. The skin on the side of my head had been broken, causing the profusion of blood, though there were no fractures. The doctor said I had an unusually hard head. The scans revealed no fractures at all. He said the problem was caused by swelling on the meninges, whatever that is. Can be fatal.

The outside world felt good, even with the insane traffic. Newf was right; the hotel came into sight after only fifteen minutes walking. "Is the GPS in the, car?" I asked as we approached our lodging.

"D'know. I ain't got no cell. I sort of lost it."

"Yeah. I sort of lost mine too." We looked in the car and found the GPS in the glove box. "Tomorrow," I said, "we're going to do a little pay-back, okay?"

"Great."

In the morning after a couple of leather eggs, a plate of lumpy oats, and some cold-incinerated bread, we paid our bill and put plan 'A' into action. Newf called a cab and asked for Benton Row. I sat in the car waiting with the GPS and the engine running. The Blue cab took him to the target street I followed as inconspicuously as possible. After the cab had driven away, Newf came over to the car. I let him in.

"Nah, what boss?"

"That's the one over there. Number six, that's where the bastard lives. There's at least two of them live there, him and a woman."

"So what we gonna do?"

"Wait. If she goes out, we go in, if he goes out we follow."

"What if neiver go?"

"In one hour we are going in the hard way."

"Alright!"

Ten minutes later the woman came out and marched down the street. "We're in luck," I exclaimed. The moment she was out of sight we both walked to number six. "You ring the bell, Newf." I hid beside the door, not to be seen as it opened.

The door opened. "I'm looking fer Bill Allen," Newf said attracting the man's gaze away from me.

"Piss off."

That was him all right. In one sudden movement I swung round grabbed him and thrust him through the doorway. Newf followed us in and closed the door. I thumped my victim up against the wall cracking the plaster. It was real good to see the expression on his face. Using all my weight I hurled him round and smashed him into the wall on the opposite side of the hallway. The plaster crumbled and crashed to the floor.

"Thought you'd got away with it did you?" I snarled. "I've cancelled the checks, and I want the cash back. Where's my phone?"

"Tom threw it away. The money's gorn. Doris took it."

I hit him with all my strength. I think something broke. He dropped like a stone. Pity I wanted to torture him a little. Walking into the living room, another idea struck me. "What yah think of a little vandalism, Newf."

He smiled; I picked up the TV and threw it through the window.

10

Drumvanich

Gran would surely not have approved, but as they say in
Scotland; 'what the hey?' Doing Allen's place over felt good,
made me feel less picked on. Newf had a wonderful time. I
checked to make sure Mr. Allen had not expired. There was a
little blood, though his heart felt strong.

"What yah gonna do next?" My bright-eyed
companion asked.

"I figure we'd go see this Lord Bennington. He's as
much to blame as that Allen."

"You gonna do 'im over?"

"We'll see."

The GPS easily led us to the big estate on Glen Roy
Heights. I drove passed the gates, about half a mile up the
road I parked in a lay-by. We walked back. Black thunderous
clouds were blowing in from the southwest. The sky looked
fantastically dramatic. Newf pointed to the huge brick wall
surrounding the estate. He'd found a good place of entry.

A large old tree had fallen across the wall breaking
some of the brickwork. With the rubble, wood, and tree limbs,
access would be easy. I carefully marked the spot on the GPS.
Newf, being a lot lighter than me hopped up like an elf, my
size made it slightly difficult.

A nice walk through woods, then garden, we arrived
at the rear side of the mansion. "Should we go in, or knock?" I
said.

"I fink if we knock, maybe they will be just as
surprised."

I banged loudly on the door. After several
hammerings the old undertaker opened the door. The look on
his face was worth all the effort. "What is sir doing here?" He
asked.

"I wanna see your Lord Bennington."

"Does sir have an appointment?"

With a sudden move I grabbed the guy and shook him. "I'm going to pound you to a haggis-like pulp if you don't co-operate."

"Yes, sir."

"Where's Bennington?"

"He's in the study, sir, working on some papers."

"Lead softly, one false move and I'll break a few of your bones. How many other people are in the house?"

"Just Lord Bennington and myself."

"Go, lead on."

Slowly the manservant walked down the corridor to a large hall, at least a dozen doors all closed presented a maze of choices. He walked to the one set of double doors and gently knocked. Without waiting he entered, Newf and I hot on his tail. Lord Bennington sat at a large desk. The moment he saw me he leapt to his feet and fled into a room off to one side.

"Watch him," I yelled to Newf and put chase. What a sucker move! I rushed into the room; Bennington bashed me with something heavy as I ran in. I sprawled full length on the floor. He should have followed though, but fortunately we all make mistakes. Scrambling to my feet I ran after him as he doubled back. I caught him in the hall.

After one thump he surrendered. "Alright, alright, I give up."

"In the other room," I growled and nodded in the direction of the room where we just came from. Newf and the other guy were just standing there.

"What do you want?" Bennington asked, as if he really didn't know.

"A woman was delivered here, by a Blue cab, Miss Cloey Macalister. What happened to her?"

"Happened, happened? Nothing happened."

I held him by the throat again. "I'm going to ask you once more, then if I don't like the answer, I'm going to exercise my free arm." I hauled back ready to thump him.

"Alright, alright. Let's talk this over sensibly. There's no reason to use violence."

"I figure your playing for time. Expecting someone are we?"

"No."

"What happened to her?"

He really looked frightened. For a guy his size, he looked like the rabbit left to confront the hound. "She was here, but she left."

I looked at Newf. "Find some rope or curtain cords, telephone wire 'll do. It's time to get tough with these guys. Now if either of you try anything I'll be forced to become real nasty."

In seconds Newf returned with a telephone extension cord. "I got this Bill."

"Right, take the undertaker there, and tie him securely to one of those chairs."

Newf was having the time of his life. With eyes filled with glee he secured the manservant, hand and foot, to a very heavy wooden chair. "Now that leaves you." I said to Bennington. I grabbed his hand. "I think I'll start by breaking a few fingers, and progress to bigger things."

His breath came in short puffs, like as if he'd been running. "No, please don't."

"So what happened to Cloey Macalister?"

"I told you, she left again."

"Not by taxi?"

"No, no. Um, er... Well."

"I'm going to find out anyway. When I do I'll be in a payback mood. I don't like Scotland or it's people. Now before I really loose my rag. What happened?"

I thought he was going to cry. "Cloey left here with Meall McLean," he finally blurted out.

I sighed a sigh of relief. "So who actually owns this place?"

"I'm the caretaker. It was bought in the name of Lord Bennington, my real name's Albert Baxter."

"So who owns the place?"

"I believe it was left to the Garstons."

"Left, but I thought Justin said you bought the place?"

"Well I did, but in the name of Lord Bennington. You see I used Garston money. They paid me to do it."

His answers were dumb enough to be true. Why would they buy a house from themselves? "I don't see why they'd buy a house they already own. You are beginning to make no sense."

"That's all I know, honest."

"So who's Lord Bennington?"

"It's a man, he's not a lord. His first name is Lord."

"So why didn't he buy the house?"

"He's, well, he's. You see he's dead."

I sure as hell wished Gran was there. The Mad Hatter's tea party was a university conference compared to this conversation. "You must think I'm stupid, if you think I'm going to swallow all this shit. None of it makes any sense. Who owns this place?"

"I told you it's in the name of Lord Bennington, but it's actually owned by the Garstons."

"Why would they buy a house they already own? It makes no sense buster. I think I'm going to break your jaw. How's that sound?"

"I'm telling the truth. Check for yourself. Ask the Garstons."

"So how come you bought the house?"

"I didn't, it's only a paper thing. The Garstons hold the mortgage. They write it off on a monthly basis. I'm only the caretaker."

"What about him?" I said pointing to the tied up undertaker.

"He works for them same as I do."

I thought for a moment. This guy seemed to be telling the truth. We still had the same problem, who would believe us? "Alright," I snarled. "You're free to go. Agent Newf and myself will be making our report to DI McIntyre and then return to Canada. There's nothing we can do here."

I nodded the okay to Newf and we left the way we entered. "You fink they'll come after us?" he asked as we ran through the trees.

"Nah! They've got too much to hide. I figure they'll just keep quiet not wanting any real fuzz digging around here."

Moments later we sat in the car, there was a comforting feeling just being inside the vehicle, almost like being home. "What next?" Newf asked.

"I've got a real brill idea."

"What?"

"We will go to see McIntyre. I figure he'll give us a carnet-de-passage."

"Wha's 'at?"

"A sort of passport."

Newf looked at me with the puppy-dog face. "You lost your passport."

"Don't worry, you'll see what I mean." With care and deliberation I drove back to the hotel. I needed somewhere to park the car. There's no way I was going to drive in central Glasgow.

We took a cab to downtown; it dropped us at the police station. I asked the desk sergeant for DI McIntyre.

"Sorry sir, he's out on a case."

"Well he told me not to leave town without informing him."

'Oh, he says that to everyone."

"Well I'd rather not antagonize him. Could you write on a piece of monogrammed paper that it's alright for us to go to Drumvanich Island?"

The sergeant smiled. "You go to your island and don't worry, sir. Mr. McIntyre won't mind."

"Sure then he'll throw me in the can. No way. Call the chief constable get him to write me a pass."

The sergeant smiled. "If it'll make you feel better." He pulled out a pad of paper. "Name?"

"Reyner, William Reyner."

"Address?"

The Banoch Hotel, here in Glasgow."

"Where you going?"

"Drumvanich Island."

He looked at his watch for the date, did a little more writing, then tore off the top sheet and handed it to me. Man! Even better than I'd dreamed. Form 2314 Area Pass. A real police form, even had the station stamp. I don't think Newf understood what I wanted it for, but he'd soon learn.

Back at the hotel I paid our bill and asked: "How would I get to Drumvanich Island?"

The receptionist looked at me as if I'd asked something unforgivable. After a few moments he said: "I've nay heard o' such a place ask at the tourist office."

I remembered seeing one on the way to Bennington's place. After packing the car and making a call to the consulate in London we set out for the tourist office. The information centre turned out to be quite a large locality on the main road to Greenock. They had maps of everywhere and everything.

"Excuse me Miss," I said to the girl at the pay desk. "I would like to go to Drumvanich Island.

She smiled and thought for a moment. "There's a passenger ferry leaves from Grennock, Tuesday, Thursday, and Saturday."

"Oh, great. How long's the trip?"

"They return Wednesday, Friday, and Sunday."

"Oh! Takes a day there and a day back."

She handed me a pamphlet. "You could take your car if you leave from Portree. A car ferry leaves there Mondays and Thursdays."

Now that sounded better. "Is the island big enough to drive on?"

She laughed musically. "I think you'll need your car."

"Where's Portree?"

She opened a map and pointed. "Take the A828, to the A82 to Fort William and the 830 to Mallaig. There you can take the ferry to Armadale and drive up to Portree. It's beautiful scenery, you'll love it."

She was right about one thing, the scenery is unsurpassed. Magnificent gentle mountains, one with snow on top. The sky looks lower up there, you can almost reach up and touch the clouds. Fort William turned out to be a real interesting town, with everything a tourist could ask for. Mountain tours, excellent stores, but no room at the inn. Every hotel and inn we tried was booked solid.

Undeterred, we continued the trip to Mallaig. Man, what a beautiful and spooky place. Mist gently rolled in off the sea and clung to the hills. By the time we reached Mallaig the sun hung low on the horizon. We found a bed and breakfast, and then drove downtown. The shipping office was one of the most obvious places, with huge hoardings.

The sign gave the times of the ferries. The one I voted for left at nine in the morning, that would give us plenty of time to sleep and still catch the boat. In the morning we loaded and awaited the voyage to the Isle of Skye. Newf absorbed the happenings like a sponge sucks up water. I don't think I've ever seen him so enthralled. We ate on the boat, the journey lasted only about forty minutes.

Skye was not what I had expected. Apart from the narrow roads, you'd think you were on the mainland. On the way to Portree we encountered sheep wandering all over the place. Clouds blow over the fields and creep over the hills like giant ghosts. Portree is a total picture-postcard. A beautiful village on the seashore with silver sands and a dramatic sky.

A ship lay moored to the pier. A quick look at my watch, 'Wednesday.' Maybe that's the ship. As quickly as possible we parked the car and walked to find lodging and the ticket office. Bed and breakfast looked good, and the landlady very pleasant. The attitude of the people seemed very different from that of the people on the mainland. Not so much of a hurry, no money grabbing.

The shipping office people were so laid back, it's amazing they make any money at all. Once I bought my ticket the girl said I could board anytime I liked.

"When does the ferry leave for Drumvanich?" I asked.

"Tomorror."

"What time?"

"Ooo, probably in tha mornin."

"I'm booked into a B & B what if I accidentally oversleep?"

"Ooo, dina worry. We'll take yee anyhoo."

We explored the village, drank in all the rustic antiquity and slept like logs. Early next morning we had a very hearty breakfast, paid our bill and set out for the dockside. When we arrived a man met us, asked for our ticket then pointed the way onto the ship. Fortunately the weather was perfect. Apparently if they don't like the look of the sky they just don't sail.

Around noon, most of the sailors woke up and obvious activity occurred. Winches and things started, and in moments the rumble of the ship's main engine began. Very soon after we were ploughing through the green water in a northerly direction. I had the GPS running I figured it might be important or useful to know where both Portree and Drumvanich is.

Talk about a voyage of discovery. Both of us truly enjoyed the three and a half hour trip. Drumvanich turned out to be absolutely huge. Not the little one-mile lump of rock that I had expected. We sailed along the island for about fifteen minutes then into a huge bay. The town of Meall Kennavay was not only the port, but also the capital city.

"Notice anything about the town?" I asked Newf.

"Yeah, it's great."

"The name. Meall."

"Neat, they named her after the town, I suppose."

After the ship safely docked we unloaded. Again there was a marked lack of hurry. The town had a population of probably six or seven thousand. Beautiful stores lined the main street, which was only just wide enough for one car. A very large and ancient cathedral towered over the town, standing in its own cemetery. At least six hotels or inns. We stopped at the P&O inn.

The inn looked very antique, Tudor I think. Huge dark wooden beams supporting the low ceiling. The barroom floor must have seen millions of guests over the centuries. The huge flagstones were uneven and worn hollow at the bar, where countless boozers dragged their feet. The air smelled sweet yet sort of acrid. The barman looked the part, very full of figure, and red-round faced. "We're closed," he growled in a low voice, as if not wanting to frighten us away.

"I'm looking for a room."

"Oh! Aye, lad. Where'd you leave it?" Great peals of laughter, the tears trickled down his face. His great weight shook and wobbled with the convulsions of uncontrollable mirth.

"To stay in," I growled.

It only seemed to add to the hilarity of the situation, the fat man laughed till he coughed. For a moment I thought he was going to choke. Eventually he calmed himself down. "Sorry lad," he said with a deep sigh. "A laugh does-nay harm your heart."

"Do you have a room?"

He burst out laughing again, though I couldn't see the humour. "Do I have a room," he mimicked and wiped the sweat from his forehead and the tears from his eyes. "Aye, laddie, I have a room," And he started laughing again.

"For Christ's sake don't tell him a joke, Newf, it'll kill him."

"Will yee, be stayin' long?" The fat man said controlling his mirth.

"Maybe a few days."

"One fer, tha tooo o' yah, or one a piece?"

"One room two beds."

"That'll be twenty-five poon' a night, each, in advance."

"What?"

"Alreet, ten poon a night each, in advance."

I gave him twenty pounds, he laughed and handed me a key. "You could 'o had it fer five, dee yee no haggle?"

"We're looking for the family Garston," I said changing the subject.

He laughed again. "Dee yee no ken where yee put them?"

"They live on this island."

He roared with laughter to the point I thought he was going to have a heart attack. Eventually he calmed down. "Gees to Betsy, I' love yee sassenachs. A laugh a minute."

"Well do you know where I can find them?"

"Aye, laddie."

"Where?"

"Well, there's a whole load o' 'em in the cemetery." He roared with laughter again. An' there's a few in Balgowan. Here's the key ta, yee room. Tha front door's never locked, but dina mak' any noise."

"Where's Balgowan?"

He smiled and pointed east. The room was very nice, though a little on the small side. Our window looked out on the port. Newf wanted to explore the town, I wanted to get in the car and explore the island. I had no idea the place was so big. A good ten minutes drive out of town in an easterly direction we found a huge stone circle, rather like Stone Henge, though it had no capstones.

We stopped for a while. The air seemed quite chilly a stiff breeze coming in off the sea. No tourist information, nothing. You either knew what you were looking at or you just admired the scenery anonymously. Sheep wandered all over the place, on the roads and even in the villages and town. The people seemed friendly but spoke a thick dialect and were very difficult to understand.

One very noticeable thing, no night. The sun sank down below the horizon yet it didn't get dark. A strange unearthly glow settled over the countryside. It turned into the perfect magic isle. Sleep came with great difficulty. North snored like a trooper; all I could hear was the ridiculous nasal and guttural sounds coming from sleeping beauty.

Breakfast was excellent, though delivered between raucous peels of laughter. Our fat landlord found us to be the joke of century. Each time I asked him where I could find the Garstons, he would laugh himself to tears and make a point of not replying, just pointing.

We took the car, and drove in the direction pointed out by the landlord. Again we found the huge ring of stones and beyond hills. "I didn't realize this island could be so big," I hissed.

"Well, we got all day. Follo' the road, 'as to go somewhere."

Newf was right. Maybe there would be another village farther on. We drove for fifteen minutes, over a hill and into another coastal valley. One very noticeable thing, no trees. Lots of vegetation, green hills and all, but no trees. At the next and only junction I saw the sign. Like a spear through my heart. The thing represented some hidden horror.

"GARSTON HALL 2 miles."

"We've found it, Newf."

He smiled. "Told yah."

The road looked unused, the hills desolate and to cap it off a sea mist blew in depositing water on my windshield. Suddenly just round a rocky corner the place came into view.

Unbelievably, a real medieval castle nestling almost on the cliff edge. Somehow it looked sinister, swirling mist and not a living thing in sight. The fog seemed to absorb the sound. I climbed from the car to survey the scenery.

The great grey walls of castle grunge towering above us. The only entrance a huge gate with portcullis. The gateway had a tower on either side, one with a human sized door. I walked over to it, no windows or doorbells.

"Go, then, bash it," Newf said.

Knocking on that door would be as useful as spitting in the ocean. Nonetheless I closed my fist and banged on the heavy oak door. Almost immediately it opened. A tall good-looking man in his thirties stood there with a huge smile on his face. "Excellent, excellent," he said.

"I'm looking for-."

"You've found it," he interrupted.

"I would like to speak with--."

"You'll speak with me," he interrupted again.

I did notice he was carrying a buff envelope and spoke with an English accent. "It's about Cloey Macalister."

Smiley handed me the envelope. "For your own good, I would suggest you go home and forget about Scotland. A mere crack on the head might not be the only thing you get." With that he backed up and slammed the heavy door shut.

I stood there like a twit then slowly walked back to the car, the envelope in my hand. "So what's in it?" Newf asked.

Tearing off the top I looked inside. The absolute shock, man! My passport, my wallet and even the cash. Nothing at all was missing.

11

Scouse

The puzzle seemed to be growing more complicated. Though my money and passport had been returned to me, how the hell did they get it here on Drumvanich Island? The drive back to town remained very quiet. My mind was filled with all the possibilities and intimations. If only I were Sherlock Holmes, then maybe I would be able to make sense of it all. I parked the car and we walked in the P & O.

Newf and I wandered into the cosy, there being fewer people in that room. "I'll get yah a drink," my companion said trying to cheer me up.

"Sure. Large bitter." I gave him a ten-pound note.

Newf came back with a grin on his face. "I know somfin' you don't"

"What?"

"That geezer at the castle. 'E were 'ere last night, lookin' fer us." He sat.

I took a beer and washed my throat down. "So?"

"Cuz, 'e knew we was 'ere."

"How did he get my wallet? How did he know what I looked like?"

"Gees, Sherlock, It don't take no bloody genius. You was mugged. Someone walked up be'ind yah, BASH. Dreamsville. They takes the body dumps it. Probably finking yous dead. They don't know yous 'ead is made o' rock. They takes the papers and buggers off 'ome to the castle. A few day's later you turns up."

"So how did he know who I am?"

"Cuz o' the passport picture. Your photo."

"Alright. Why did he give me the money and everything back?"

"Scared the shit art o' yah, din' it?"

I shrugged. "Didn't really scare me, just confused me."

"Scare, confuse. Eiver way, you didn't attack the castle you retreated to fink abart it."

Sure wished Gran was there. She had that uncanny knack of figuring out these people puzzles. "Why didn't they kill me? Why did they give me back my things? Why did they buy a house they already own? And what happened to Cloey Macalister?"

Newf shook is head. "We'll 'ave to find art."

"Well we didn't need my carnet-de-passage." I took the piece of police paper out of my pocket and ripped it in half.

"What you do that fer?"

"I was going to use it as an official document, to scare the Garstons. Sort of wave it in their face, make them think I came on official business. But that's a goner now. I think we should go home. Give up on this quest. We're never going to get anywhere, we don't even know who the enemy is or what we're looking for."

Newf grimaced and shook his head. "Don't give up now. We must 'ave them rattled. Let's go somewhere they won't expect. Do a little digging, then maybe go 'ome. What we needs is a gun."

"No. No guns. Alright, if we stay, what are we looking for?"

"You still got that list of people we found in the law office?"

"Yeah, sure."

"Well 'ow about tryin' the next on the list?"

I thought about it for a moment or two. "Alright, we'll try the next nearest, then take the plane home." I took the paper out and read a few names, then decided that Liverpool had to be the nearest place. Ester Jane Annison, Blackwall Mews, Birkenhead, Liverpool.

"We'll take the ship. Okay?"

"Let's go to the shipping office and buy a ticket."

When we got down to the harbour, there was a big ship in, but the one we came on had already sailed. The man in the ticket office smiled and apologized a great deal.

121

"I'm sorry, bu' if yee want ta goo ta Portree yee'll have to wait till Sunda'."

"What about that one in port?" I asked impatiently.

"Oooch, she's gannin' ta Dundee."

"Is that Scotland, I mean the mainland?"

"Aye. I'm sorry, bu' it is."

"Good. I'll take that one. When does she sail."

"In aboot two hours. Yee ken she's gannin ta Dundee. Aboot 22 hours sailin' time."

"Great."

"Will yee be wantin' cabin, or chair?"

"What?"

"Will yee be wantin a cabin?"

"I guess so, what's usual?"

"I'm sorry, yee ken. Yee can sleep on a chair in the common rooms or yee can have a private cabin."

"Oh," I said beginning to understand his strange way of speaking. "A cabin will do fine. I do have a car."

"Aye, well I'm sorry yee canna tak' the car in tha cabin. It'll have to be loaded in tha hold."

The ticket for Newf, me and the car required a small mortgage, though we, or at least I was glad to get off that island. Newf had to enter the ship by the passenger entrance; I drove the car aboard. The crew were very friendly and helpful. I found Newf in the cabin.

"What a neat boat," he said greeting me. "They got everyfing. Come-on, I'll take you to the dining-room."

"I take it your feeling hungry?"

"Yeah. Come-on, Bill. It's a great ship. They've even got a cinema."

"First I want to know where Dundee is."

'Why?"

"That's where we're headed. If we leave at noon, it'll be ten in the morning when we get there. We've gotta find a map."

"There's a store on a deck, er-, I fink it's toward the back."

"Stern."

"What?"

"They call the ass end of a boat the stern. Come-on let's go find a map of Scotland."

Newf was right; at the stern was a very large open deck with a bar and a trinket store. I asked for a map. The girl smiled sweetly and indicated the wall of the barroom. A huge chart of Scotland almost filled one wall. Holy mackerel, Dundee was not only on the wrong side of Scotland, it turned out to be around three hundred miles almost five hundred kilometres, from Liverpool.

We retired to the dining room, lunch was already underway. "They call it the galley," I told Newf as we entered.

"Alright, let's eat in the galley."

The voyage, though uneventful had its interests. The scenery though once we left port still held some fascination. The timing was all wrong; the journey took only nineteen and a half hours. At 7:30 am our ship drove carefully into the harbour at Aberdeen. The entrance is almost like a river; well I guess it is a river. We berthed without the aid of tugs or anything.

Newf had to leave via the passenger exit; I walked down to the hold and eventually drove my car off the ship. I found Newf wandering in the street, still in sight of the ship. At that time of day Aberdeen didn't seem very busy and the streets are well organized. Within fifteen minutes we were motoring through spectacular countryside enrout to Liverpool.

It's a funny thing, Drumvanich felt like a bad taste in my mouth, something not quite real, something from a bad dream. Scotland, away from that island looked and felt clean and fresh, exciting even. With two meal and rest stops we entered the outskirts of Liverpool at just a little past 4pm that same day.

Another giant seaport town but totally different from Aberdeen or for that matter any Scottish town. Liverpool seemed to hustle and bustle in a more friendly way. The accent of the people sort of a nasal singsong instead of the staccato spit-in-your-face brogue of the Scots. A small B&B at the Bootle end of town suited our purposes. A very nice middle-age lady, Mrs. Simpson, ran it.

Man what a town. We drove to a place called the Pier; it's sort of down town on the water's edge. You see this huge place, the Royal Liver Building. With it's giant clocks and eagles.

"I wonder where Birkenhead is?" I said to Newf, more as a question than a statement.

"Over there," he said pointing across the water.

"Now how the hell would you know that?"

"It's elementary," he said giggling. "Look, the Birkenhead ferry."

He was right. A small office at the end of a wharf or pier proclaimed to be the ticket office of the ferry. I walked over and asked the girl: "How much to Birkenhead?"

She smiled and handed me a small pamphlet. "The quickest way's by the Mersey tunnel," she said.

It was easy to find a good restaurant for our evening meal. And for the first time what seemed like weeks, had a comfortable and undisturbed night. Both of us awoke fresh and ready for a new adventure. I bought a map at a local newsagent. Armed with map and GPS, what could go wrong?

After only an hour and a half we found the street and the Blackwall Mews. A long curved street with a single building, like the biggest townhouse you've ever seen. Georgian architecture. The Mews is in fact a couple of dozen attached, or row houses, mostly apartments. Lovely places and obviously upper class. Parking in front was angle and clearly marked. Opposite the row stood some form of park or gardens, with an iron railing fence all around.

Having nothing better to do, I knocked on the door. After about a minute a young lad in his early twenties opened the door. He was wearing overalls almost like a grease monkey. "Yeah?" He said his black hair glistening with grease and his eyes deep blue and sparkling.

"Hi! I'm William Reyner, I'm looking for Ester Jane Annison."

The kid smiled. "Wrong house, mate."

I looked at the number on the door. "I don't think so."

"Well this house belongs to the trust. It's for summer rent. If you in't rentin' there's nothing here."

I pulled out my wallet and removed my GPS quick guide. I flashed it quickly before his eyes. "I'm on official business, may I come in?"

The kid scratched his ear, smiled and said: "So what's GPS."

"It's er-, it's the er-."

Newf interrupted. "Grounds Police Service. It's a sort of Royal detective agency that checks on the feft of lands and property."

The youth lit up. "Neat. Come-on in. What can I do for you folks?"

The interior looked most impressive, almost up to Cromlet style. The foyer even had a painting of Cromlet castle, and would you believe a guilt staircase, with marble stairs. The ceiling looked amazing with almost life-sized angels holding up the corners. The floor some form of ground stone with brass inlay.

"Like it?" Asked the boy in his nasal dialect.

"Yeah, sure."

"So what's a yank doing lookin' at Pool property fer?"

"I'm not a Yank. I'm from Canada. We're checking certain dealings. Are you the only tenant in this house?"

"I in't a tenant, I'm the superintendent. Lord Greenley'l be here Monday. He's rentin' it fir a month."

"Who do you think owns the house, then?"

"I know, who owns it. It's the Trust."

"What Trust?"

He sighed as if we were boring him. "The bloody Trust. The Cromlet foundation and housing trust. Look." He pointed to a framed certificate on the wall near the back of the door.

I read it and it looked very official. "So the house belongs to Cromlet. What happened to Miss Annison?"

"The old bird is a real preservation freak. See, she gives this place to the Trust, they maintain it and look after it while she bogs off on an extended world cruise."

"So she's still alive?"

The kid laughed. "Sure she is."

"I think we're barking up the wrong tree," I said to Newf.

"So when did all this 'appen?" North asked.

The kid shrugged. "I reckon, say 98. Yeah, 98. I've only bin here for a year an' it must have bin at least a year before that."

"You don't know where I could find Miss Annison, do you?"

"No. She's still voyaging. Don't come here no more."

"She's really rich is she?"

The lad smiled. "Rich, huh. She's got more money and houses than I got pimples. Made millions with shops, and importing stuff. They do say she even owned a few ships. Our-kid knew a millionaire once."

"Oh, really?" I said just making conversation. The young man seemed lonely and needed someone to talk to. "You here all alone?"

"Yeah. As I said our-kid knew a self-made millionaire."

"Oh, yeah." We wandered into the front or sitting room.

"Yes. He made is money with cat's eyes. Invented them see."

"Cat's eyes?"

"Yeah, you know. Those things in the middle of the road, that light up at night."

"Oh!" I said, "those things."

"Yeah. See, he was driving home one night and a cat walked down the middle of the road, see. His headlights reflected in the animal's eyes. He suddenly realized the value of it. Thousands of people would be saved just by planting an imitation cat in the road."

"I see."

"Cause, if the cat had bin walkin' the other way, well, I mean."

"He'd be poor today?"

"Oh no, he'd have invented the pencil sharpener."

Newf roared with laughter. I realized the lad was taking the micky, but I couldn't see the humour in it. "So you think Miss Annison's still alive and well?" I said changing the subject.

"Yeah. Sold the place and sailed the world."

"I guess we've done here," I said and put out my hand for a shake.

The young man took it in both of his. "Pleased to meet you. Mr. They call me Scouse."

"Mr. Scouse?"

"No. Just Scouse."

"He's a millionaire," Newf said with a huge grin.

Scouse's eyes lit up. "Wow, I wish I could win the lottery and be a millionaire."

Just as we walked out the front door, I was struck with an idea. I turned to Scouse and asked: "How'd you like to make some money?"

"Yeah."

"If you can find out what happened to Miss Annison. Like exactly where I can find her, I'll pay you."

"How much?"

"Well don't ask the Trust. I'd rather they didn't know I'm asking questions."

"I'll get fired then. It's undercover stuff."

"No. Alright, I'll make it worth your while. How much do they pay you for care-taking here?"

"Seventy-five a week, room and board free."

"Hmm, three hundred a month. I'll give you two month's pay. Six hundred pounds. How's that sound?"

"Scouse at your service, sir. How shall I let you know?"

"How long'll it take you?"

He thought for a few moments. "Don't know, couple o' days maybe."

"Alright. You know that large building, the one with the clocks, at the pier?"

"You mean the Liver Building at the Pier Head."

"Whatever. Meet me there at dead on noon, in exactly two days. If you've got the information, I'll pay you, if you don't, well don't come."

He nodded and smiled. "It's a deal."

Newf and I climbed in the car and motored in the direction of our lodgings. "Do you fink 'e will come fru?" Newf said quietly.

"Sure he will, I figure he'll do anything for six-hundred." At least I hoped he would. Back at our digs I phoned a local travel agent and arranged a flight back to Canada for Monday. It worked out well, there was a plane leaving Manchester at nine Monday morning. If all went according to plan, we could see Scouse, then head directly to Manchester and fly the next morning.

While in Liverpool we decided to do the tourist thing. We visited the Walker Art Gallery. I thought the place was marvellous, but Newf found it boring, except when we found the nude section. I suppose it boils down to education. The cathedral was a different story. I could barely contain him. Especially when we went up the elevator to visit the upper tower. Actually they only let you go about halfway up, but you still get a terrific view of the city.

The Liver Building's interesting too. The huge clocks, they said were the biggest in the world, being half an inch greater in diameter than the Westminster clock. The guide lady said the big hand on each face weighed in at just over a ton and a half. Again you get a spectacular view of the city. We visited Birkenhead and anything we found on the tourist map that looked interesting.

Amazingly the time flashed by and suddenly it was Sunday, our clandestine meeting with Scouse. I parked the car near Pier Head and we walked to the Liver Building. For a big tourist day, there weren't very many people about. The street almost empty. Time dragged, I figured any minute we would get arrested for loitering. Scouse failed to arrive.

"So what' yah fink?" Newf said looking rather bored.

"D'know. Let's walk once round the block."

"Then what?"

"D'know. If Scouse don't turn up, we'll leg-it."

There was nothing to do, but hope he would turn up. As we walked slowly round the block, Newf said: "You know, we could go to the Mews. That's where 'e lives."

"No, he just works there. I bet he hasn't found anything, that's the reason he's not here."

"So do we still fly, tomorrow?"

"Sure. No point hanging around. I don't think there's anything we can do. Cloey Macalister vanished. I'll bet Miss Annison has too."

"Look!" Exclaimed Newf pointing.

There across the street, at a roadside hot-sausage stand stood Scouse. We sidled over. About halfway he spotted us, a huge grin spread across his face. "I thought you chaps were lost," he said.

"Us? I thought you weren't coming."

"You did say the front of the Liver Building, didn't yah? This is the front. I've bin here for almost half-an-hour. I thought you'd reneged on our deal."

"Alright," I said. "Let's walk and talk."

"D'you bring the money?"

"Sure. Did you bring the information?"

He smiled and walked toward the docks. "I got good stuff. It'll cost you."

"How much?"

"Well. I know where Miss Annison is. I know how she got there, and I know when. I don't know how. I figure the information's worth at least a thousand."

"Our agreement was six hundred, and that's twice what it's worth."

Scouse thought for a few moments. "I tell you what, I know three things, where-how-and when. How about I tell you one for two hundred and fifty. If you like it I'll sell you the next bit for three-fifty. If you like that then the last bit for four hundred?"

"How about I take you apart? If I like what I see, I'll maybe let you live?"

"Oh alright. She's dead. Died in 1998, just after she gave everything away. There was no sea voyage, that was just to keep people from asking questions."

"And where is she?"

He stopped walking and scratched his nose thoughtfully. "Well, she's buried in a village you'll never have heard of. Apparently she went there, she went for a holiday, tits-up, and stayed."

I sighed trying to show my boredom. "So where's this village?"

"It's in Scotland, a place called Pitcalver."

That statement shook me. "Pitcalver? I've just come from there. Are you sure that's where she died?"

"I have it on excellent authority. Here." He handed me a small piece of paper. "That's the grave number and row, you can easily check it out. Now what about my six hundred?"

I felt sorry for that lad; he actually thought six hundred pounds would solve his life's problems. "Here." I handed him an envelope with the six hundred in it. "It's all yours, you earned it." Then I gave him my business card. "If you're ever in Canada, drop in, I'm sure I could find you a nice job."

His eyes lit up. "Thanks Mr. Reyner. I hope everything works out alright, see yah." With that he commenced running down the street.

Newf. and I just stood watching him disappear into the distance. "What do you make of that, Newf?"

"I fink we should get the car and 'ead for Manchester. You know where it is?"

"The car or Manchester?"

"Bofe."

"Sure."

The drive to the huge city turned out to be totally uneventful. A hotel fairly close to the airport seemed appropriate. Next morning the agents took my car and credit card details, with the promise to return it to Reading. We were early, booked in, dumped the luggage and wandered around.

There are things that people do, that on second thoughts you wish they hadn't. Newf bought a newspaper. As it turned out, there was no time to read it. At that very moment the PA system announced that passengers for the flight to Canada should make their way to gate 24. We walked in the general direction and eventually found the gate.

Quite a crowd of people were queering up. As we arrived a woman in a bright red uniform came over. "First or business, sir?"

"First."

"Please follow me." She led us through a more private entrance. Only one customs inspector. He smiled and waved his magic wand. "Good morning, sir. Please pass through the sensor."

Moments later we were sitting in the luxury of a 747 first-class cabin. "'Oly mackerel," gasped Newf.

"What?"

"Look."

He opened the paper and showed me page two headlines. 'Body found in Mersey.' "So?"

"So, look at the picture."

Gees. The picture at the bottom of the page was none other than the lad Scouse.

12

Home Sweet Home

Man I wouldn't have believed it, but Canada is home. When the pilot announced we would be landing at Pearson in fifteen minutes, it was as if I hadn't been home in years. I hired a taxi to take us to Dundas. Gran and Spadafora were obviously at the tea garden. The heat seemed unbearable, at least fifteen degrees above England and twenty above Scotland. The sweat sheer poured down my face in rivers.

At least the new house had air-conditioning, though Gran never used it. I turned it on, needing time to acclimatize. It was already late afternoon; Gran would be home in a short while, no point in trying to make supper. After a while we heard a car out front. Like a shot I switched off the air and went to the front door.

"Hi! Gran," I yelled.

She smiled a warm, 'I knew you were home,' smile. "How was your trip dear?"

"There's lots to talk about. Where's Mr. Spadafora?"

"He's helping Dagwood clean up."

"How did you know I would be here?"

"Come along dear. I'm sure you have heard of a telephone."

"Yeah, but!"

"Would you like some food, dear?"

"Sure, Gran."

In her amazing and inimitable manner, Gran whipped up a meal in less than half-an-hour. She didn't eat, just sat there admiring Newf and I eating. I was fair bursting to tell her all about out adventures. "Gran," I said with a mouthful of food. "There's a few things I want to ask you."

"I'm sure they will wait until you have finished your food, dear."

"Sure." I chewed and swallowed. "There's one thing, one real bad thing."

"Which is?"

"Well I paid a guy, Scouse to do some research for me, and. Well, he, er-."

Newf interrupted. "Some body dun 'im in."

"Oh dear. Did you get the information you were looking for, before he came to an untimely end?"

"Well, yeah."

"Scouse is merely a name for a person originating from the Liverpool area. Where was this person from?"

"Liverpool."

"Did you find Cloey Macalister?"

"Well, not really, Gran."

"Not really. Did you or didn't you?"

I exhaled in a small hurricane. "You're missing the point Gran. We questioned Scouse, then someone killed him and threw him in the Mersey, whatever that is."

"And your point, William?"

"They killed him because he helped us. I paid him for the information. He had my card. Man they will know everything."

Gran glared at me. "They may know everything, though I fear I know nothing. You will have to tell me more clearly what happened."

"Yes, Gran. See, we were looking for Cloey, just as you said. She went to this house in Glasgow, and vanished. Lord, whatever said she left with Meall. So we went to Drumvanich Island. They are a real creepy bunch. I got my passport back and my money."

Gran blinked a few times, raised her eyebrows and said: "Dear, William. Organize your thoughts then illiterate in a coherent manner."

"Well that's it."

"That's it. You mean you went all the way to England and Scotland, visited numerous establishments and that's it?"

"Well, Scouse was murdered. The article said he'd been stabbed and thrown into the Mersey."

"So you said, William. The Mersey is the river or sea-way between Liverpool and Birkenhead."

"Oh! That's where we left him." I suddenly saw the inferences. He was murdered right where we left him. "There's this list, Gran." I handed her the piece of paper with the names we found in the lawyer's office."

She examined it for a few moments. "Just what is the significance of these names?"

"We went to see McWittie and Annison, both dead, both gave everything to the Garstons. Well sort of."

"Sort of?"

"Yeah. One left it to the trust, that's Cromlet, and the other gave everything to the Garstons, through fart-ass."

"I beg your pardon?"

"Oh! Sorry, Gran. I meant Edward Cameron, who's actually a Garston."

"Do you have any conclusions?"

I thought about it for a few moments. "Well, not really, it's all too complicated. You see nothing makes any sense. Some one bashed me on the head and stole all my papers and money. I found the money on Drumvanich Island, and the papers."

She sighed in a way that showed her annoyance. "William please write all your adventures down in chronological order. Miss nothing and then present it to me. Maybe then I may understand your incoherence."

"Yes Gran. Do you happen to know what a sassenach is?"

She smiled. "Indeed. It's someone from the south, south of the border."

"Oh! I thought it was something rude. So any idea where the Westminster clock is?"

"Of course. It's at Westminster."

"Well you see the lady said the Liver clock is bigger than the Westminster clock, like as if the Westminster clock was famous."

She sighed again. "And you a university man. William, have you ever heard of Big Ben?"

"Sure, who hasn't?"

"Big Ben is actually the bell, the clock is the Westminster clock, sometimes known as the parliament clock."

As usual, Gran knows everything. I can't imagine how such a little lady could have so much knowledge. She's like a walking encyclopaedia, with quick index.

It took me almost two days to write a diary of our adventures with Newf's help. Gran and Spadafora read it with interest. I guess it was almost a week after I'd landed, that we all got together. Newf and I just returned from a drive in my beautiful Rolls. It was Sunday supper, or as it would have been in England, tea.

Spadafora was his usual quiet self. He listened intently, but added very little. Gran poured the after meal tea. You could tell by the expression on her face she was about to come up with some extraordinary theory or something. "How's Priscilla?" She asked.

"Who cares?"

"I see. Do you think the Garstons killed, Cloey Macalister?"

I shrugged. "Well, maybe. Though I'll bet they murdered Scouse."

"Then it's time we found some physical evidence." She sat down. "What we have to do is find authentic evidence allowing us to formulate an hypothesis. Something we can present to the authorities. Something they will believe and follow up upon."

I thought for a few moments, there was nothing that I could think of. "There isn't any, Gran."

"It exists, William, we merely have not found it up to this point. Do we have any theories at all?"

"Yeah," North put in. "It's obvious. They's nicking money from rich people. They knocks them off and pretends to be them. Then when no one's lookin' they gives all the money to Cromlet then ups and dies."

"Upping and dying, does not seem a very favourable way of becoming rich," Gran said.

"Gees, Mrs. H. They don't really die. It's a scam. They goes 'ome. I'll bet there ain't no bodies nowhere. Like as not, they's still walkin' around."

Gran digested, Newf's theory, you could see her mentally unravelling the bad English. She'd got to the sate where she no longer corrected what he said. "I see. Someone replaces the rich person, then makes provisions to pass the estate to Cromlet, or the Garstons, then disappears after the event."

"That's what I said, didn't I?"

Gran sat thinking again, then after thoroughly digesting the speculation she said slowly: "I believe our task is simple. We must prove the whereabouts of the missing well-to-do characters in our unfolding drama."

"What?" Newf said, showing his ignorance.

"The corpus dellicti. The body in question. We must find out what happened to the real people. Miss Cloey Macalister for instance. Where is she?

I shrugged. "Dunno."

"Very well, William, you and young North should go to Donjon and put your cards on the table. We have, Miss Macalister's passport. You can point out the discrepancy in the physiognomy."

"In a fizzy-who?"

"Oh dear! William. The face, the face, boy."

"Oh!" I think she looks up these words in the dictionary the day before, just so she can make me look stupid. I mean who uses words like that, physi-whatever. "Alright, Gran, Newf and I will go over there tomorrow and sort this woman out. I think she's Meall McLean. That's how they got rid of Cloey."

"Yeah," Newf agreed. "Meall's the only one missing from Cromlet."

It was all arranged, after a good night's sleep, we would take my nice shiny new Rolls and investigate the broad at Donjon Towers.

We had breakfast at around ten, Gran and Spadafora had already left for the tea garden. "I reckon, now we're back in a civilized country, Newf, you can drive. You can be my chauffeur again."

"Great, do I get paid?"

"Ten bucks a day."

"Is that all?"

"Well your room and board's thrown in."

"It's a deal. Can I have a new uniform?"

"You've got a hat, that'll have to do." Man I could see the disappointment in his eyes. Honestly, he's like a big child. "Alright, we'll think about it."

We drove off in the general direction of Galt. I switched on the GPS and dialled up Edie's store. Real neat gadget a GPS, come up with the details instantly, even a map of how to get there. As soon as we reached the outskirts of the town I began giving directions. Like magic we arrived at the rundown corner store. This time both of us walked over and entered. Mr. Edwards came from his hiding place and smiled when he saw me.

"Good-day, Mr. erm, Reyner is it?"

"Good memory. Sure, call me Bill."

"What can I do for you, Bill?'

I sighed and showed him the passport. "Do you know this lady?'

"Sure, that's Miss Cloey Macalister from the Towers."

"Great," I said. "That's all I wanted to know. Do you still do any work for her?"

"Nah. She ain't called me since she got back from Scotland."

"Okay, thanks. I'll see if I can throw some business your way." We left and walked back to the car. "So what'd you think Newf?"

"'E ain't got no reason to lie. The woman in the Towers is a fake. Let's go duff her up a bit. Squeeze the troof art o' 'er."

"Come-on then James, to the Towers." I reset the GPS and we were off again. Not exactly what we expected though. Newf drove up the driveway with the swamp over to our right, just up the hill a bit and the house should have appeared. Man, what a shock. The place had gone; nothing but a pile of rubble.

We parked the car and climbed out. The Donjon Towers had had a serious fire, some time ago. Bulldozers had virtually levelled what had remained. "So now what do we do?"

"D'know. Ask the fire chief. Or maybe it'll be in the paper."

I stood surveying the rubble for a moment, almost unable to comprehend. Why? Was it a genuine accident, or was it to cover something up? What happened to the woman? "Come on Newf, let's find a fireman."

Finding the fire-chief turned out to be a little difficult. You'd expect to find him in the fire station. His office is in city hall. When we arrived his secretary told us he was attending some meeting or other. "I'm just trying to find a few details on a fire," I said.

"Like what, sir?"

"I've been a broad, well today we thought we'd visit an old friend, when we got there the place has gone. Just rubble."

"And?"

"I wanted to ask the fire-chief what happened."

"What is the address, sir?"

"Oh! It's Donjon Towers, RR, something."

She rustled through a large book. "When would this have been?"

"In the last couple of months."

"No, I'm sorry, no fires mentioned with a Donjon Towers. Why don't you ask at the courthouse, they have all the building records? Ask for Joyce Brown, tell her I sent you."

"Thanks."

Leaving the car parked at city hall we walked over to the courthouse. Joyce Brown worked in an office just down the hall, from the front door. Poor kid, talk about harried, even her hair was having a bad day. "What?" She said looking up from a pile of paper on her desk.

"Hi, the fire-chief's secretary said you may be able to help us."

She looked up and smiled sweetly. With obvious difficulty she tried to innocuously straighten her hair. "I'm sorry, I've been, there, under the desk. We've got a mouse, you see."

"Oh dear."

"Yeah, well what can I do for you?" Her eyes were a little disturbing, sort of wild and darting, as though she expected the mouse to appear on the desk.

"I'm trying to find out what happened to Donjon Towers. Miss Cloey Macalister's place."

"Hmm! What's the address?"

"Well that's all I know."

"Hmm! Donjon Towers. I think I remember that name." She walked over to an over stuffed set of bookshelves and extracted a volume, replaced it and took another. Opening it she walked slowly back to her desk. Suddenly she dropped the book and shrieked an ear-piercing scream.

Newf turned to run, while I ducked, not knowing what to expect. Then I saw it. A little brownish furry body skulking near a leg of the desk. When I advanced, it scurried away. "Sorry," I said. "Your pet's run off."

"I told them we had a mice," she sniffled. "If it's not removed I can't stay."

I picked up the book and handed it to her. "What you need is a cat."

"Yeah. Hmm! Now let me see." Wearily she placed the book on her desk then surveying the underside settled uneasily into her chair. "Donjon Towers, oh yeas. Here it is. So what do you want to know?"

"Well, what happened to it, and the owner?"

"Hmm! It was sold to North Coast Development Company. They cleared the site."

"And what happened to Miss Macalister."

"Doesn't say. She paid all her taxes and made a legal sale. It's out of our hands. Why don't you speak to the lawyer who handled the sale?"

"Sure, who?"

"Hmm! Oh yes, here it is. Edward Cameron."

My blood ran cold when she said that. "Edward Cameron, what's his address?"

""Hmm, sorry, doesn't say."

As usual, Newf and I were up a gum tree. I knew where to find Cameron and it wasn't in Cambridge. The only thing left to do was report to Gran. Maybe she could figure out what to do next. "Come on Newf, let's go home."

"That broad frit me when she screamed like that."

"Yeah, me too. What do you think?"

"D'know. I reckon Meall's gone 'ome. I bet she's at Cromlet. They got rid of Cloey long ago."

"So you think the woman at Donjon's Meall McLean?"

"Sure she is. They done away with Cloey at Lord, fingamy's place. Meall came 'ere and disposed of the cash and property, then buggered off back to Scotland."

We drove to Gran's tea garden, figured we may as well get something to eat. Yet another surprise, when we walked into the kitchen from the back way someone was helping Dagwood, but not anyone I knew. "Hi," I said.

"You shouldn't be in here sir," the pretty young girl said. She had gorgeous blond hair and deep blue eyes.

"It's alright, where's Gran?"

"Gran?"

"The lady who owns this place?"

She eyed me up and down suspiciously. At that opportune moment Dagward walked in carrying a tray of dirty dishes and stuff. "Ah! Mr. Reyner, sir. Mrs. Hubert thought you'd drop in. She's in the tea-room."

"Thanks Daggy."

Somehow I'd lost Newf. Gran sat at a table with a couple of old biddies. When she spotted me, she excused herself and came over. "Let's talk outside in the garden," she said.

Spadafora looked smart, but it seemed strange seeing a cop with a waiter's tray and a white towel on his wrist. He smiled and nodded, but didn't say anything.

"So what's up, Gran?"

"Sit, William."

I sat. "Alright, you first."

"You've found nothing," she said.

"Almost true."

"Then elucidate, boy."

"I do wish you wouldn't call me boy, Gran. Do I look like a boy to you?"

"Yes. Though I'll try to remember. What did you discover, William?"

"The house was sold by none other than our old friend the farter."

"I beg your pardon?"

"I mean the father, you know, Edward Cameron. He sold Donjon Towers. The developer has-."

She interrupted. "Pulled the place down."

"Right, how did you know?"

"Someone told Dagwood, he told me."

"Yeah. Well, Newf and me-."

"I, dear. North and I."

"Alright. Newf and I went there, there's nothing but rubble. The courthouse said it had been sold, and Cameron was the lawyer who did all the legal work."

Gran smiled one of her all-knowing smiles. "Excellent, William. I'm sure now we have enough circumstantial evidence to convince the authorities that something skullduggerous is afoot."

"Something, you mean murder. I reckon they've killed loads of rich people and stolen the property."

"Yes, indeed, William. Alas we have no evidence. We only know Mr. Cameron seems to be involved in a lot of property transfers. I fear there's no law against that."

"Yeah, but the majority of the transfers is to Cromlet. Doesn't that sound a little fishy?"

"Hmm! Yes, William, but again, people who make these endowments, well it's a sort of attempt at eternal remembrance, you see."

"Alright, how about Scouse. I'm sure they murdered him."

"We'll have to prove it, William. Guessing is neither here-nor-there."

"So, what'd you recommend?"

"I think it would be nice if you and young North went back to Britain and did some intelligent digging."

"No."

"You could probably visit Priscilla."

"No."

"Have we lost interest in that exciting young woman?"

I sighed. "She's marrying some dink from the upper crust of English society."

"Still, would make a nice little holiday, especially now that you know your way around so well."

"No."

"We'll see dear."

Missing my companion, I decided to see where he had got to. For a skeleton with skin stretched over it, Newf could pack more food away than anyone I know. There he sat at a small table in the kitchen area, a plate piled with various and sundry offerings.

"Hi. Bill," he said as though we had only just met for the first time that day.

"What are you doing?"

"Brenda's give me some leftovers. Mrs. H. won't mind."

"You're sure about that?"

"Sure."

"Come-on, it's time to go. You are still my chauffeur, aren't you?"

Reluctantly Newf rose from the table. "Fanks, Brenda. I gotta go, the boss's calling."

Back in the car, chauffeur North sat with his special peeked cap awaiting instructions. "You're beginning to annoy me Newf."

"Why?"

"You were all keen to drive now you want to stay and talk to that broad."

"I don't like Brenda called a broad."

"Please, Newf Let's go home. I've had a real bad day, what with you and Gran, I'm developing a nasty headache."

"She wants you to go back to Cromlet, eh?"

"How did you know?"

"Brenda told me."

"How the hell does she know?"

"Cuz, Mrs. H talks to 'er. So are we going?"

"Drive."

"Right. Are we going to Scotland?"

"I don't think so."

For the rest of the journey home, Newf was very quiet. Now and again I saw him in the rear-view mirror. Man, was he ever deep in thought. "So what's the deep thinking, Newf?"

"Brenda said if you go to England it would give her the chance she always needed."

"What the hell's that got to do with anything?"

"Well are we going, or not?"

"No. No. No. Now what part of 'no' don't you understand?"

He parked the car in the garage, which I find very annoying. As we walked to the house he handed me an envelope. "I fink you should look at this."

As we entered the house I opened it and pulled out two airline tickets. In stunned shock I stared at them. Toronto to London, and in mine and Newf's names. "Where the hell did you get these?"

"Your Gran gave them to Dagwood, to give to us."

"Why?"

"So we can go to England and finish the job we wuz doin'."

"I'm going to kill you Newf. And I'm not going to England, Scotland, or anywhere near Europe. Do you understand? There is no way, you or anyone else can make me go."

It's a very strange thing, in the morning just after Gran had left for work, the phone rang. Now I'm no easy mark, but. "Hello."

"William, darling. This is Priscilla, oh William dear, I need you. I really need you."

How fortunate that I had the very tickets needed to make the trip.

13

Round Two

After only being in Canada for just over a week, we were on our way to England again. Gran's a crafty, senior citizen. Priscilla had phoned while we were at Donjon; Spadafora nipped out and acquired tickets. We would have gone prior to this, but being peak season there just was no earlier flight available. Newf knew all about it, the wonderful Brenda had told him.

Priscilla had not clarified, why she wanted to see me so desperately. She called and begged me to go as soon as possible. Funny though after that call I tried dozens of times to call her, with absolutely zero success. The very last time I called the operator said the number had been disconnected. Night flying is boring, and with the stress and worry I couldn't sleep. Newf's a second cousin to a rabbit; started snoring fifteen minutes after takeoff.

Typical of England, it started raining only minutes after crossing the coast. London looked dark and grey as a mantle of fog settled over the whole land. I gave the lady my passport at the immigration desk. With a sweet smile she flipped it to the visa section, pressed a little button and said: "Welcome to England, Mr. Reyner."

"Thanks." I put my hand out for the passport.

She smiled, at that moment a very large and burly policeman behind me said: "Mr. Reyner, sir, would you please come with me?"

It wasn't really a question, more of an order. There's no point resisting, though I had the urge to run. He pointed the way. "Newf, call Gran, do something," I barked.

"Not to worry, sir," the policeman said. "Just routine inquiries."

He led the way through a door and into a corridor, then into a small office. A plainclothes man smiled kindly. "Please take a seat, Mr. Reyner."

"What've I done?"

The civey looked kindly and smiled a lot. "We're investigating the unfortunate demise of Patrick Devlyn. I understand you knew him?"

"I did? I mean did I?"

"You last spoke to him, in Liverpool about ten days ago."

I almost fell off the chair with the shock. "You mean Scouse?"

"Yes."

"Well, yeah. Me and Newf had a deal with him."

The plainclothes man sat opposite me and still smiling asked: "Was he alive when you left him?"

"Well, sure he was."

"What exactly was the arrangement you had with him?"

"Needed information, that's all. I asked him to find something out for me."

"I see, sir, and did you get this information?"

"Yeah, sure."

He stroked his pursed lips thoughtfully and stared into the corner of the room. His thoughts would appear to be distant, as though what I said set off a whole new train of ideas. Slowly he focused his attention on me. "Well, sir, what exactly did Mr. Devlyn tell you?"

"Tell me? I... er. He looked into the disappearance of Ester Jane Annison for me. Nothing real difficult."

"And?"

"And, well, she's dead."

He nodded. You were arrested in Glasgow a few days earlier, sir. Would you like to tell me about that?"

"I think I should call my lawyer."

"Really, sir. And why is that?"

"Well, either arrest me or let me go."

He smiled, just like Gran. "What have you done that requires the assistance of a lawyer?"

""Nothing."

"Then shall we stop playing footsie and answer a few harmless questions?"

I shrugged.

"Very-well. Exactly where and at what time did you leave Mr. Patrick Devlin?"

"I don't know, why you questioning me. Newf was with me. He's probably got a better idea of the time than me anyhow."

"Newf?"

"Oh! His real name's North. He's the guy who travels with me."

He sighed inordinately loud. "I'm still waiting for an explanation."

"I can't remember, I think it was three o'clock, or not long after. He gave me what I wanted, then he went his way and me and Newf drove to Manchester, we had a plane to catch."

He stood up slowly with his hands behind his back walked thoughtfully round me and the table. I could feel the anxiety building up in my breathing. Any minute I'd have to explode or something. He stopped walking and turned to me. "So who is Cloey Macalister?"

"Why?"

"Come now, Mr. Reyner, your not going to pretend you've never heard of her?"

"No, you just surprised me with that question. She's a, or she was a woman who lived near my home in Canada. You see she disappeared. I thought she vanished at Cromlet Castle up in the Highlands."

"And?"

"Well that's it."

"If this woman disappeared in the Highlands of Scotland, what exactly did you expect to learn in Liverpool? Maybe you were lost, or suffer from a severe lack of geographical knowledge." He sat down again and glared at me. "Well?"

"It's ever-so complicated. You see I think there are several people missing. I was in Liverpool looking for Miss Annison. She was the owner of stores, ships and stuff, a very rich woman. Just the sort the Garstons would be looking for."

"Your story is ridiculous enough to be true. So how many people are missing?"

"Not sure. At least three. I have a list, didn't check them all out yet. You see the cunning thing is the missing people seem to have gone of their own free will. The money always lands up at Cromlet, which is owned by the Garston family."

"Whose employ are you in?"

"Well, no one."

"Sort of a good Samaritan, are we, a knight errant? What's in it for you?"

"Nothing. I'm learning to be a detective, it's just practice."

He pulled a grimace and raked his ear out as though the words irritated the lining of his auditory apparatus. Then he pinched his nose and scrunched up his eyes. "Mr. Reyner, tell me why the Glasgow police suddenly decided to let you go."

"I don't know, why don't you ask them?"

"Did you discover the whereabouts of any of these missing people?"

"Well, yes, I guess so. Scouse said Miss Annison is buried at Pitcalver."

"And is she?"

"I don't know, never got around to check it. Now are you going to charge me with something or what?"

"I believe 'or what' is the order of the day. Where are you going this time?"

"First to see my girl, well, a girl. She called me and said she needs my help."

"Then?"

I shrugged. "Haven't made up my mind yet, sort of play it by ear."

"Commendable, commendable. I have done a little research myself. I would strongly recommend you stay away from Drumvanich Island."

He got up and smiled at me then put out his hand. I shook it. "Is that it?"

"Certainly, Mr. Reyner. And try to stay out of trouble."

The constable led me out of the room, didn't even go near immigration. At the end of the long corridor we entered a sort of luxury lounge. Newf sat with his feet on a small table and his nose stuck in a magazine all our luggage beside him. He looked up and jumped to his feet. "Hi Bill."

A uniformed lady handed me my passport and walked away. The cop pointed to a door. "The exit, sir."

"Thanks."

Once out of the airport, the air smelled clean and fresh. "We gotta get a car," I said.

"Where from?"

"There's a car rental place in Reading that have the best choice, we'll take a taxi there."

Even though we'd arrived at high season, the car rental place had a couple of the expensive ones available. Newf refused to drive in the big city; it unfortunately was left to me to get us out into the country. What with the traffic and the insane traffic circles it took almost an hour to reach the green belt then two more hours to reach West Lavington.

The gate to the hall had not been closed by the previous person entering. I drove up the long golden coloured drive to the house. A different servant let us in this time, a woman.

Priscilla came running, she met us in the hallway. With her usual exuberance, she flung her arms around my neck hugging and kissing. I couldn't get a word in edgewise. Eventually she said: "I'm so glad you came, I feel so much better now."

"What's the problem?"

"Daddy has vanished."

"Oh!"

"Well you're a private detective and all that. Mummy wanted to hire someone from London, but I want you."

"Okay, can we sit somewhere and you can bring me up to speed."

"Oh! You're so efficient, William, I just knew you would be the right person."

She dragged me into a large ornate room that had a huge bay window overlooking the gardens. A giant fireplace and one wall sporting a full width bookcase. Three easy chairs were arranged around a coffee table in front of the fireplace. I sat, she arranged herself on the floor at my feet, still holding my hands.

"Well?" I asked.

She snuggled close to me; somehow I felt it was an act. "Daddy left for a meeting and just never came home."

"Where was the meeting?"

"In London, dear William. Mummy phoned, but they said he never got there."

"Any ransom demands?"

"No. Nothing, daddy just vanished."

"What about his car?"

She began to whimper. "Vanished too."

"What about the police, have they been informed?"

"Oh, yes. Mummy called them almost immediately. I don't think they care, that's why I called you. I knew you would solve it, you're so clever."

I felt like a piece of toast, buttered on both sides. I couldn't even find Cloey Macalister, now she wants me to find her father. "Alright," I said in my most manly voice. "I want you to write down everything that happened that day, like a diary. Don't miss any names of people or places. Newf and I will start as soon as we get the information."

As if stung by a bee she leapt up and rushed into the room adjacent. Moments later she returned with that goofy geezer she called her boyfriend. "Godfrey didn't think you would help," she said.

I looked at the goof and had a very strong urge to pound his head in. "Well he's wrong," I growled.

"I'll have the information for you first thing in the morning, William dear. Please bring, your little friend. We'll have breakfast together."

I assumed that was the end of the interview. My little friend and I left with a sour taste in our mouths. "You drive," I growled under my breath.

"What yah fink?" Asked my little friend.

"Don't know, Newf. I am beginning to think the old man couldn't stand the pressure any more and ran off with his lady-fair."

In moments we were on our way to a nice B & B. "I fink, we's bein' used. That nit Godfrey's just a bozo. I would 'ave thought she'd remember my name. I knew 'er afore you did."

"Yeah. I'd think I'd rather look for Cloey, who cares about her 'DADDY,' for crying out loud?"

"What yah fink the cops wanted at the airport?"

"What do you mean?"

"You wuz whisked away and interrogated, why?"

"Dunno."

"I fink it's very queer."

"Why?"

"Well, 'ow did 'e know yous gonna be on that plane? "Ow come 'e didn't ask me nothin'. I fink 'e's a fake."

"You think everyone's a fake."

We stopped outside the B & B, but Newf had planted a seed in my brain. He was right, how did that cop know I was on that particular plane. Thinking back on it the whole interview made no sense. The whole world had begun to make less and less sense. People disappearing all over the place, even buildings vanishing. Cops that might not be cops. And why did that detective let me go in Glasgow?"

"Cause a mystery's only a mystery when yous don't know the answer," Newf said softly.

* * *

Why did she pick breakfast? Man, I began to wish I'd gone straight to Scotland. I didn't really want to look for Daddy. The maid led us both into the breakfast-room, gees; even I didn't have a room especially for one meal of the day. Goofball was already seated holding Priscilla's hand, enough to turn your stomach. We sat on the opposite side of the table. A stern elderly lady sat at the head.

The maid leaned close to me. "English or French, sir?"

"What?"

"English or French breakfast, sir?"

"Oh, um! English, I guess."

"I'll 'ave French," Newf said.

"I have the information you requested, William. There isn't very much. We really don't know anything."

"I think it requires strength, not brains," Godfrey said.

He spoke as though he had a mouth filled with marbles or something. I mean, what a twit. His name should have been God awful instead of Godfrey. "Yeah," I said. "If you had any you'd be in there."

He smiled. "I had a friend, haw, haw. He was very strong, really strong."

"So 'ow strong was 'e?" Newf snapped impolitely.

"Oh, haw, haw. He was so very strong. When he wanted a cup of tea, he put a tea bag in his mouth and drank boiling water. Haw, haw, haw."

The woman at the end of the table said nothing. You'd think she'd passed away, and no one had noticed. "Where's this information?" I said putting out my hand.

Priscilla pulled a scrap of paper from a little pocket in her blouse and handed it to me. A quick read revealed, she didn't know very much at all. The date and time he left, his supposed destination, and the car type and number. That's it?" I asked.

"What else is there, William?"

"How about a photo?"

"Grandmamma will give you one after breakfast, won't you dear?

The old lady grunted, I think she was showing her distaste for the entire proceedings. I know I began to feel very hungry, and there was nothing on the table to eat. "What did the police say?"

"Oh, nothing, they took all the particulars and said they would report if anything should turn up."

The maid walked in with a table-trolley. The smell of freshly cooked bacon flooded the air. She gave the old lady a bowl of horrible looking brown oats. Godawfull got an egg with soldiers, and Priscilla, just three pieces of toast. Newf got a small sample of marmalade, a croissant and a glass of milk. Then she opened the silver cover thing and extracted a large plate with sausage, bacon, beans, two fried eggs and stewed tomatoes. She placed this feast in front of me. I got more food than the rest of the company put together.

She then placed a large toast rack and a triangle of butter beside my plate. "Coffee or tea sir?"

"You should have tea, William," Priscilla said.

"Sure, tea, please."

Though the food seemed plentiful and tasted excellent, I felt out of place, sort of like eating on display in a museum. You never really knew if Grandma was dead or alive. I think she ate by osmosis, for I never saw her move a muscle. After breakfast we all shook hands like a bunch of diplomats planning the next war.

Newf suddenly turned as we walked back to the car. "Where's your old man gas 'is car?" He yelled at Priscilla.

She shrugged. "Fornstone Motors, I suppose."

"That was a daft question," I said as we climbed in.

"Nah! I reckon that's where we should look first."

"You think he's still gassing up his car do you?"

"Gees, Bill, use yah finker."

Newf seemed to like driving on the wrong side of the road; I think it came natural to him. In less than ten minutes we found Fornstone Motors. We pulled up in the forecourt and walked to the office. "So what'll we learn here, Newf?"

Newf gave the garage-man a nice smile and asked: "'Ave yah seen a rolls wiv this plate number." He showed the piece of paper with the number on it.

The garage-man glared back. "What if I 'ave?"

Remembering my adventures in Scotland, I said: "Could be worth something to you."

"It's Critton's car. So what of it?"

"We're looking for, Mr. Critton," I said.

He eyed me, then Newf, and then eyed the car. "It's a rental. Why you looking for 'im?"

"His wife and daughter can't seem to find him."

The garage-man laughed heartily. "'E don't want to be found, poor sod."

"How do you know?"

"'E's got a gob an' I got ears."

"So you're saying he got lost on purpose?"

"Cause 'e did."

"Do you happen to know where he went?"

The garage-man looked around surreptitiously then leaned forward and whispered: "Might."

"What would persuade you?"

He smiled. "Wife needs a new coat."

"Ten pounds?"

"She won't shop at the Sally-Ann."

"Twenty five pounds?"

"Ah! She won't shop at no flea market neiver."

"A hundred pounds?"

"Well there's the VAT, and the taxi fare. You're getting close."

"Two hundred, that's my last offer. But it better be good."

"'E's gorn to see 'is mum in Bristol, She lives somewhere in the Heights." He put out his hand for the reward.

I counted out two hundred pounds and handed it to him. "What Heights?"

"'S'all I know. I heard 'im tellin' the geezer driving another car that was 'ere at the same time."

The Cloey Macalister case had a connection in Bristol. I figured we could kill two birds with one stone. "You wanna drive to Bristol, Newf, or shall I?"

"I'll drive."

A short consultation with the book of maps and we were on our way to the city of Bristol. The English countryside is very beautiful in those parts, and Bristol wasn't that far away, at least by Canadian standards. We arrived in early afternoon. Compared to London, Bristol seemed quiet though just as old. A very beautiful city with steep hills and Georgian buildings.

"Pull into that gas station, Newf."

"We don't need gas."

"We need guidance. Pull up to the pumps anyway."

The young lad ran round and opened the filler cap. "How much, Gov?"

"Fill it please," I said and climbed out. "Where's the Heights?" I said nonchalantly.

"Don't rightly know. Never 'eard o' it. I'll ask the Governor, 'ell know."

After the fill up I followed the lad into the office. The Governor reminded me of Pete's uncle in Stoney Creek, but this time I was the paying customer. I settled the bill and the lad asked the boss if he'd ever heard of the Heights.

"He stroked his clean shaven chin. "Heights, I reckon you mean Clifton, like Clifton Heights. It's a bit of a ritzy area up by the Brunell Bridge."

"How do I get there?"

He gave us directions. Man, he was right, you couldn't miss it. Just down the road a bit we spotted the huge suspension bridge he'd talked about. It took longer to get there than I would have thought. Man what a gas, we had to cross it three hundred odd feet above the Avon River. A huge iron suspension bridge built in 1853, scary.

A phone book quickly revealed the most likely place, and with a couple of inquiries we arrived at the mansion sized house. This one looked new, well new for Bristol, probably Victorian. No gates or security, just a big driveway that turned into a circle near the house. Lawns and gardens with a cherry tree grove to one side. We parked and rang the bell.

A parrot-faced man in a tuxedo opened the door. "Good day gentlemen, to what do we owe the pleasure?"

"I'm, er, I'm looking for Mr. Critton."

"Do you have an appointment, sir?"

"No, just tell him I've just come from Priscilla."

"Please wait sirs." The parrot-faced penguin walked away leaving the door open, in a few moments he returned. "Mr. Critton will greet you in the drawing-room sirs. Please come this way." He led the way into a beautifully decorated modern room with desk, easy chairs, and a large table. The room looked as though it was used as a sitting-room-cum-office.

Just ten seconds later Critton walked in. I recognized him, and he recognized me. "Mr. Reyner, I should have guessed. You solved that dreadful affair with the TOD. I should have realized I couldn't hide from you.

"Hide sir?"

"Yes, please take a seat and relax. Geeves bring me a whisky. What would you like?"

'Oh, he's driving, just orange juice for Newf, and I'll have a, er. Do you have any beer?"

Critton smiled a very friendly smile. Funny I thought he would be a real stuck-up twit. "Bring Mr. Reyner a Guinness, Geeves."

I sat on one of the luxurious easy chairs. "I'm sorry, sir, but Priscilla pressed me into looking for you."

"Didn't take you long."

"No sir."

"And I suppose you are looking for a reason?"

"Yes, sir."

"Well if it were anyone else, I would try to bribe you into silence. Though I doubt I have enough wealth to bribe a person of your monetary stature. Is there anything I can do to persuade you not to report my position?"

I sighed, what an awkward spot to be in. "Sir, I'll do whatever you think best."

A flush of relief flooded down his face. "Thank god, you're a reasonable man. You see I just can't stand it any longer. Have you ever lived in a hen house?"

"Hen house?"

"Yes, a precocious daughter, an indulgent wife and mother-in-law who would diminish the evil of Lucritia Baugere. Even the bloo-, even the servants are female. Being the only man in that house is sufficient to stress the patience of the Pope."

14

Narrow Escape

I felt very sorry for Mr. Critton, poor sod. Fancy a man of his age running away from home, especially when it's his mother-in-law who holds all the purse strings. He seemed a very gentle and friendly man, wanted me to call him by his familiar name, Herb. I promised to keep his secret, at least for the meantime; we had other business to look into anyhow. He seemed a man of leisure, certainly knew his wines. The house had a fully stocked cellar, wines dating back to the mid-nineteenth century.

"Well Herb," I said. "Thanks for your help and hospitality, but Newf and I have some bad guys to catch."

He smiled. "It's a pleasure talking to you. I wished Priscilla had taken with you instead of -. Well it's all water under the bridge. Would you like to stay the night? It'll save you the trouble of finding lodgings."

I looked at Newf, he nodded in the affirmative. "Yeah, sure. Thanks."

He rang the bell, and Geeves came into the room. "Ah! Would you tell Molly to prepare two rooms, our guests will be staying the night."

"Certainly, sir."

"Please feel at home, here. If there is anything I can get you, just, well, just ask."

"Thank you." Funny thing, when I met him in Canada he seemed a very stuck-up kinda character. "There's a case here in Bristol we're looking into."

"Oh!" He said brightening up. "Do I know of it?"

"I wouldn't think so, you see it wouldn't have hit the papers. It's a case of a missing person."

"Oh! Well you're excellent at finding people. Didn't take you long to find me."

"Ah! Yeah! This is different. I believe Mrs. Marion Brindle has been abducted."

Herb smiled. "I doubt that. She's a very prominent woman, especially since her husband vanished."

"Her husband vanished?"

"Oh, certainly. It's been in the papers for months. Disappeared on a trip to Scotland, not a trace found. They thought it had to be foul play, not a thing. Never even found as much as a hair, so-to-speak."

"When was this?"

"Oh just last year. Even now it's still in the paper. She keeps kicking up a fuss about the incompetence of the police. Oh yes! You definitely have it all wrong. She's alive and well, it's her husband that's missing."

Another puzzle didn't make any sense for him to go and she's still around. Nonetheless her name is on the list I found at Cameron's place. Maybe, she's the next target. "Very strange," I said and sipped my Madera.

In the morning, as bright as a pair of fleas in the sunlight, Newf and I were up, shaved, dressed, and prepared to go by seven. Surprisingly the household was awake and active. Breakfast already filling the air with pleasant odours. Not a single female servant in sight, though I knew some existed somewhere in the huge house. Breakfast had already been set out in the dining room; Geeves conducted us to our seats.

Herb appeared smartly dressed. He walked in and took his seat. "Good morning."

"Hi."

"Have you decided whether you are going to inform Priscilla of my whereabouts or not?"

"Yes I have." He seemed a real nice guy. "I'm not. I can't lie to her, so I thought we'd do our research here then probably go home."

"Excellent. I have a job interview. Geeves will give you anything you need if I'm not around." He stood up, smiled ever-so lightly then shook our hands. He left us to our breakfast.

Mrs. Marion Brindle lived in the penthouse of the Grand hotel. The reason became obvious; the security had to

157

be better than that of the Royal Mint. No way would they allow us into the upper reaches of the hotel. Wouldn't even call Mrs. Brindle to ask for an appointment. The obvious thing, would be to do a clandestine entry

We walked to the shopping area of the city and found a store where we could buy white coveralls. I bought a nice looking toolbox just to complete the ensemble. I packed the uniforms into the toolbox and struck out for the hotel again. With nonchalant confidence we walked to the elevator and pressed the button. No one bothered us.

The car stopped and the doors opened, we walked in and I selected the basement parking area. Once in the garage we donned our new clean coveralls and called the elevator again. Now looking like efficient hotel maintenance staff, I pressed the penthouse button. No response. Zip, nada. The dumb elevator needed a key to go to the top. Unperturbed I selected the highest public floor.

"So why we going there?" Newf asked.

"Simple my friend. There has to be a fire route and a stair route. We'll pretend to be maintenance staff and wheedle our way in."

"Like she's gonna confide in the hired help."

"We'll play it by ear. Now buck up and play the part."

"What'd yah expect we gonna learn, then?"

"I bet she's been replaced. She's another of them Garston cuckoos."

"Like as if she's gonna tell us that."

"Shut up, Newf. We're looking for anything that may help."

I was right, on the tenth floor; we exited the elevator and looked for the stairwell. Sure enough there were stairs going in the up direction as well as down. At the top of the stairs a locked door barred the way. No problem for Newf. In moments he frigged the lock and we opened the door. It felt exciting to be doing a little covert work again.

The door led to a short corridor with another door, at the end. I figured this would be the apartment entrance. I knocked and stepped back. After about a minute the door opened and a woman in her mid fifties glared at us. "Yes?"

"We're plumbing maintenance. Someone on the floor below reported water leaking in through their ceiling."

"Then why haven't we been informed?"

"It's an emergency, only just happened."

"So what do you want?"

"I need to inspect your pipes."

You could see the suspicion in her eyes. "Alright, main bathroom's that way. Make a mess and there'll be trouble."

We walked in the direction indicated. We were in, but what to do next? Obviously there would be no telltale papers in the bathroom. "You bang around a little, make it sound as if you're actually doing something and I'll do a little snooping."

"What if yah gets caught?"

"I'll worry about it when and if it happens. Now get to making some noise."

Carefully I spied the hallway outside, the woman had retreated to somewhere else. Carefully and slowly I crept out and tried the handle on the next room, it opened easily. Inside I found a bedroom, though it looked like an unused one. Probably only for visitors or something. Across the hall lay a more inviting door, it was locked.

I slipped back into the bathroom. "The room across the hall's locked, it needs your expertise."

Newf quickly slipped across and did his thing with the lock. In moments we were in. Just as the door swung open the house-woman turned up and caught us red handed. "What are you doing?" She yelled.

Instinctively, I grabbed her and clapped my hand over her mouth, and held one arm tight up her back. "Quiet, and you'll not get hurt."

She stopped struggling and I released her mouth. "You'll pay for this," she hissed.

"Sure, now you be a nice lady and no one'll get hurt. Where's Mrs. Brindle?"

"Out."

"So you're alone?"

Her eyes flashed with anger. "What of it?"

It was about then I realized she had a slight Scottish accent. "Search this room, Newf, the mistress and I have another engagement." I let go of her arm. "One false move and I'll start breaking a few of your bones, alright?"

"What do you want?"

"I know what you're up to. I know all about the Garstons, and Cameron. Now I want to know what happened to Mrs. Brindle."

"She's not here."

"I already figured that. Where is she?"

"Shopping."

"Bull shit. She never leaves here. I doubt she even lives here, I doubt she even lives. Where is she, buried up at Cromlet?" We walked into the living room, a well-appointed chamber with all the accoutrements of living. For a millionairess, the place seemed meagre.

"So what do you want?" She asked angrily.

"Evidence, something to prove what you're up to. So who are you? Are you a Garston?"

"I have no idea what you are talking about. I am only the housekeeper."

"How many other servants are there?"

"Oh lots, they'll be here soon."

"Now sit and shut up." I yelled for Newf, he came running. "Find something to tie her up with. We've got work to do."

Telephone extension cords are usually the easiest thing to use, but this apartment only had one phone and that was cordless. Eventually he ripped a cord from one of the curtains. Together we secured her to one of the chairs, giving us a totally hands free approach to the search. She didn't put up any resistance, not even a scream or two.

I suppose it was only to be expected, the whole suite turned out to be squeaky clean. No pictures, no papers, not a single document. After a good half hour's search I decided it was about time to make our get away. We exited the same way we entered in exact reverse. As soon as we reached the car I made a phone call to the hotel and told them about the prisoner tied to a chair in the penthouse.

"Where too guv?" Newf said sitting behind the wheel.

I sighed. "This whole expedition is a waste of time, we should go home to Canada and give up."

"You could 'o bashed 'er around a bit, you know squeeze 'er a little."

"I'll squeeze you a little, drive back to Critton's place, maybe they'll offer us a meal or something."

"Right-you-are. Then what?"

"I think I'll make a report to Priscilla, then we'll have a look at the one in London."

"London?"

"Yeah, there's one missing in London, then we'll catch a silver bird home."

We drove the rest of the way in near silence. I guess Newf had some thinking to do. I did, this case was no fun at all. If the Garstons were really behind a tyrannous endeavour to steal from the rich, they sure hid their tracks well. Maybe Newf was right, I should buy a gun from somewhere and go sort out the Garstons in their lair. Go do someone a real injury and make them talk.

Man you could see why they called it the Heights. Didn't matter which way you approach there's a good-sized hill. The Clifton Bridge must be the highest point in the city. Newf enjoyed it; he handled the car like he'd been driving in Britain all his life. Up the hill across the bridge and into the residential area. It really is a beautiful and old city.

Critton wasn't back from his meeting, but Geeves welcomed us with open arms. You'd think we were long lost relatives. He offered us a meal and said: "Would sirs like to partake of the household entertainment?"

I shrugged. "Like what?"

"There's a perfectly well appointed games room in the bodega."

"Oh! What's that?"

"It's the cellar, sir. I do believe you Americans call it a basement. If you'd follow me."

We did, an' man he was surely right. The entire bottom of the house had been turned into a large playroom. With a full sized pool table, even a five-pin bowling alley. I should have thought of something like this when we had our house rebuilt. The balls on the pool table were odd though.

"Look at this," I said showing one to Newf.

"So?"

"Well they're useless."

Newf shook is head. "Ain't yah ever 'erd of snooker."

"Yeah."

"'Ave yous ever played?"

"No."

"Thought not. Them's snooker balls. I'll teach yah 'ow to play."

I guess it was a bit of a cheek, imposing on Mr. Critton like that, but I figured after what his daughter put me through. Well, it felt right. I offered to pay for the inconvenience, though he wouldn't hear of it. Funny thing, never saw hide nor hair of any relatives. Only Herb, and Geeves occupied the house while we were there. A manservant is a great thing, I figured maybe I'd train Newf, though we'd have to find him an appropriate name.

The following morning and after an excellent repast, we were ready to return to London and look at one more missing person before going home. "You wanna drive, Newf?"

"Where to?"

"Priscilla's house, I guess. Then we'll find some digs."

"Sure, but I ain't doin' no drivin' in London."

"No problem."

We bid our host ado and set out on the long drive. Down the drive and onto the street. I suggested taking the southern route, but Newf wanted to cross the Clifton Bridge once more. It's slightly uphill to the huge iron structure. On the other side there's, three choices of direction, two downhill and one still uphill. The lights were with us and Newf made a right turn down the steep hill into the town.

"I fink we's got trouble Bill," he said.

'Why?"

"There ain't no brakes."

"Oh! Christ."

Quickly the car built up speed, Newf leaned on the horn to alert other road users. Fortunately there's not too much pedestrian or vehicular traffic at the early hour. "I fink we's in real trouble, Bill."

"Use the gears. Look there's an empty space brush up against the building."

Holy mackerel, we leapt into the air as the wheels struck the sidewalk. With a fearful crash the side of the car collided with the solid stone building. Sparks and flames lit up the entire left side, then I think we must have slipped into a doorway and struck solid stone. The vehicle spun round and cartwheeled, then smashed into a parked car on the opposite side of the street.

The stupid airbags deployed, dam near knocking my head off. I think that's why Newf lost her. It's difficult to drive when the cab's full of dusty face-stinging safety gear. It's amazing how silent the world seems immediately after a smash-up. For a moment I just sat there, sort of dazed.

"Newf, you alright?"

"I fink so."

I don't remember how, but I must have climbed from the car. I remember standing there looking at the terrible mess. Bits of glass, and plastic all over the road. People began to arrive on the scene, though all I remember is confusion. My head still spun like a top. I can't remember what happened to Newf. Then I found myself lying down looking at the ceiling of an ambulance. At that moment I felt no pain, though confusion clouded my intellect.

By the time we reached the hospital I had fully regained my memory. Newf lay on a litter on the other side of the vehicle. They had an oxygen mask on him and a drip thing attached to his arm.

"Is he alright?" I asked and attempted to sit up. The restraints kept me horizontal.

"Nothing to worry about, sir," the friendly attendant said. "You're both in good hands."

I didn't want all that fuss they make. I could easily have walked into the hospital, but they forced me to lie on that stupid gurney and wheeled me in. In moments all those white-coated individuals were probing and prodding. I had a terrible pain in my chest, beyond that I felt great.

After ten or fifteen minutes I was forced to submit to x-rays, then half an hour later the pretty nurse said I could leave after completing all the documentation. Still my only concern was Newf, where was he? And how well had he fared? No one seemed very interested in my questions. Eventually I found the inquires area. A dam silly computer, not a person.

After tinkering with the stupid computer for a few moments I gave up. What a waste of time. I walked back to the nurse's station and eventually attracted one's attention. "I'm looking for Newf. I mean, North, Mr. East, He came in about an hour ago, a traffic accident."

She smiled. "You'll have to ask at reception, sir."

With a sigh of resignation I asked: "Where's that?"

"Down the hall, follow the overheads, sir. You can't go wrong."

I heard one of them giggle and say something about, I should get a compass. What a dumb hospital. She was right, there were signs, and the overheads, as she called them were guiding arrow, red for emergency blue for waiting areas and yellow for inquires.

"Hi!" I said to the man in the telephone-box-like inquiries office. "I'm looking for my friend, we were in a traffic accident about an hour and half ago. I can't find him."

"Ah! Mr. Reyner?"

"Yeas," I said with surprise.

"The police are looking for you. Where've you bin?"

"Where have I been?" I've been marching all over this God-damn hospital looking for my friend North."

He picked up a phone and mumbled a few words. He put it down and looked at me. "The cops'll be here in a minute, if you'll wait."

I'd expected a genuine English Bobby, instead this flat hatted, leather jacketed traffic warden turned up. "Mr. Reyner?"

"Yeah."

He motioned his head for me to follow him. "Over, 'ere, sir."

We walked to the side where there was less human traffic. He took out his notebook. "So, where's my friend?" I asked.

"He's being detained, just for a while sir. I understand you were passenger in the vehicle concerned?"

"Yeah."

"Would you like to tell me what happened?"

I sighed. "Why don't you ask the driver?"

"We did. Now I would like your version, sir."

"I really don't know what happened. We left Critton's place, came over the Clifton Bridge and turned right at the lights. That's when we lost the brakes. Newf did a fine job. We didn't hurt anybody, did we?"

The constable shook his head. "The car's been taken to Wright's garage. They're looking at it there. Until this is cleared up, you'll have to stay in this city. At what residence, sir?"

"Stay, we can't stay, we've got work to do."

'Work, sir? I thought you and Mr. East were on holiday."

"A sort of working holiday officer. How long've we got to stay?"

"Long enough."

"Like how long?"

"Until you're told otherwise sir. Now, would you like to come down to the station and make a full statement?"

"Right now?"

"Today sir, anytime today, sir."

"Oh sure. Can I go now?"

" Yes, sir."

I walked back to the kiosk and asked the guy where I could find Newf. The instructions were fairly simple and in no time I found him in bed on the second floor. He sat there reading a magazine with some bandages on his woodenhead. When he spotted me his face lit up in welcome.

"Hi, Newf. I've been looking all over for you." I sat on the chair beside him, feeling a little over used.

"Did yah bring me any grapes?"

"I'll grape you in a minute. No. What are you doing taking it easy here?"

"I cuts me 'ed in the crash, didn't I? They examined and couldn't find nothin' in it."

"They only had to ask me, I could have told them there's nothing in your head. So when'd you get out?"

He shrugged. "Just observation, she said. They'll let me go when they're sure me 'ed's alright."

"Oh gees! I guess your here for eternity, then."

"I ain't 'avin' no baby."

"Eternity, not maternity, you twit." I think the accident had killed his solitary brain cell. "You still got your cell phone."

He shrugged. "D'know. They took all me clobber."

"Alright. I'll have to get another car, this time I'll drive. I also gotta get us some digs. I'll come back later, don't move till I do, okay?"

"Sure boss."

The rental company had an affiliate garage in town. Surprisingly they were not unduly upset by the accident. I had to sing a few papers and in under an hour I drove out with an almost brand-new car. Next, somewhere to stay. That wasn't difficult either. I got a room at the Avon Hotel on the Southport Road. Funny thing, Bristol and me clicked, I began to like the city, to spite the hills.

I parked in the cop-shop parking lot and walked in. A sergeant at the desk told me to wait. After an interminable half hour he leaned over and said: "Jorden 'll see you now. Second door on the left."

Jorden looked too old to be a cop. Too scruffy and uncouth. He nodded toward a chair. "Sit," he said.

I sat. He pulled out a packet of cigarettes and lit one. "So who's after you?"

"Pardon?"

"Don't come the funny with me. I said who's after you?"

I really had no idea what he meant. "After me? Like how do you mean?"

He sucked hard on the cigarette and blew a cloud of smoke. "Stop all the farting around, someone's out to get you, who?"

I shrugged. "D'know. Why?"

"Yah car had the brake line sawed through, it weren't no accident, son."

166

15

Change of Attitude

The police began to see sense and reason; they released Newf
and myself. Poor old Newf had been given a clean bill of
health and released from the hospital. We'd only been delayed
a couple of days. The question now, should we return to
Canada, London, or Scotland? After collecting my companion
from the hospital I asked him: "You wanna drive?"

"Sure. I banged my 'ead, didn't break me arm."

"Alright I direct you to our digs."

"You goin back to Brindle's place?"

"What for?"

"Cuz them's the ones 'oo tried to kill us. I fink we
should go there and duff that broad up a bit."

I sat silent thinking for a few moments, just giving the
appropriate directional instruction. Gran would know what to
do. When we stopped in the hotel parking lot I used my cell
phone. It only rang twice, and Gran answered it. "Hallo."

"Hi! Gran. It's me."

"Oh! William. How are things proceeding?"

"Quite well, I guess. Sorry I forgot to check the time
before I phoned."

"No problem, dear. The time here is almost half past
six p.m."

"Great, what do you think we should do, Gran?"

"Do, William, do?"

"We've discovered nothing. Oh, I found Priscilla's
dad, no sweat. Some one tried to kill us, they cut the brake
lines on our car."

"William, I have expressed upon you before, care,
stealth, and persistence. We must gather intelligence, evidence
is an absolute necessity. Whatever you do, don't leave the car
unattended, there is two of you."

"Right, Gran. What do you think I should do now?"

"Evidence, William. Investigate the next on your list, and take exceptional care, William. Do the police have any clues who sabotaged your car?"

"No, Gran."

"Very well, William, do not go to Scotland without consulting with me first. And do, please, try to phone in sociably acceptable hours."

"Yes Gran." I folded up the phone and put it in my pocket. "Newf you stay with the car. I'll go get our stuff and pay the bill."

"Why've I gotta stay in the car?"

"'Cause we don't want another show like the other day. If anyone comes near the car phone me. I'll come and dent their ego."

He smiled and returned to the car. As quickly as possible I collected our gear and paid the hotel bill. In less than thirty minutes we were rolling.

"Where too, boss?"

"Head out, say easterly. We're going to London."

"Right yah are. But I ain't doin' no driving' in London. Okay?"

"Sure Newf. I'll take over as soon as we get close. Till then I'll navigate with the GPS."

"Where 'zactly are we goin'?"

"First, let's go to Priscilla's, then we'll go to Rhoda Holmes's place."

"She's the next on the list?"

"I guess you could say that."

"Well, this time, Bill, let's start out tough and keep it up. I fink you should beat the shit out o' 'em. Then they'll be more ready to talk."

"Yeah, yeah, Newf, you drive, leave me to do the thinking."

I had a lot of thinking to do. Priscilla worried me; who is this twit Godfrey? Oh! Who cares? Someone wanted to play rough, they tried to kill us. Scouse has already been murdered. I can't believe anyone or any group could disappear, kill, and sabotage so many people without leaving a trail a mile wide. How would they make their next attempt to kill us? The thought struck me, giving the way of international terrorists, maybe it wouldn't be safe flying home.

After getting lost twice, well not lost, say misguided, we arrived at Cottenham Hall around 7 p.m. God-freak let us in. Surprisingly he seemed pleased to see us. We all met in the sitting room. Thank goodness grandma wasn't there, just Priscilla and God-whatever.

"I found your father Priscilla, he's safe and well."

"Where is he?"

"He asked me not to reveal his whereabouts."

"Why?"

I shook my head. "I don't know, it's family stuff. Anyhow, he's safe, there's nothing to worry about. I told him I'd only keep his secret for one month. So if he doesn't come home by then, I'll tell you where to find him. Can we stay the night here?"

"Certainly not."

Somehow I felt like giving her a good thrashing. You know when I think about it, she cost me a fortune. I hired a boat for her once, and I mean a boat complete with crew. She drives like a nut. Godfrey's welcome to her. What the hell do I care? "Your old man's in Bristol. He left cause he can't stand living in this house with you and your mother and grandmother. Said he never wants to come home."

She smiled. "Spiteful, William. Will you please leave now? I don't want to hear your lies. Go away, or Godfrey will throw you out."

"God-freak, old boy, you're welcome to her. She's selfish, indolent, and a genuine tease. If I were you I'd pack and leave. Good-by all. Come-on Newf this dump's beginning to smell."

"Wow, neat, Bill. You sure told 'em. You drive."

"No sweat."

It felt sort of better, like a weight had been lifted from me. I really loved Priscilla, I still probably do; yet somehow she aggravates me and scares me. To change the subject, we found a small inn on the outskirts of London. The problem remained, what to do with the car. I figured, that maybe we've given the enemy the slip anyhow.

First thing in the morning I personally checked the car; pumped the brakes hard, and checked for any limpets or other nasty devices. I even looked at the steering linkage. Everything looked all right to me, no sign of any outside interference. I would drive, as Newf had a fear of London traffic.

"Where to?" Newf asked as he climbed in the passenger side.

"What we need is a Who's-Who. Let's see if we can find a library in the village."

No, the village did not support a local library. On the outskirts of London we found just what the doctor ordered, a large local-studies library. The young lady quickly looked it up in the appropriate book. "Oh yes, sir here we are. Rhonda Holmes, wife of the later Sir Allen Holmes. The address is given as East Paling Manor, sir."

"Thanks. Any idea where that might be?"

"It's rural London, the greater London area. I'll look it up for you." She pulled another large volume from the shelves and quickly ascertained the exact location. "There you are, sir," she said pointing to a small red dot on the map.

"Thank you." I walked back to the car where I'd left Newf on guard. Didn't want any unexpected surprises, you see.

I jumped in. "We've gotta go round to the North Circular. We need northeast London. Shouldn't take long."

'Then what?"

"We'll make an entrance and find out if the lady's in."

It took almost an hour and a half to get to the right area. The house is not visible from the main road. An unoccupied gatehouse, then a long winding drive through the trees and eventually an open meadow with the biggest house I've ever seen. A monster three and four stories tall, chimney stacks as tall as small industrial flues.

The place looked clean and well cared for, though I did notice a definite lack of staff. We parked in a courtyard, stables and garages on two sides, green houses on the third, the main building on the fourth side. We entered through an arch between the stables. Not a soul to be seen.

"'Oly smoke," Newf said duly impressed by the splendour and age of the place. "Which way's in?"

"D'know. I'll park by the house."

"You wan' me to keep guard o' the car?"

"No, I may need your moral support, you come with me."

"I don't know if it was the front, main, side, or back, anyhow I banged on a very large-wooden door that had hundreds of iron rivets or bolts through it. It looked like a church door, being arched. At close quarters you could see the stonework had lasted through many centuries. After two or three vain attempts at waking someone with very loud banging we tried the door. It was locked. A smaller entrance at the top of a short flight of stone steps looked a good chance. Newf started the banging, then I took over for a while. Still no one on the inside noticed us, and this door also resisted our attempts to open it.

"Newf, do your thing."

"You wanna break in?"

"No, I want you to unlock the bloody door."

"It ain't locked."

"Then open it."

"Can't rightly do that, it's bolted from the inside."

There was no lack of choice, at least another six doors were in clear sight from our viewpoint. "Okay, let's give another a good try. How'd yah know it's bolted?"

"Easy, ain't got no keyhole."

The next one we tried had a keyhole and after minutes of fruitless banging, Newf opened it with his magic touch. Creaking like the entrance to a mysterious dungeon, the door opened. The interior looked inadequately lit, a plain unfinished wooden floor and walls of unfinished stone.

"What'd think?" I whispered.

"There ain't no point in speakin' soft. There ain't nobody to 'ear us."

Gingerly we inched down the darkened corridor. It appeared to go forever. Some eight or ten meters in a heavy door with rusty rivets stood to the left. The opening device was a huge latch, also very rusty. Newf lifted the latch and the creaky door swung aside. An empty room, completely empty, bare walls and stone floor. The far interior shrouded in total darkness offered anything but an invitation.

"You got a light, Bill?"

"No."

"Let's find another door."

"Wait, my eyes are becoming accustomed to the gloom." I walked into the darkness to investigate further. At the darkest end lay six steps up and another door, a modern looking one in fair condition. "Look, this one's got a keyhole."

"Is it locked?"

I tried the handle, it was locked. Quickly Newf did his thing and the door swung silently open. Beyond lay a hall of some magnificence. Intricately painted blue walls and polished wood floors with scattered Persian rugs. Paintings of long dead ancestors hanging on both sides. Fully furnished and decorated, the place looked lived in, or at least museum-like. No windows, though the ample light was supplied by small electric chandeliers hanging every six meters or so.

"Take a butchers at this," Newf growled in surprise.

I turned and saw his back in a doorway. Looking over his shoulder I too was amazed. The giant and splendiferous room put even Cromlet to shame. Golden models of sailing ships a meter tall standing on antique tables all around. A blue rope with gold thread seemed to describe a path through the room.

"I fink, we's broke into a museum," Newf said walking in to examine some of the treasures.

"What about alarms?"

"Don't see none. Uh-oh! Look, see." He pointed.

There was a TV camera in every corner of the room, near the ceiling. "Christ, I think we've been spotted."

Quickly I ran to the next room following the rope. I had some insane idea I would find a sword or something to protect myself.

"Bill," Newf called from behind me. "Bill, it's too late."

I turned; a young lad in a smart robe stood watching us from an arch to one side. He didn't look unduly alarmed. I'm tall and muscular, which usually makes people feel a little

172

uneasy. He smiled, and rubbed his hands together. His eyes sparkled; he looked about my age but thin and not quite as tall as me.

"We're lost," I said weakly.

"You must be Reyner. I've half expected you."

He stood there dressed kinda strange, with soft shoes, and a robe. He looked like someone from the east, though his face spelled London. "Who are you?" I growled in my most aggressive voice.

He smiled sweetly and moved toward us slowly and gracefully. "You may call me Demise." He stopped about an arm's length in front of me.

"Where's Rhoda Holmes?" I snapped and closed my fists in preparation, just to intimidate him a little.

His broad sickly grin persisted; his eyes sparkled, and never seemed to blink. "She's dead and gone. This place belongs to Cromlet. I am the caretaker."

His honesty staggered me at first, sort of took the wind out of my sails. "So how was it all arranged?"

"You are by far too nosy, Mr. Reyner. But as this is your last day on Earth. I may as well tell you. The Garstons infiltrate, and eliminate. That's why they are called the Edinburgh Cuckoos. Nothing and no one can defeat them. They have almost infinite wealth and power."

"So what about Cameron, Edward Cameron?"

Demise gave an all knowing-smiling nod. "Edward Cameron died years ago, John Garston took his law degree in the same name. Just another little diversion. Now if you would follow me we have two more coffins to fill."

I figured this wimp was either joking or had a gun under his silly looking robe. "I need more information."

He sort of slowly melted into a Kung-fu stance, moving his arms slowly in the air. I mean, what a twit. I outweighed him by thirty percent. I didn't really want to hurt him. I thought a good punch may do him real damage, so I hauled back and went to hit him on the chest. He grabbed my arm spun round and threw me over his shoulder. I hit the hard floor with everything, stars flashed before my eyes, and I was some pissed off. As soon as I could I leapt up and took another swipe at the idiot. This time I intended to knock his block off.

Oh gees! That damn floor was real hard. Again I found myself staring at that beautiful ornate ceiling. For a moment I wasn't quite sure where I was or what was happening. It sounded like an alarm bell ringing in my head, and nothing wanted to respond to my wishes. Desperately I struggled with muscles that did not want to respond. I staggered to my feet and looked about the blurry room, blinking to clear my vision.

Ah! There he stood, still grinning like a Cheshire cat. I felt like a drunken man, my breath was short and every muscle ached. A trembling started in my legs making it hard to remain vertical. "Right you bastard, you're a dead man." Again I swung hard at the grinning face.

This whistle thing got louder and louder, I opened my eyes and could clearly see the magnificent markings of some wonderful map. My vision seemed clear, though I couldn't fathom what I could be doing looking at this strange pattern.

"Are you alright, Bill?"

Somewhere in the distance someone was obviously talking to me. I moved my head painfully to one side. Now I know what it is. I could see the ceiling. Suddenly I realized I was lying horizontal. Newf came into view.

"I fort you wuz a gonner, Bill. That geezer kicked the shit out o' yah."

I sat up, oh the pain! My head began to swim with the effort. "What happened?"

"Well, ol' Demise over there, well 'e dinged you up good. So I 'ad to put 'im down for yah."

I looked at Newf, he was dead serious. "You put him down? You? You couldn't put a gnat down and this guy tosses me around like a toy."

"Well 'e were busy doin' you. I figured after 'e'd fixed you up then 'e come and do me. So when 'e was sort 'o busy wiv you, I 'it 'im."

"You hit him? You couldn't knock the skin of a rice pudding."

"Well, 'e 'ad 'is back to me. I picks up that golden ship there and beamed 'im like."

"How appropriate. I'm sure Gran would have some smug remark for that. Sort of took the wind out of his sails, eh? Sank his ship, pushed the boat out, or something akin." I looked around; Demise lay on the floor, quite a bit of blood, and a priceless antique golden ship lying in ruins beside him. "Is he dead?"

"Nah. I only winged 'im."

Feeling worse than something the dog dragged home, I staggered to my feet and walked over to examine this Demise character. He was alive all right, the injuries looked superficial; mostly his ear. "Tie him up Newf. We don't want another enactment like the last."

I still felt woozy, any sudden movement causing my head to spin. "When he comes round I'll kill the bastard. I'm sure he done me an injury. You got any aspirin or anything?"

"Nah. I ain't got nothin' to tie 'im up wiv, neiver."

"For Christ's sake, Newf, use your brain, and before he gets up and clobbers the pair of us."

I sank down onto a table, unable to think straight. My prime interest was to get this character disabled permanently. I sat and watched the body while Newf ran off to find some kind of restraint. After a few minutes he came running back with a dog lead.

"This'll 'ave to do," he said.

"Great, Newf, tie the sod up, never mind his feet. I want those hands tied behind his back. Roll him over."

Newf enjoyed himself; this kind of thing really turned him on. He secured the guy's hands and left him face down. "Turn him over and tie his shoelaces together."

"Wha' for?"

"So he can't run or kick."

I carefully checked Newf's work, then decided it was time to find water. "Where's the bathroom?"

"Feelin' sick?"

"No. I need to wash my face and freshen up, maybe find some aspirin for this head of mine."

"It's a big enough 'ouse. Gotta be 'undreds o' barf rooms."

"You stay here and watch the prisoner. I'll go find a bathroom or washroom. If I call come running, you may have to rescue me again. And thanks, Newf, you did a fine job."

I think I swelled his pride a little. "Don't be too long, Bill. Yah never know someone may come."

The trouble with a building of that magnitude, there's so many rooms it would take all day to look in them. Carefully I noted where I travelled, in order to return. Eventually I found an office, with bathroom. Nothing in the medicine cabinet, I looked in the desk drawer, nothing of use there either. The filing drawers looked interesting. Just like any office the files were alphabetical. Under which would I search?

Nothing really mind blowing, maybe it was my headache that made the search dull and annoying. Maybe I was just being stupid, as if they would leave incriminating evidence. The documents all pertained to the house, repairs, and income. On the way back, disappointed and head throbbing, I suddenly noticed a safe. Now if there's anything to learn, there would be the place. Eventually I found my way back to Newf and his prisoner.

"Did yah find any aspirin?"

"No I bloody didn't." I looked at Demise, he sat up glaring at me. Man if looks could kill. "Where'd you keep the aspirin?" I growled.

"Drop dead."

"Wrong reply. I think we should torture him, Newf. I think the old fire in the hands will work. What do you think?"

"Nah! I fink we should drag 'im to the kitchen. There's lots of lovely fings there, like a blender, toasters are good. It's real neat when yous tie a hand in the toaster then turns it on. I get a real laugh outa that'un."

I looked at Demise with my most evil smile. "Yeah, I think the kitchen would be the best place. Oh by the way Newf, could you open a safe?"

"Don't know, maybe."

I watched Demise's eyes as I said: "Maybe we should just kill him and go for the safe." He showed no sign of concern. Not exactly what I had expected. If my head would just stop throbbing. It tends to make a person slightly short tempered and we were getting nowhere. I kicked the prisoner. "I think we'll kill him anyway. He's just a burden."

"No," Demise said. "What do you want?"

"A bloody aspirin, first."

"There's some in the first-aid room."

"First-aid room?"

"Yes. Release my feet and I'll show you where it is."

"Just tell me, I'll find it on my own."

He shook his head. There's maintenance staff coming soon, you going to hold them prisoner too?"

"Untie his feet, Newf. If you make a run for it or try anything clever, I swear I'll kill you on the spot. Is that clear?"

"Certainly."

Newf untied his shoelaces and took the shoes off. "You won't need these."

"Come on. Lead the way." I picked him up by the scruff of his neck. "One false move, that's all."

The first-aid room wasn't even very far away, I'd explored in the wrong direction. Just a small room with a litter and a medicine cabinet. "What's it used for?"

"First aid."

"Idiot, I mean why would a house need a first-aid room?"

Demise smiled. "When Mrs. Rhoda Holmes died in 1975, she left everything to the National Trust. This house is open to tourists, almost every day."

16

The Mechanic

Gran always says; "Use your brain, William." I do try to, but sometimes things just aren't that simple. Now, Demise must think I'm totally stupid if he thinks I'm going to believe his bull about the National Trust. To start with he said he'd expected me; why? His real name turned out to be Norman Morley, don't know why he said it was Demise. His driver's licensee had all the info. I kept it.

We made our getaway, more or less the way we had entered. Poor Demise, or Norman would have to stay in a closet until someone found him. The safe was of no interest, Newf couldn't open it. The only interesting piece of information we collected from Demise was a more-or-less slip of the tongue. He said it must have been the mechanic who sabotaged our car, though he wouldn't elaborate.

Newf jumped into the driver's seat. "I fink we should get the 'ell art o' 'ere."

"Yeah, you're right. Where to though?"

He started the engine and backed around, then drove out of the courtyard. "Well, Bill what about the last name on your list. D'yah fink 'ee's the mechanic?"

I pulled the book of maps out of the glove box. "I doubt it. The mechanic must live in Bristol, and the last name's in Peterborough."

"Where to then?"

"Don't know just drive, if you see a pub, we'll stop for eats."

"Okay."

I needed time to think. Demise was just the housekeeper, it seemed that all the houses had someone to look after them, but why? Somehow the enemy were able to track us, even when we made erratic decisions. That had to be a clue. Who killed Scouse, and why? The only people who could know our whereabouts were, the taxi driver in Glasgow and-.

"Newf, I think we should go back to Scotland. I think we should find Mr. A Williams the taxi driver."

"Why?"

"'Cause he must know the Garstons. It was at his house they bashed me on the head."

"You really fink 'e'll still be there?"

"Well I bet he's the mechanic, he's got a car."

"Nah. Priscilla's dad's closer to 'ome. We was at 'is place when they fixed the brakes. I reckon 'ee's gotta be in on it."

"That's ridiculous, Newf. How would he know I would even be in England? What possible reason could he have? I think your nuts. It's gotta be the taxi driver. Head for Scotland."

"Okay boss."

"Why you stopping?"

"Pub. You said find a pub. I found one."

Fortunately Newf didn't drink and as he intended to do the driving, I felt that I could imbibe. The pub turned out to be a modern theme pub. I prefer the old ones. It had everything to do with aircraft or flying. Propellers, even bits of engines hanging on the walls. I guessed the owner must have been a flyer or something. Pictures of all kinds of fighter pilots all over the place. The pub had the most unlikely name of "The Battle of Britain."

Round the back they had a really nice garden that backed up to a small river. A young girl told us to make our order through the ordering window and relax in the garden. While I waited for food I examined the book of maps.

"Hay, Newf. The A1 highway passes right beside Peterborough. What d' think? Should we take a look-see?"

"I'm watching our car. I ain't gonna let some twit fix it while we eat."

"What about Peterborough?"

"What abart it?"

"Shall we give it a look?"

"Okay, sure."

Gees, sometimes talking to Newf is like talking to a water pump. He chunters on and acts like a drip. I figured I'd better call Gran. The cell-phone wouldn't work, I guessed we were in a dead spot. No sweat I'd phone later.

Peterborough's a nice place, sort of flat compared to Bristol. We'd been here before, Newf liked the place. A large and lazy river gently wended its way under the main bridge and passed a large park. A spectacular and ancient cathedral looked down over the lush greenery of the park. We drove down the main street and stopped at a municipal parking lot.

"So where, now?" Newf said switching the engine off.

"Well I've been doing a lot of thinking. I reckon we should try something slightly different. This time let's phone and tell them we're coming."

"What?"

"Let's pretend to be from the Garstons, doing a property check or something."

Newf blinked, then the light of dawn struck, like a lightning bolt. "Alright! Let's pretend we's looking for us. We'll tell them two dangerous Canadians are on the loose. I fink that'd be real sweet. Take the rats with their own bait."

"We'll have to find a phone book, all I have is the area he lives in."

Leaving the car unattended we wandered down the main street. I spotted a phone-box and checked out the directory. James Edward Burton, the Grange, Thorney Road. I made a note of the number. "Let's get back to the car."

"What'd you find, Bill?"

"You make the call, your accent's a little more believable than mine. I'll try to keep my mouth shut, they'll recognize my North American droll."

Newf's eyes rolled up and he pulled a grimace as he put his brain in gear to come up with a line. "Okay, Bill. Let's say we's security tryin' to find the Canadians and do 'em."

"Go on then."

I showed him the number and dialled it on his cell. "'Allo! "Yeah, this East. I'm calling from our organization. What?" He listened for a moment, then smiling said: "Nah! Nah! We've come to give yous a bit o' support. There's a couple o' troublemakers on the loose. The Mechanic almost got 'em in Bristol. We's bin called to finish the job. They's probably on their way to you right now." Again he listened for a few moments, then, "Right, we'll see yah soon. It's East, and Rigby." He closed the phone and grinned like a Cheshire cat.

"What's East and Rigby?" I asked.

"Me 'n you."

"I'm Reyner, not Rigby."

"Same initial. Yous don't expect I'd use your real name, do yah? They know you. Demise knows your name. Thay's all know it by now."

"So what they say?"

He smiled that smug smile, rather like Gran when she's figured something out. "They said they was expectin' us, but we's a day early."

"A day early?"

"Yeah. I reckon they's got some one commin to 'elp guard the place, and nail us but good. We'll get there first. This time we're a jump up on them. What yah fink?"

"I think we aughta get there before they do some checking. Where is it?"

"I didn't ask. I fort you knew."

The book of maps came to our aid once again. The Thorney Road seemed easy enough; We'd have to ask someone where the Grange is. Amazingly it only took fifteen minutes to find the road. I saw the postman, if anyone would know he surely would. Just ten minutes later we arrived at the Grange. A big-old Victorian house at the end of a short earthen drive. The place looked deserted, the grounds a little overgrown and no flower gardens.

"Well this place isn't for visitors, there isn't even any parking. "

As we pulled to a halt at the front door a tall gentleman in a black suit came to greet us. "Welcome," he said as I climbed from the car.

I nodded, stuck out my hand for a shake and in my best British accent said. "Hello! Rigby."

"Jeremy Goodlaw," he replied with a huge smile. Somehow he looked relieved to see us.

Newf introduced himself. "I'm East, the brains of this art-fit. 'ee's the muscle. Quick off the mark too, loves to bash people's brains art."

"You'd better come in," Jeremy said and led the way.

"So this is Burton's house," Newf said following our host in through the front door.

Man! What an odd place. The building on the inside looked utilitarian. Plain wood floor unpolished. Nicely decorated walls and ceiling, but in a row by the front door were a dozen bells. On a stand near one of the four other doors stood, what looked like a small jet-engine turbine. Above the entrance door hung a chromium plated six-cylinder crankshaft.

I didn't say anything; I poked Newf and directed him to the crankshaft with my eyes. "Neat decor," he said.

Jeremy seemed pleased to explain. "Mr. Burton was an inventor and mechanical genius. That's how he made his money. He used to work with Frank Perkins in the early days."

"Perkins?" I said in surprise.

"Oh, Frank's factory's not far from here. He was the one who worked with Rudolph Diesel, they developed the diesel engine together."

That didn't ring true; surely everyone would know someone that famous by sight, though I'd never heard of either. I'll bet Gran would know. Our host led the way into a cosy room, one of the smallest in the house. The room had been furnished as a small live-in apartment.

"Make yourselves at home. Would you like a cup of tea?"

Now he spoke the language I understood. "Sure."

"You American?" he said tinkering with the electric kettle.

Dam! For a moment I put my guard down, and he spotted the accent. Trying hard to speak like Newf, I said. "Nah! Zealand." Had to try and remember to drop the occasional 'H'. "'Ow did you know, we were coming?"

"Edward phoned. He keeps abreast of everything. The Canadian fellow was in Bristol only a few days ago, then London. You see there's a pattern to his whereabouts. It was obvious he'd be here next."

"You keep sayin; 'ee, I 'urd there were two on 'em." Newf said.

"Oh yeas! But Edward said the larger of the two, the Canadian was the dangerous one."

I began to feel a little hot under the collar. Was this a trap? Did this innocuous little Jeremy know who we really were? I decided to keep my mouth shut, let Newf do all the talking.

"I thought you would be here tomorrow," Jeremy said.

"Nah! We was close-by and fort we'd come over. So what's the plan? You want us to stay and catch these foreigners when and if the' comes?"

"Well, you're the security expert. I'll leave all the planning to you."

"What abart food and accommodations? Are you takin' care of us, or would you rather we bogs off uptown?"

"It's up to you." Jeremy placed the cups, milk and sugar on the table. "I hear they roughed poor old Norman up a bit. Still I believe violence begets violence, don't you?"

I nodded and Newf said: "That's why we's 'ere. The two of us'll soon make short work o' them. "Ow long you worked 'ere?"

Jeremy smiled that coy smile, I began to think he was a puff and had taken a liking to Newf. It was just the way he looked at him. "I don't like all that piggin' violence, really. I just do my job."

"What 'zactly is your job?"

Jeremy got up to answer the kettle. "Well this is my gaff, they pay me for just being here. The house is empty now. All the good stuff's gone to Pitcalver. I've never seen Cromlet, but I will."

"I 'ave. It's just another big 'ouse wiv lot's a stuff in it. I prefer the open road, lots of adventure an all that. I fink it's a real pity abart poor Devlin, you know, Scouse."

"Yes!" exclaimed Jeremy. "I was very shocked when I heard about that. I still think the Canadian killed him. The police insist he was murdered for the money he'd been given. But he was a gambler, always taking chances and always owing people money."

"I'm surprised the Garstons haven't landed in jail afore now."

"What for?" Jeremy said showing real incredulity.

"Oh come orf-it. They's take money from the rich and gives it to the richer."

"Nonsense," Jeremy snapped. "The Garston family are saints. They spend their lives persuading the rich and idle to be useful. They share their fortune with everyone in need. Even Robin Hood had nothing on the Garstons. Why, they're saints all of them."

"Don't they knock orf the rich to make the richer even richer?"

Jeremy looked astounded. The mere suggestion that the Garstons could be criminals offended his dignity. "Haven't you ever been to Cromlet?"

"Yeah."

"Did you see any sign of cruelty, or violence?"

"Nah."

"Even the village of Pitcalver is supported by the Garstons, the entire island of Drumvanich is supported by their ingenuity. Hundreds of people owe their existence to the Garston family. What on earth made you think they could possibly do anything illegal?"

"What abart this 'ouse. What 'appened to the geezer 'oo owned it?"

Jeremy smiled. "Like all those who see the truth, J. E. Burton saw the light before he died. He gave everything to the Cromlet Institute, and lived here until he died of old age. The perfect example of how the Cromlet institute works. Why, they wouldn't harm a flea. That's the problem with this Canadian bloke. They do say he makes his money out of other people's misfortune."

I kept my mouth shut. Though I would love to have defended myself. I've never harmed anyone. Well not a good guy, anyhow. Newf grinned as he said: "Yeah, them rich Canadians is right dummies. What you fink he's tryin; to do?"

"Destroy us. They want to take away our heritage and wealth. Even I'd be out of a job if they got their way."

"What abart the tamperin' wiv their car, then?"

"You have to fight fire with fire. I understand they didn't take the hint in Glasgow. So the mechanic gave them a serious warning."

"Why'd they call 'im the mechanic?"

Jeremy shrugged. "D'know, he used to be wealthy, but they say he lost his money on poor investments, and pandering to his precocious daughter."

I almost choked on my tea as something clicked in my head. Man I really wanted to ask a question, but I was terrified Jeremy would get a hint from my accent. Newf seemed to be doing all right on his own.

"I fort the mechanic wuz a right screw-up, that's why we's bin called in. Do you know him?"

"No. Mr. Cameron likes to keep us all informed. He usually phones once a week. He called yesterday and told me you were coming. He said the Canadians are dangerous and thought they'd be coming this way."

"So you don't know the mechanic?"

"No, I've never met Mr. Critton."

I almost jumped up. Man! How could I be so stupid? Where was the car parked when someone tinkered with it? It all began to make sense, Herb Critton wasn't lost. Gees, he used Priscilla to get me back into the country. How I wished Gran was there, she'd know just exactly how to proceed. I drank my tea and sat in silence. All I wanted to do was get out of there, but Newf kept talking.

"So you reckon thems Garstons ain't got nofin' to 'ide?"

"Well of course not. They run a respectable and very clever industry. Did you know they even cater for the tourists? This place isn't much use in that way, but most of the inventions are stored. Cameron said he want's to start a museum to show how clever Edward Burton really was."

"Where is this geezer, Burton?"

"Oh! He died."

"So where's 'ee buried?"

"I think he rests in the village, Pitcalver. I know a lot of them finish up there, because it's a lovely place, and Cameron takes care of them all. That's where I'll go eventually."

"So, you want us to 'ang around until the Canadians turn up or you want us to sort of 'ide art side?"

"You fellows are the experts, you just tell me what you want."

"'Ow did yah know we was 'ere?"

"The intruder alarm told me." He smiled and brushed his hair back with one hand. "I invented that."

"So you's a inventor too?"

"Only in a small way. I have a digital surveillance camera. The computer does a checksum every second, that's how it knows the picture has changed. And a changed picture means someone or thing has arrived."

"Oh!" Newf said totally confused by the explanation. "Then it sounds a alarm, do it?"

"Yes. The computer tells me whether it's front, back or either side."

I stood up, and indicated to leave with my head, still afraid to open my mouth. Newf seemed totally at home and enjoying himself. "I fink we should check the art-side." He stood up and joined me.

The grounds were nothing to speak of, a few old disused flowerbeds and a path all the way round the building. As soon as we were out of earshot, I said: "I thought you were never going to shut up."

"Found art 'oo's mucked wiv the car, didn't I?"

I sighed. "Yes you did, and on our way back I'll repay the favour. Now we know all we need let's get the hell out of here."

"We don't know nofin'. I votes we stay an' grill 'im some more."

Slowly circling the house and pretending to point and look, I said: "What the hell else do you expect to learn?"

"I fink this geezer believes all that crap abart the Garstons bein' nice guys. What do you fink?"

"I think the Garstons are deadly dangerous, especially if you're rich and alone. We should call Gran and ask what to do next."

"We should pump this geezer for all 'ee's werf. There ain't nofin' to lose. You could always do 'im up a bit, if you 'ave to."

"I sighed again, very deeply. "Alright. We'll go back inside, but this time lets get something incriminating, not just friendly chit-chat."

"Like what?"

Together we walked to the rear door and entered. Jeremy sat in the cosy room; somehow there was something strange about that lad. He acted too cool, too comfortable, as though the had great moral support. He grinned as we entered, and said: " Would you like to see the inventions room?"

"Sure," I said forgetting I was supposed to keep quiet.

Jeremy said nothing; he stood and began walking from the room. Newf and I followed. He walked to the rear end of the hall, which ran from front to rear of the entire house. One door had a padlock on it. He unlocked it and opened the door. Beyond lay a darkened staircase.

"After you," I said. It looked suspicious to me.

Jeremy flicked a switch and the stairs became lighted. He walked down and we followed. At the bottom he opened a very heavy door, it looked like metal. For a moment he disappeared inside then put the lights on. A scene straight out of Frankenstein. I've never actually experienced anything like it. A totally Victorian laboratory. Do-dads and gismos all around, like some fantastic movie set.

"Does any of it work?" I asked.

Jeremy smiled; he thoroughly enjoyed the fantastic display. "It only works if you know how to run it. The Garstons would have moved it all but they're going to wait until they find someone who understands it first."

I couldn't believe what I was seeing. "So what exactly did he invent in here?"

"He worked on many things. One experiment he worked on was television. He believed the eyes of corpses could reproduce synthetic or electrical pictures."

"Gees, how gruesome."

"There ain't no dead-uns 'ere, is there?"

Jeremy laughed. "No, there are no dead ones here. Yet."

I didn't like his answer, and walked to the exit. If anyone was leaving I intended to be the first. Suddenly a noise like an electronic ding-dong sounded upstairs. "What's that?"

"Oh, only the… the… er. It's the kettle boiling. I must have left the sensor on." He made like to he was about to go upstairs.

"No," I growled and bared the way. "I'll go first, Newf you go last." Nervously I backed out of the laboratory, keeping an eye on Jeremy. I felt sure he was up to something. There's no way I was going to wind up locked in a mad inventor's basement. I quickly ascended the steps and awaited the others at the top.

"You's a bit jumpy, Bill. I fink nah would be a good time to show our 'ands."

I grabbed Jeremy by the scruff of the neck. "Listen, chummy. We are the Canadians. Now let's all walk into the cosy and do some serious talking."

Jeremy seemed unperturbed. "Certainly, let's do some real talking." He led the way to the cosy door then stepped back and waved his hand for us to enter.

As soon as I cleared the doorpost I saw the reason. An ugly and menacing geezer sat on a chair facing the door with a shotgun pointing my way. I backed up quickly, the front door opened and there stood another.

Jeremy giggled. "Sorry Mr. Reyner. You really didn't think we were that stupid, did you?"

17

The Cuckoos

One does not have to be a rocket scientist to grasp the situation, when someone is pointing a shotgun at you. Does the word 'captured,' mean anything? I thought to myself as I stared down the barrel.

"You're making a big mistake," I said trying to make light of the situation. "I'm supposed to make a phone call about now. If I don't there'll be more people looking for me than you can count on your toes with your boots off."

The gunman smiled. "Doesnay matter, laddie, dead is dead."

"I think I grasp your meaning."

I just knew it would come to this, somehow it always does. I could be even richer if I'd been paid for every time someone shoved a shotgun up my nose. I tried to get close to Jeremy; the thought being that the gunman wouldn't shoot his own. After all he was there to protect.

Jeremy turned and smiled. "Did you think I was so stupid I couldn't tell you fellows from the real thing?"

"Exactly," I snapped and made my play. I rushed Jeremy and tried to put him between me and the muzzle of that gun. I suppose looking in retrospect, it wasn't the best thing to do. The gun went off with a deafening explosion. At first I couldn't be sure what had happened. Deafened by the bang and blinded by the flash and falling plaster, both of us crashed to the ground.

Somehow I kept moving, using my momentum to roll over and regain my feet. I grabbed a chair and spin it round in the air catching the gunman squarely on the shoulder with it. In a split second I was on him and thumped him hard in the face with my fist. He went down the gun skated across the floor. Newf the little darling, quick and nimble as ever leapt over and grabbed the weapon.

The next thing I heard was the second barrel exploding close to my ear. More plaster, smoke and dust. I ducked and fell over the table. As I looked up I saw the second intruder crumple and slither to the floor. The battle was over, now to assess the damage.

Quickly I examined the first gunman, bleeding and broken but alive. The second guy didn't look so lucky. He'd caught half the buckshot from a scatter barrel in his stomach area on one side. He looked a right mess, though he remained conscious and bleeding. Jeremy lay dead, he stopped the shot intended for me, this time from a choke barrel.

"What nar?" Newf hissed still clutching the empty gun.

I exhaled in a loud rush of air. "God knows. Jeremy's dead and this one looks like he won't last very long. Tie up the sleeper while I think."

Newf put the gun on the table and ripped out the phone wire to tie up sleeping beauty. My head still spun from the rush of adrenaline, the room stank of gun-smoke and plaster dust. I looked around at the mess, God! For a five second punch-up, you wouldn't believe the devastation. I walked over to the guy bleeding on the floor and knelt down to examine him.

"I think you're a dead man without help," I said softly.

"Drop dead, sassenach."

I grabbed his chin, trying to reinforce my meaning. "You're a dead man, get it. I'm leaving here. Without a doctor, you'll die. About two, maybe three painful hours, then, well, I'm sure you get the picture."

"They'll come for us."

"No they won't. What's your name?" I could see he was already beginning to fail.

"Dave. Why don't you finish the job?"

"Tell me who sent you?"

"It don't matter. The Garstons will get you for this."

"Who sent you?"

"Cameron. He knows everything."

I stood up. "Get a pillow for this guy, Newf. He's dyeing. We may as well make him comfortable." I flipped open my phone, for a moment I couldn't think who to call. I didn't know the emergency number. I dialled for the operator.

A guy answered. "How may I help you?"

"I'm calling from the Grange on the Thorney Road in Peterborough. There's been a shooting, one guy's dead. Call the police and ambulance, and be quick." I closed the phone.

"I fink we should get art o' 'ere, like nar."

"Sure Newf." We ran out of the building, my only thought, to get away from there. I jumped in the driver's seat, and had to drive over the garden. The idiots had parked blocking me in. A sweat broke out when one of the front wheels bogged down in the soft soil and began wildly spinning. With care bordering on panic I managed to back out and eventually pass the spot. I gunned it and rushed down the short drive to the street.

The phone operator must have been quick to call the appropriate authorities, as I drove toward downtown Peterborough a cop car dashed by with lights flashing, and only two seconds behind him came an ambulance.

"Wow!" Exclaimed Newf. "Looks like we made it in the nick of time."

"I'll feel better when we reach the A1 highway and put some distance between us and that house."

"Where we goin'?"

"Pitcalver. I want to see that graveyard. Then I think I'll give Mr. Cameron a little visit. I'm sick of being shot at. I don't like it."

"I reckon you fink they's bad guys then?"

"Yes of course they are. I knew that all along. I've got a score to settle with Priscilla's dad too. We'll take care of him on the way out."

"The way art o' what?"

"Out of this country, you twit. Did you bring that shotgun?"

"Nah."

"Christ, we're still unarmed. Doesn't matter as soon as I get that Cameron in my hands I won't need a gun."

"I'm a bit 'ungry, Bill. When we gonna stop and eat."

"How can you be so thin, you're always hungry and eating?"

I guess it must have been about halfway to Glasgow when we stopped. The sun had already begun its decline and the shadows were lengthening. We found one of those service centres, J. Arthur Rank or something. A huge place on both sides of the motorway, we'd left the A1 behind long ago. The meal was okay, nothing to shout home about. Newf enjoyed it. I had a beer, and a doughnut.

"I think you'll have to drive the rest of the way, okay?"

"Alright, Bill. Where we goin'?"

"I think we'll give Glasgow a miss. We can always get them on the way out. What I think is, we should go directly to Pitcalver."

"Why?"

"I'm sure our answers all lay at Cromlet. We'll go to the Cuckoo inn and partake of Ellen's hospitality."

"Yeah, that sounds good. Then what?"

"I'm still thinking. I guess we shouldn't go to Cromlet in daylight. Yeah, we'll hide the car. The village is small enough to notice a new car."

"What?"

"We'll arrive at night. It'll be dark, see. We'll park the car in the forest and hide it then walk into the village and stay with Ellen." Somehow I think Newf didn't understand. Man! He could be thick at times.

Newf drove and I navigated, we passed through Glasgow without difficulty, it had just started to get dark. A hundred kilometres to go, about two hours driving, maybe more. Things sure look different in the dark. The GPS was a Godsend, leading us through the darkness directly to our target.

"We're about three kilometres from the village, Newf. Let's pull over and look for somewhere to hide the car."

The road which is only wide enough for a single vehicle seemed to wind into the distance forever. The moon was about half and gave enough light to see fairly well.

"Look over there, Bill, trees. I fink we could 'ide the car there."

"Great, I'll walk ahead, don't run me over."

I walked toward the trees, Newf drove the car. The headlights gave plenty of vision. The ground seemed firm but a bit rocky in places. We got the car well into the trees, a couple of hundred meters off the road. "This'll be alright," I shouted.

Newf stopped and switched off the engine. "This is excitin', eh, Bill?"

"Sure." I marked the GPS so I could find the car again. Then called up Pitcalver. "It says we're two point six kilometres from the village. It's that way." I pointed.

"Alright, let's go. I fink I should o' brought that shotgun."

"We're not going to kill anyone. Let's keep our voices down."

In moments we found the road again and walked in the general direction of the village. The night seemed warm and the air thin. For the first time on this case my adrenaline was up. I wanted to prove to Gran I could be a good detective.

"Ah shit!" I exclaimed.

"What's wrong, Bill?"

"I forgot to call Gran. Gees, she'll kill me. I'll call her now."

"Why don't you wait till we get to the inn?"

I walked back and used the car's dome light to see the phone's dial pad. The phone rang and rang; I thought she'd never answer. At last a voice said: "Hallo."

"Hi Gran. I've got important news."

"My goodness William, can't you phone at a sensible time of day? I barely got into the house. Have you any idea what time it is now?"

"No, but I've got news. I tried earlier but we were in a dead zone. Gran we need your help."

"Very well, William allow me a moment to get a piece of paper."

Gees, she put the phone down and walked away. Man how annoying can a person get. My phone beeped, indicating a low battery. "Hurry up, Gran."

After a few moments she returned. "Go ahead, William what seems to be your problems?"

"Well, Gran first my battery's getting low. We went
to Peterborough; there was a terrible fight. Jeremy was killed,
and I wouldn't be surprised one of the other guys has died by
now. Mr. Critton is a bad-guy. He's the one who cut our brake
line on the car."

"Calm down, William. Who's Jeremy?"

"I don't have time to explain, Gran. We're in
Scotland, we're going to get the truth out of that bunch at
Cromlet."

"William," she said demandingly. "Do not go into that
house. Return to London now."

"Sorry, Gran. We've started it, we'll finish it."

"William, sometimes you do not use your brain.
Please return to London. Call me at a sensible time, say in one
or two hours, until then stay out of trouble. Now do as your
told, do you hear?"

"Yes, Gran." I should have known she'd be in a real
bad mood at that time of day, just finished work and all that. I
closed the phone up. "She can be real ornery when she wants.
Says we should go back to London."

Newf glared at me. "I ain't goin' back to no London
after all we's bin froo. I'm goin' to Pitcalver, what abart you?"

I had to think about it for a few moments. With a deep
sigh I said: "What the hell? We're here, let's go to see Ellen,
then we'll go back to London. What, yah say?"

"Sure, boss."

"If we're not attacking Cromlet, we may as well travel
in the car."

"Sure. You drive, Bill."

We climbed in and I drove the rest of the distance.
The village had no streetlights, something I'd not noticed the
first time. Very few of the houses had lights on. I parked close
to the front door of the inn. The entrance was locked; I banged
on the door several times. At last it opened and Ellen's face lit
up when she saw me.

"William," she gasped. "I thought you had returned to
Canada. Come in."

I leaned forward and gave her a polite kiss on the
cheek. "It's good to see you. How've you been?"

Wow! She flung her arms around me like some long-lost lover. To say the least she was very pleased to see us. "Come in, come in." Ellen quickly hustled us in and closed the door. "Have you any luggage?"

"No. Well, yes, some."

"Alreet," she said in that sweet Scottish accent. "I'll get yah all some food, what'd like?"

"Oh, anything."

"You collect yah baggage, room two, and the other in room 5." With that she dashed off excitedly, leaving me standing in the entrance hall.

It's a strange feeling, just as though I'd never left. The inn represented a home away from home, a refuge, and besides Ellen's a whole lot better looking than Gran. It only took a few minutes to collect everything from the car and place it in my room. This time I got the larger room with a luxurious double bed and a view of the village main street.

By the time I got to the dining room the table had already been set for three people. The smell of food drifted in from the kitchen. A few seconds passed when Ellen entered.

"I'm so pleased to see you William. I'm sorry but all I can offer you is sausage, home fries, eggs and beans. Will that be alreet?"

"Excellent?"

Her eyes rolled and glistened as I answered, then with a flourish she turned and returned to the kitchen. She began ferrying hot food into the dining room even before Newf turned up. Considering the short notice, Ellen did marvellously. Newf entered like a clumsy ox, knocking one chair over.

"Sorry."

"Come on you klutz, sit, and be careful."

"Yeah, sorry, Bill."

Ellen brought the last dish and seated herself. "Oh I forgot the drink. What would you like?"

"Whatever you have."

"How's lager sound?"

"Great."

"Glass or bottle?"

"Bottle'll do okay."

Quickly she dashed off and returned with a small case of six bottles. From her apron she took an opener and placed it with three bottles on the table. "Come on laddie, help yee'sel."

Without further prompting I loaded some of the excellent food onto my plate, then opened a couple of bottles. I gave one to Ellen. "Cheers," I said and drank some of the liquid.

"I hear you have caused quite a stir at Cromlet."

"I did. I mean I did?"

"Aye, there's quite a buzz. We've all been told to report your presence at first notice."

"Oh! The car, what'll I do about the car."

"No one will know who it belongs to. I do get visitors, you know."

"Sure. So what's all this buzz we've created?"

"I heard you killed a guardian in Liverpool, then gave one in London a thrashing. Is there any truth in the stories?"

I laughed. "Some. Scouse was murdered alright, but not my us. The other guy, well he started it, Newf finished it. Though I should tell you about our latest escapade."

"Which is?"

"Well, we've just come from Peterborough, and I'm ashamed to say we left a rather nasty mess there."

"Like what?"

"They attacked us with guns, and, well. Well one of them was killed."

"Good."

"Good?" I echoed.

"Yea they deserve it. It's aboot time someone gave them a lesson they'll remember." She looked serious.

"Now I am confused. I thought the Garston family cared for this entire area. All benevolent and all that."

She sighed and looked quite sad. "Firstly, tell me what you're doing here, and why yee came to Scotland in the first place."

I had to think about it. I felt like I'd spent almost all my life chasing shadows. Well, to cut a long story short, a woman went missing, and we traced her to Cromlet. No one's seen her since."

"So you are a detective. Police?"

"No, private investigator."

"An' you came here looking for this woman. The one in that picture you had sent by fax?"

"Yes."

"You realize you are in terrible danger? The more you know the greater the danger."

"It goes with the job."

"You're very brave. Perhaps I should put you straight on a few little points."

"Yeah."

"Well." She stopped to think and wrung her hands as if in distress. Then looking around as though expecting someone else to be in the room. Leaning forward she spoke in a low voice. "It could mean death to tell you this, but you're in too deep now. You see there are two families. The Garstons once owned Cromlet. It was a genuine inheritance. A nasty family from Edinburgh slowly wheedled their way in. At first they were house servants, then as time passed they slowly murdered the Garstons and took over their enterprises.

"One by one they removed the Garston family and installed their own. That's why they are called the Edinburgh cuckoos. Yee ken what a cuckoo is?"

"Yeah. Its a bird."

"Aye, but it's a bird that lays it eggs in another's nest."

"Now I am confused. Who lives at Cromlet?"

"'Tis the McLean Family."

"And they're not Garstons?"

"Och, noo. The Garstons live at Drumvanich."

"Alright, so what's all this crap about the McLeans capturing the castle hundreds of years ago?"

"It's noo difficult. The McLeans captured Cromlet and gave it to the English Lord who had the right to it. He in turn died and left it to the one girl who he loved."

"A McLean girl?"

"Noo, a cousin. She was Flora Garston. So you see the castle of Cromlet belonged to Miss Flora Garston."

"So how did the McLeans get it back?"

"It's terribly easy. They murdered her and wrote a will of their own. You see, then the McLeans became the rulers of the district."

"So what did the Garston family do about it?"

"Well, using the same theory of inheritance they looked for lonely rich people, befriended them and tried to gain their property."

"That's all very well, but everywhere I've been the property belongs to the Cromlet Trust."

"Of course. The McLeans infiltrate, murder the Garstons and take the property by inheritance."

I didn't understand it. Gran would have to explain it to me. If everybody was murdering everybody else, why didn't the Garstons just come over to Cromlet and sort them out once and for all? Ellen could see by the expression on my face, I was puzzled. Newf seemed to be okay, but there, he always looks like he understands, then he says "What?"

Ellen smiled real sweetly. "It's no that difficult The McLeans are a real bad lot. The Garstons are the ones paying for it."

"It was the Garstons that bashed me, and the McLeans that were nice to me. What you say makes no sense at all. Who killed Scouse?"

"I don't know anyone called Scouse. I only know the McLeans own this village, they closed the Pools office and all the other industry around here."

"Now that doesn't make any sense. The McLeans have been here sine Jesus was a kid, who started the Pools office?"

"I dinna ken. The McLeans always stayed in their castle; slowly they spread their web, and bought property here. Twenty years ago they acquired the Pools office and soon after closed it."

"I thought you said they support this entire village?"

"They do, but only when it's to their advantage. If they knew I was talking to you they'd kill all of us."

"My car's parked out front."

"Och! Dinna worry, no one knows who's driving it. We do get visitors here."

Somehow the words of Ellen echoed around in my head. Nothing made much sense to me. Even Priscilla's father turned out to be one of the enemy. I'll call Gran in the morning, the phone battery's on charge. I lay back on my bed thoughts of Garstons and McLeans fleeting through my head. Ellen's ceiling had the most amazing cracks in it. They described a strange maze or even a mosaic. I could see a castle and rivers.

A gentle tap-tap came to my door. "Come in."

Surprisingly, Ellen came in with a bottle of wine and two glasses in her hands. I couldn't help but notice she wore a frilly pair of pyjamas. "I couldn't sleep," she said.

"Oh!, Ar! Okay. I wasn't sleeping." I sat up. I hadn't even undressed ready for bed. My brain was suffering fatigue.

Ellen sat on the edge of the bed. "It's a lonely life, here in Pitcalver."

"Oh, is it? I mean, yeas I guess it is."

She handed me a glass then filled it with the sweet red wine. She sipped hers and smiled. "North said you were a millionaire."

"Did he?"

"Are you?"

"Sure."

In one gulp she finished the glass and placed it on the floor. I felt my pulse began to race. For a woman old enough to be my mother, she was very attractive and that thin material didn't really hide very much. She took my glass and put it with hers. "You seem very shy," she whispered.

The sun just showed above the horizon when I awoke. Ellen lay curled up beside me. She really is a beautiful woman. The empty wine bottle lay on its side on the dresser, the glasses on the floor. Suddenly a loud crash came from downstairs. The noise woke Ellen.

"What's happening?" She asked sitting up.

"Don't know." Quickly I went to the window and looked out. A small truck stood across the street with three armed men. Again a loud banging came to the street door. Then someone shouted. "Come out Reyner, we know you're in there."

18

The Jacobite

Before making a desperate attempt to stay alive, I usually get dressed. In this particular incident, there just wasn't time. I'd only got my trousers on when someone came crashing upstairs. Ellen screamed as our bedroom door burst open. The intruder had a hunting riffle, which discharged the moment the door opened. Before he could draw the bolt a second time I flew at him. Being strong and a couple of kilograms heavier than him I floored him in one.

"We've gotta get out of here," I shouted at Ellen. She sat naked on the bed, frozen with fear. "Ellen, let's go."

I grabbed her and an armful of bedclothes. "Come on, we've gotta get out."

Ellen seemed totally reluctant, and stiffened up. Someone came up the stairs. I grabbed the riffle, but the insurgent was armed with a shotgun and fired. The door beside me exploded into a handful of splinters and confetti. Newf appeared behind him and brought him down with a heavy candlestick. What happened next is a little unclear. Somehow we managed to reach the ground floor, only one other person in our way.

The inn seemed empty, the bad guys all crowding around outside. I gave Newf the hunting riffle, "Make sure no one enters," I hissed then fled back upstairs to rescue Ellen. She remained standing in our room next to the bed. Somehow the excitement caused her to mentally lock-up. Frozen to the spot like a stuffed dummy.

"Ellen. We've got to get out of here." She totally ignored me. I grabbed a bed sheet and wrapped it roughly around her then picked her up and ran back downstairs.

"Crikey," Newf gasped. "You gonna carry 'er."

"I did."

"No one's tried to get in, they's all standin' around artside."

"Please put me down," Ellen said softly.

I placed her on the floor, standing. She began to fidget with the sheet. "You'd better get dressed," I snapped.

She looked at me and began to cry gently. "I'm too afraid."

"Not to worry, Newf'll blow away anyone who tries to get in. I think we're safe here for the time being. Time to think and plan." There's another shotgun upstairs. Where's the backdoor?"

Timidly she pointed. "It's a heavy door, they won't break it."

"Alright, Newf, park yourself over there that'll give you a view of both ways in. I'm going to go get dressed. There's another gun upstairs, it's a shotgun. If I hear anything I'll come running. Okay?"

"Yeah, excitin' ain't it."

My brain had begun to calm down, the solution would come, but first I had to get dressed. "Where's your cell phone, Newf?"

"In the car."

"Shit, so's mine. Come on Ellen let's get you dressed first. We'll fight this battle later. Is there a phone here?"

She indicated the barroom. "In there."

"Come on. Let's get you dressed first." I dragged her back up the stairs and into her room. "Now get dressed quickly." I left and ran to my room, where I grabbed the rest of my clothes. I daren't leave her for more than a few seconds. There were still three of the enemy sleeping on the floor. As quickly as I could I grabbed the shotgun, the woman, and rushed back downstairs.

The barroom opened directly onto the street. This was the door they battered down. The probability of using the phone in full view of the enemy left a lot to be desired. "Somehow we've got to get out of here, or at least make them think we have."

"The backdoor's the only way out," Ellen whispered.

"Nah, they'll be watching that. Newf, what do you reckon?"

"Is there an attic?"

"No."

"Then that's the way art."

"She said there isn't an attic you twit."

Newf pulled a face. "Of course there ain't but there's a 'ollow space between the ceiling and the roof, ain't there?"

"Dummy, what use it that?"

"All we gotta do is penetrate the ceiling and we can break into the house next-door. Crawl froo the attic, see."

"Is there a hatch or trapdoor, Ellen?"

"No."

"I fink we should get started afore them geezers wake up."

"Alright, let's go. We'll try Ellen's room."

We rushed upstairs and into Ellen's room. I locked the door. Newf jumped up onto the dresser and examined the plaster ceiling. "It's larf an' plaster." He gave it a swift bash with the butt of the gun. Amazingly the old plaster smashed and fell to the floor. A second hit and the lath broke. Newf quickly pulled and tugged, after a few moments a large section of the ceiling fell down. He laid the rifle down then disappeared into the hole he'd made. His head poked out of the hole with a huge smile. "Pass the gun, Bill and git up 'ere."

I passed both guns up, and then helped Ellen onto the dresser. Newf grabbed her hands and between us we lifted her into the attic. I climbed up; man the darkness there gave me little confidence.

"Stay on the joists, or you'll fall froo. Look see, the wall ain't very 'igh 'ere. We can git to the end of the street."

He was right; my eyes began to accept the gloom. Light filtered in through cracks in the tiles. We could move about three houses. Quietly and carefully we inched our way along. Newf seemed to know what he was doing. At the end he picked a spot at the rear of the house and quickly kicked the ceiling in. He looked down into the hole. "S'all right, Bill, you go first."

I slipped over and with a good grip of the joist swung down through the orifice. I found myself in a small shelf-lined room. Clothes of all sorts on the shelves. Newf handed the guns down, then he lowered Ellen and dropped himself through.

"Now what?" I whispered.

"The backdoor's just over there," Newf said softly. "We've gotta get out quick, run away from the 'ouse and we'll reform in the woods at the back. Okay?"

"Yes general." I lifted the latch and eased the door open. No one in sight. Good. Tip-toeing gently toward the stairs my breath started to come in gulps, the stress forced my heart to pound.

"Who's there, came an old and quavering voice."

A little old lady opened a door across the tiny hall. "It's alright dear," Newf said comfortingly. "We're here to 'elp you, love."

She looked startled, I was afraid she'd start screaming. Ellen took the old dear's hands and whispered something to her. The old lady backed into her room and closed the door. "What'd you say to her?"

"She knows me. I told her you were from the electricity company."

Downstairs we still had the problem of how to get out of the row house without being seen. Newf looked out the window and summed up the situation. "There's 'edges and a shed. I fink we could get to the shed."

"Then what?"

"Well, it's closer to the woods. Only a 'undred meters from there."

I looked. The backyard of the inn had three or maybe four men just standing around. They looked to be armed. The shed down the garden definitely presented cover. A hedge and a few bushes may prove helpful. "Alright." I said. "Ellen take that tablecloth put it over your head, pretend it's a shawl, then walk nice and slow toward the shed. Stoop so's they'll think your the old broad from this cottage."

"What if they see me?"

"They probably will, just act like you're the old lady, don't panic. If anything goes wrong run for the woods. If all goes well, stay behind the shed till we get there."

Talk about a hair-raising caper. She took the cloth and walked slowly to the shed. Two of the guys noticed her and did nothing. The plan had worked. "Alright, Newf we'll crawl to the shed, okay?"

"Sure."

For two fit young men it turned out to be easy. We reached the shed without giving our position away.

"What next?" Ellen asked.

"From here we have a head start. You two run for it. I'll stand here; if anyone notices you I'll put a shot over their heads. When they take cover I'll run for it. Are you ready?"

"Yes."

"Go."

Newf and Ellen took off at a run toward the forest; I levelled the rifle and waited. They were halfway there before anyone realized what was going on. He yelled. I think the others were about to run, but when I fired they scattered like mice. I ran hell-for-leather.

Newf and Ellen encouraged me. Newf took a shot in the general direction of the bad-guys. Man that shotgun was loud. I didn't stop, just kept running into the woods. Ellen and Newf followed. After several minutes I stopped and leaned against a tree for support. "Are they coming?" I asked breathlessly.

Ellen seemed a lot fitter than me, she smiled and said: "They will nay chase us."

"Why?"

"There's nowhere to go. We canna live in the hills for long."

A very short time later the trees thinned and gave way to high ground. The hills stretched out ahead of us forever. "What's out there?" I asked.

Ellen shrugged. "Hills, rocks, maybe a few sheep."

"For crying out loud, it's Scotland not the Sahara. We'll walk across the hills and find civilization. Then we'll get a car and go to London."

"It does-nay look far, but people die out there every year. You'll get lost and the nights are harsh. What'll you eat?"

"Eat? We'll be across, find a town or something within a few hours."

She snickered. "I dinna think so. Without a compass you'll walk round in circles until you fall on your face."

It was my turn to laugh. I pulled out the GPS. "With this I can find my way anywhere, anytime." I turned the instrument on.

"How will that help?"

"As soon as it finds a few satellites we'll know where we are."

Moments later I asked the instrument a question. Pitcalver lay two kilometres to the southeast. Man I was exhausted and we'd only made a short distance. I changed the scale on the display to see where Glasgow was situated compared to our location. We were going the wrong way. Ellen was right we were heading into the unpopulated area. Which way to head? I had to think about it for a few moments. "Alright," I said, having finally made up my mind. We'll head west."

It's not as easy as you think making headway across the Scottish moors. The ground's rough, stubble, rocks, dips and shallows. Sometimes the thistles and grass are as bad as the rocks. At one point we had to head north to circumnavigate a cliff. By mid afternoon I began to think Ellen could be right. We were all thirsty, hungry, dirty, and exhausted. In a straight line we were only nine kilometres from Pitcalver, yet best part of a day's walk.

I sank to the rocky ground. To walk back would take just as long, we couldn't reach civilization in daylight. Ellen sat beside me. I could see she didn't want to go any farther. What a motley crew we presented. A stupid leader, an exhausted woman, and Newf. I looked around, Newf had disappeared, and I was the one with the GPS.

Quickly I jumped up and called. "Newf, Newf, where are you?"

The funny thing I hadn't noticed him go. Running quickly to the next rocky promontory, I climbed up and called his name. He answered. Moments later he came into sight. He'd been just beyond in a gully.

"Where the hell have you been?"

"Sorry boss, just exploring."

"Aren't you tired?"

"Nah. But I've found shelter."

"You have? Where?"

"When I was down there I saw a 'ut in the distance. Over that direction." He pointed.

"Okay, we'll head that way." I called Ellen and again we all set out, this time heading toward a possible resting place.

I would never have believed travel could be so difficult in such a small country. At length we saw the refuge, a low stone hut with a thatched roof. It looked to be in good condition. "'Tis a crofter's black house," Ellen said softly.

"Is it alright?"

"I would-nay wish to spend a vacation there. Though in this situation, I suppose it will do fine."

As we approached, the rickety looking door opened and an old man carrying what I thought was a stick came out. He raised his weapon and shouted something totally incomprehensible at us.

"Jesus preserve us," Ellen hissed.

"Why, what's wrong?"

"I did-nay get all he said, but he thinks we're the English."

"So?"

"So he say's he's going to kill the lot of us."

I checked the rifle. There was one round left. "What about your shotgun, Newf?"

He cracked it and grumbled. "Two spent cartridges. I could always 'it 'im wiv it."

"Come on walk slowly we can pretend to be armed. Ellen, call and tell him we're friendly."

"He's crazy, won't listen to reason."

"Then threaten him."

She shouted something in a peculiar foreign language. I could see the old man had a sword he seemed very active for an old one, dancing and jumping and waving the weapon. "Does he realize I have a gun?"

Ellen shouted something at the old fellow. Whatever she said seemed to calm him down. He stuck the tip of his sword into the ground and leaned on the weapon with a huge grin on his wrinkled face. "What did you tell him?"

"I told him I have a message from Charlie."

"Who the hell's Charlie?"

"Ouch! Tis the Bonny Prince."

"What?"

"He thinks the battle of Culloden Moor has-nay been fought yet."

History has never been my strong point. "I think you should do all the talking I don't understand."

The old man jabbered on in his strange dialect, then suddenly broke off into English. His accent was so thick, that it made little difference, I couldn't understand very much at all. Ellen translated for me. "He says we are welcome to share his lodging, and wants to know the message."

"So what are you going to tell him?"

She spoke lively with the old man for a while, the words bandied back and forth. "I told him Charlie's coming, that the English are camped at Pitcalver. The clans will be coming as soon as the word's out."

I sighed a sigh of relief, but didn't understand the situation. "Will he feed us?"

"As long as he believes we are from the Prince he'll protect us with his life. He's as mad as a hatter. Thinks he's a Jacobite."

"I don't care what he thinks as long as we can get some food and shelter."

Ellen whispered in my ear: "Wants to know why we're not wearing our tartan."

"It's camouflage, tell him it's because we're hiding from the English."

She told him in his own language. He swirled the sword around and slipped it into his belt. With a huge grin on his face he slapped me on the back and spoke in a very thick dialect. I couldn't understand a word. He led us all into his little house. The place smelled very strong of some acrid scent. "What's the stink?" I asked.

Ellen laughed. "It's the peat."

"Why's he burning peat in this weather?"

"Cooking."

Though as mad as a hatter, our host turned out to be very generous. There was no shortage of food. I have no idea what the concoction was, but it tasted great, and satisfied my hunger. Newf got stuck into it, but there again, he'd eat anything. Ellen arranged for us to stay the night with the Jacobite. At least it would be warm, dry, and we'd be well fed. He even had hooch, I think it had to be some form of homemade whisky. Tasted like firewater.

He had no phone, and it would be a day's walk to the nearest one. Somehow I had to get a message to Gran, or the police. Tomorrow, perhaps we would reach civilization. At least the Jacobite would know the best way off the moor. Newf enjoyed it, for some reason he got a bang out of living rough. I guess it was sort of romantic. The only people in the world, or at least that's how it felt. I couldn't help worrying about the McLeans, were they following us?

My bed for the night turned out to be a pile of old rags. I hoped they were not populated by anything. The hut or house had alcove-like dugouts in the walls, these were our beds, the building had been constructed of stone collected from the moor and piled up. I think the cement was earth or mud. Man, the door didn't fit; you could walk a medium sized dog under it.

Even as bad and inconvenient as everything turned out to be, I slept like a log. The musty smell of the burning peat, and absolute quiet would put an insomniac to sleep. The old man snored, so did Newf, but somehow that only made the house seem friendlier.

The old man served breakfast at the crack of dawn. Wild birds eggs, and some form of fried meat, not bacon. I have no idea what it was, though the taste seemed somehow familiar.

"Tell the old man we have to reach Charlie's army. We've got to tell them that the English are at Pitcalver, Ellen."

She relayed the message to the old geezer. You could tell by the expression on his face he understood the importance of the mission. He gabbled on waving his arms and pointing occasionally. I've no idea what he said.

Ellen smiled and said: "He tells me that the Price's army is that way." She pointed northeast. "That's why the English are at Pitcalver."

"What's in that direction?"

"Culloden moor and Inverness."

"How far?"

She shrugged. "A dam-sight farther than we could walk."

I had to think about it. Using the GPS I could take us off these stinking badlands, but, and that's the big one. I don't know what's out there, rivers, bogs, mountains; this old geezer knows the terrain. "Ask him how long it would take to get there."

Ellen asked him, he smiled and gesticulated. "He says we could easily make it by nightfall, he knows the best way, through Dead-Man's pass."

"Gees, I don't like the sound of that."

"It's only a way through the mountains, they're no high, but there are cliffs and crags."

"Alright, we should get moving before you-know-who catches up with us."

She relayed the bit about moving. You could see the change in the old guy's countenance. He brightened up immediately and collected his huge sword. Ellen translated the stream of guttural sounds into English. "He says we should move at once, the Prince will be needing our help."

"Sure. Let's go. What about food?"

Either he understood what I said or he anticipated the need. Quickly he took dried meat from a hook in the ceiling, and handed it to me. Man, talk about out of date, he pulled a leather water bag from another hook and handed it to Newf. Moments later we were all hustled outside, and the trek began.

For an old one, he was certainly sprite. The thought of defeating the English must have acted as a galvanizing force for we could barely keep up with him. He kept up a continuous jabber, occasionally waving his sword and shouting at the hills. By noon we had reached a small pass through the hills. I can only describe it as a crack in the earth, about five meters wide with cliffs either side.

After a tiring walk through the canyon we came to an open expanse or rocky plane. About thirty meters ahead stood a cairn three or four meters high. "What's this place?"

Ellen asked the Jacobite. "He says this is called traitors rest."

"Traitors rest, what sort of name is that for a place?"

The old guy walked sprightly to the cairn, we followed him. He leaned his sword up against the pile of rocks and began excitedly jabbering in his thick guttural droll. Ellen watched him with a grim look upon her face. When at length the old man shut-up and leaned his back against the cairn, Ellen translated. "He says this is the place where seven traitors were executed for betraying the revolution. He says they are buried under the cairn."

"He wants you to swear on the death of the traitors that you support the revolution."

"What revolution?"

"The Jacobite revolution."

"No problem."

"He also said this place is cursed and a man holding the stones can only speak the truth."

I laughed and leaned with both hands on the rocks. "I believe in the-." I stopped and turned round. Ten or fifteen armed men had followed us into the area. The Jacobite began to laugh most heartily as he collected his sword and confronted me with it.

19

Last Will and Testament

The first thing I would do if I became President is pass a law that would make being a Jacobite punishable by death. The old devil howled with joy and laughter, swinging his huge sword like a real pro. After a few minutes of celebration he came over to me. I thought for a moment he was going to use that sword of his. He gabbled on and pointed to an antenna mast on a distant hill. Ellen translated. "He says that even Jacobites have mobile phones now."

None of the armed men were known to me, but Ellen seemed to recognize several of them. We were treated courteously as they gently placed shackles on our ankles. After about fifteen minutes three four-wheel drive Land Cruisers arrived. We were hustled into them, one of us in each vehicle. I couldn't imagine why they were so gentle with us, but it seemed someone wanted us undamaged.

The mystery of who were the bad guys quickly resolved itself. The three vehicles drove directly to Cromlet castle. Cameron, or whatever his real name was came out to greet us. You could see he really was an old man, probably as old as the Jacobite.

"Take them to the holding area," he growled and punctuated the sentence with an enormous backdoor draught.

Not quite as gently this time, we were taken into the castle and along the long corridor to the wax dummy room. A section of the floor in there, opened revealing a staircase down into the bowels of the earth. The area seemed well illuminated by electric lights behind strong metal grills. The floors were stone and walls made from huge stone blocks. At one end the room had been divided off with a very strong iron-bar wall.

A very efficient prison, with only one cell. In the jail, there was a toilet and sink, no bed or chair or table. "In," growled the toughest of the guards. He pushed me through the doorway.

Newf was thrust in after me, but Ellen had already been filtered out. She had not even entered the dungeon. The heavy iron door slammed noisily closed. I felt like an animal in a veterinary's cage.

"So what you fink they'll do wiv us?"

"I don't think it's an invitation to supper. I would guess we'll probably be joining those dummies upstairs."

"The wax uns?"

"Yeah."

"Wish I'd known that old geezer 'ad a cell phone."

"Yeah, me too. I find it hard to believe that Stephanie's one of the bad guys. I thought she was genuine and honest."

"Yeah, well you would, she wears a bra."

"Meaning?"

"Oh, come-on Bill, anyfing that wobbles up front, an' your all eyes and no brains."

"How do you mean?"

"Gees, Bill. How about Priscilla, she's nofin' but trouble. I fink Ellen's also one of them. And now you fink Stephie's coming to our aid."

"I didn't say that."

"The fing is, Bill, we's gotta get out of 'ere. An I reckon we shouldn't put no faith in any female."

"Well for a genius like you there shouldn't be any difficulty getting out of here."

"I can get us art of 'ere, Bill, but I can't get us art of the 'ouse."

I didn't know whether to laugh or cry. "Alright, how you gonna get us out of this jail?"

"Easy, I'll pick the locks, then 'ow you gonna get us art o' this 'ouse?"

I had to think about it. The best bet would be to wait for nightfall. "When all the McLeans are tucked up tightly in their little beds, we'll simply creep out of the house and go find my car."

Newf laughed. I don't know where he got the mirth; the tears trickled down his stupid face. "I gotta 'and it to you,

Bill," he said as soon as he could speak. "You 'as a good sense of 'umor."

"Well, you got any better ideas?"

"Nah, I fink yours'll work."

Moments later the door at the end of the room opened and two armed men walked in. One stayed by the door while the other came over to the cage. "You," he said pointing to me. "You'll come wi' me." He waved the handgun menacingly.

I backed away from the bars as my jailer opened the gate. He beckoned. Obediently I obeyed taking small steps so as not to injure my ankles on the manacles. As soon as I cleared the cage door he slammed and locked it. He locked the dungeon entrance as we left. I took careful note of the way, noticing where windows and doors were, and light switches.

At the top, in the waxworks, some of the McLeans were building a new display. Stephanie saw me and pretended she didn't know me. Just along the corridor from the wax-room we entered a small office opposite a large window. I entered alone, the guards closed and stayed outside the door. Cameron, or whatever his name is sat at a very expensive looking desk. He greeted me with a handshake and a minor anal eruption.

"Sit," he said gruffly.

"Haven't you ever heard of Beano, or Gasex?" I asked.

He lifted one cheek and released a gurgling cascade. "Shut ye mouth, laddie."

I sat on the only chair unoccupied. "So what do you want?"

He smiled. "I thought you would see sense."

"See sense, what do you mean?"

"Well laddie. Mostly we are hospitable, but you have forced our hands. I'm afraid you'll have to go without a holiday."

"So what do you want?"

He squeezed some mucus from his nose then wiped it on his collar, then squinted at me. "Son, laddie, I want your money."

I laughed. "You moron I wouldn't give you a red cent."

"It would be easier for you if you comply."

"Comply, how?"

He pushed a piece of paper across the desk. "All you have to do laddie, is sign the document."

I read it. "It's not legal, you'll need at least two witnesses."

Poppa McLean, or John Cameron, whatever his name was laughed, farted and said: "I'll have as many witnesses as I need as soon as yee sign, laddie."

"What if I don't?"

He sighed, and took the papers back. "It does-nay matter. If you sign all'll be alreet, if no, well then I'll have to get nasty."

"You are bloody nasty. You must be the origin of the saying 'old fart.' My Gran will soon see you behind bars."

He laughed and let fly again. "Your Gran is on her way here now. The silly old bag is following our plan to the letter."

"What do you mean?"

He sighed as if I had become boring. "Are yee no rich, laddie?"

"Yeah."

"Very well then. All I want is yee money. Yee house is-nay worth a brass farthing. You should-nay of rid yeesel' o' that island. Now that would have been something to own."

"Okay, you explain. What'll happen when... if I sign that paper?"

"We'll let yee go, laddie."

"Go, go as in free?"

"Aye."

"But what about Gran. Where does she come into this?"

"She'll have to sign over all her property too."

"And what if we don't?"

He pouted his lips and strained. The result was a minor earth tremor. "Then, we'll have to, to," he thought, his eyes rolled up toward the ceiling. "Well shall we say there's loads of room in yon cemetery?"

"You can't get away with it. Gran's a genius when it comes to detective work. I'll bet she's got it all figured out already. I reckon your only avenue is to let us go."

He laughed. I don't know why, but the strain of laughing caused a severe anal exhaust. The man had to be filled with gas. I've never met anyone who could let fly as often as him. When he stopped laughing and turning the air blue he said in a serious tone of voice: "Listen laddie, you're a dead man. You have only one way oot. You do as I say and there's a possibility you'll live. On the other hand, without yee signature, you're dead for sure. Are we now communicating at a level that yee wee brain can handle?"

"I need time to think about it."

He seemed polite and gracious. "Laddie, yee have all the time in the world. As soon as you've made a decision, we'll se aboot food and water for yee and yee companion."

"Where's Ellen?"

"Dinna worry aboot the lass, she'll come to nay harm. You can go back to yee cell and have a nice long think."

Although I didn't see it, somehow he signalled the guards. They entered the room and hustled me back to the dungeon. Cameron had said his peace, now it was all up to me. The heavy iron-barred door slammed closed. Newf lay back relaxing. Somehow he didn't look as afraid as I felt. These guys were not playing, they were for real.

"Did you learn anyfin'?" He said sitting up.

"Yeah."

"What?"

"We're dead meat."

"That'll 'elp. I fink we should blow this place, and not wait too long."

I sat cross-legged on the floor, if it's possible, my brain hurt. Maybe just fear; it was like being a condemned man, and the hangman just arrived. "You're no bloody help, Newf. If you had the brains to carry you cell-phone we wouldn't be in here."

"Yeah, an' if you'd use your brains instead of uver part's we'd never 'ave been caught in the first place."

"Shut-up, Newf, I have to think."

"While you're finking, do you mind if I leave."

215

"Leave?" I looked up. He had the manacles in his hand.

"Nar, if you've finished wiv the self pity bit, shall we go?"

"No, there's too many of them out there. Let's leave when it gets dark. Maybe they'll feed us in the meantime."

"Maybe they'll blow us away in the meantime."

"Alright, I've got a plan. Can you fix the lock on the manacles so it'll open if I pull it?"

"What for?"

"So we can put them on and make it look good, but when they take us upstairs, open and phooey, gone."

"Why not just take 'em orf nah and git?"

"You may not have noticed, but there are several doors between us and the outside world, all of which are locked."

"No problem, I'll open 'em."

I put my face in my hands, I had to think. Gran always says; "Rash action brings rash results. Think, William before you act." Sensible things to do are always obvious when it's too late. They call it hindsight. "I'm sorry, Newf. I guess I'm not a very good leader. I always seem to do the wrong thing. I wish Gran was here, or even Mr. Spadafora."

Newf got up and walked over to me. "Not to worry, Bill. I fink yous a great leader. We 'ave lots o' fun don't we? An' in the end we gets the bad guys." He sat on the floor beside me. "I fink we should figure art a plan, cuz Gran ain't gonna show-up wiv no seventh cavalry"

I looked at him, for the first time I saw in his eyes, honesty and admiration. He didn't seem scared. "I guess I could always go berserk," I said.

Newf laughed. "That's more like my Bill." He started work on the manacles around my ankles. "So you fink you could take 'em all down?"

"What all?"

"All the geezers in this 'ouse."

"Yeah, but, well, I couldn't hurt Stephie."

"They're off. Should I unlock the jail door?"

"Sure, what the hay! You know! All they want me to do is sign my last will and testament, then they'll let us go."

Newf laughed heartily. "Sure, Bill, they'll let us go alright. But you know where we'll go."

"Yeah, that's why I wouldn't sign. I figured while we're alive we can still think of a way out."

"Good finkin', Bill."

Newf unlocked the heavy iron-bar door. At that moment we heard voices in the outer hall. "Slip your anklets on, Newf and pretend we're still prisoners. Just follow my lead." I stood holding the iron-bar door closed and awaited our visitors. The outer door opened and two men walked in, both were armed. Fortunately neither expected trouble. One propped his rifle against the wall and sauntered over to the jail. The other nursed his shotgun and picked his nose.

As the first guy bent down to unlock the iron-bar door, I pushed it as hard as I could. The iron clanged as it contacted his head. The other geezer tried to ready his gun, but I was out and running. The shotgun went off, I felt the blast, he felt my fist.

"Two down. They'll have heard the gun, Newf." I grabbed the rifle, checked and cocked it. Whoever came down the hall would get blown away. No one came. I stood trembling with the excitement and the anticipation.

"I fink we' should disable these geezers."

"Use the manacles, attach his right leg to his left, and both right hands together."

"Smart finking, Bill."

Newf dragged the smaller of the men to the other then manacled them together. If they awakened they'd have difficulty doing anything. "Check and make sure they don't have the keys."

I did a quick check to see if I had any holes in me. Everything seemed to be attached in the correct places and no trace of blood. Not a sound came from upstairs. Could it be they didn't hear the gun going off? I eased myself through the door and inspected the hallway. Slowly I crept toward the stairs, gun in hand. Not a single sound came from above.

"Are you ready, Newf?" I whispered.

"Sure."

Gingerly we crept up the stairs, to the waxworks floor. As I poked my head through at first the room seemed empty except for all the dummies. One step farther and a dummy moved. "Mr. Reyner," it said. "I do hope you haven't harmed any of our men."

I recognized him. Pointing the weapon his way I said: "Alright, backup, or I'll blow you away."

His expression remained stern. "You are a dead man if you do not comply with our wishes, Mr. Reyner. Do you have enough ammunition to shoot us all? Do you have any ammunition?"

I glanced around, there was probably a dozen of them including Stephanie. "You're Aulay, aren't you?"

"Fine memory you have. Now would you please hand me that empty rifle?"

I drew the bolt halfway and looked. A shiny brass-cased round lay in the breach. "It's loaded," I said snapping the bolt closed and pointing the weapon at Aulay. "You'll be the first to go."

Not a single change of expression, a perfect poker face. "Is it a live round, Mr. Reyner?"

He was playing a game of nerves. Slowly I slid the bolt back again, and kept a close eye on Aulay. Sure enough, as the tip of the round came into view I could see the crimping of a blank. The rifle had been loaded with blanks rendering it totally useless. Of course I could use it as a bat and bash a few brains out. "Newf, keep these gentlemen covered, your gun's loaded."

Aulay grinned a great smirk of pleasure. "Nay. Do we look like fools to you?"

I almost messed my pants as Newf's gun fired close behind me. If it had been loaded with real cartridges, Auley would have become a wall decoration. "Alright, alright," I said. "I know when I'm beaten." I dropped the rifle on the waxworks floor. Even a bat would be of little or no use against real guns. Although, dead is dead, what did I have to lose. Two of them came to re-arrest me, I put my hands up as if surrendering.

Now, this is where it helps to be both strong and agile, it also helps if you're stupid. He did the wrong thing. He poked me in the gut with his shotgun barrel; I grabbed it, ripped it to one side and brought my knee up fast enough to ruin his day. There wasn't enough time to turn the gun round and use it, so I continued my pirouette and dinged the second fellow across the head with the butt.

It was about then that all hell broke lose. I'm not sure who did what to whom. Somehow I managed to dive to one side, turning the gun round. As I landed I fired at Aulay. This weapon had been loaded with real buckshot. Aulay flew back with the impact and several more guns went off. The noise was deafening. Newf had taken a handgun off one of the dead or dying in the middle of the floor. After a vicious and deafening ten second exchange, no one remained standing.

I guess it was about then that I discovered blood all over my left side, though I couldn't feel any pain. My gun was empty as I lay among some damaged display dummies. "Newf," I called. "Are you alright?"

"Sure, 'ow abart you?"

I climbed to my feet, still clutching the empty weapon. "D'know." The pain slowly began to seep into my left arm and side. I'd been hit by buckshot. One guy still kneeled in the centre floor groaning and bleeding. "I think we're the only survivors."

Newf emerged from one of the displays. The room looked foggy as the gun-smoke hung in the still air. I kicked the injured man down, then walked over to Aulay. I took a gun that lay on the ground. Poor Aulay was finished, caught him square in the head. He had only two companions near him, both dead.

"Some one's commin'" Newf yelled.

I covered the door, waiting to blow whoever it was away. It turned out to be one of the girls, weepy Flora. She saw me and the gun, let out a shriek and fled back down the corridor.

"We need a phone, and quick," I said and began creeping toward the main entrance, the way Flora had run off.

"Where we goin'?"

"Just up here's Cameron's office, there's a phone in there." We reached the door, it was locked. "Open it, Newf and quick."

He bent down and looked at the situation. "Can't, the key's in, on the uver side."

I guess I was in no mood for stupid delays, I pointed the gun and fired. With a deafening bang the door opened. Cameron stood my his desk, quivering with fear. "Don't shoot, laddie."

We entered. "Guard the door, Newf." I walked to the desk, Cameron cringed away from me. Keeping the weapon trained on him I lifted off the receiver and dialled '0'. "Hallo, operator, this is William Reyner, there's been a gun fight here at Cromlet castle. Send the police and ambulance, quick."

"Your address, please, sir?"

"Address, for Christ's sake there's a dozen armed men trying to kill me, what's my address got to do with anything?"

"Please remain calm-." The phone went dead.

"Shit, they've cut the line." I slammed the receiver down. "I hope for your sake Cameron, that she sends help."

"Surely we can come to some amicable arrangement, laddie."

"Half your murdering crew are in the waxworks, dead, the other half seem to have run away. Is there any other way out of this room?"

"No."

"It's like being rats in a hole, here. Newf, is the way clear?"

"Yeah."

"I think we should get back to the waxworks. There's better cover there, and more than one exit."

"I fink we should make a run for it."

Suddenly a loud voice came from outside. "Everyone in the house, lay down your arms and come out. The building is surrounded."

"I don't think so. We stay here, they'll have to come in and get us."

"I don't like 'im," Newf said waving his gun at Cameron.

"Yeah, me neither." The phone rang. I looked at it. "That's weird, they cut the line, how come it's ringing?"

"Well ain't yah gonna answer it?"

"No."

"Why?"

"Cuz, I don't give a shit who's on the bloody phone. Let's get to the waxworks before they try rushing us."

Newf walked over and picked it up. "Yeah, yeah, sure." He turned to me. "It's for you, Bill."

"Me?"

He handed the phone to me. "I fink the fight's over."

"What?" I yelled into the receiver.

"William I have told you to be more polite when you answer the phone," Gran said.

"Gran, Gran, is that you?"

"Sometimes, William you show the aptitude of an oaf. Of course it's me. I thought I told you to stay away from Scotland. When will you learn to do as you are told?"

"Gran, we're in real trouble, call the police. We're trapped in Cromlet with a bunch of killers, and the castle is surrounded."

20

Just Deserts

I put the phone down, and looked at Newf with a puzzled expression. "Yeah?" He said prompting me to speak.

"That was Gran. At least I think it was Gran."

"Wha' she say?"

"She said we should stay put and relax, the police are going to empty this house."

"How's she know that?"

"Beats me."

"Everyone in the house, lay down your arms and come out with your hands up." Came a very loud voice from outside.

I felt totally uncertain. As usual nothing made any sense, I didn't ask Gran the right questions. "Shall we go?" Newf asked.

"Gran said to sit tight, we'll sit tight."

Suddenly gunfire broke out, yelling and screaming punctuated by loud bangs. I grabbed Cameron: "The battle's over," I growled. I could feel him tremble.

"I'll give you anything you want, anything. Just let me go."

"I notice you haven't farted lately, why?"

"Let me go, please let me go. I'm not a McLean. I'll tell you anything, give you anything, just let me go."

"You stay."

"It ain't 'alf quiet, Bill. What you fink's 'apening?"

The door opened and several armed men wearing dark blue uniforms rushed in. "Drop the weapons and stand where you are."

I dropped the rifle, Newf dropped the revolver. Cameron jumped forward. "I'm only a visitor here, these men are killers."

The policeman we met in London sauntered in through the open doorway. "Well, well, well," he said calmly. "So Mr. Cameron, you're only a visitor are you? I don't think so. I believe your real name's John Garston McLean. And how are you Mr. Reyner?"

I nodded in shock.

He sauntered over to me. "Take this animal away," he growled indicating Cameron. "Well, well, well, Mr. Reyner, seventh cavalry to the rescue, eh?"

I felt week, the relief, maybe the after-effects of the adrenaline. "Where's my Gran?" I asked softly.

"Well, well, well," the plainclothes cop said. He clasped his hands behind his back and strutted like a general after a serious victory. He stopped and looked me straight in the eyes. "You're a good lad, a good lad. This is tremendous, well, well, well."

"So where's my Gran?"

"Oh, she's outside. As soon as we have secured this castle, we'll see her. I see you're injured. Is it serious?"

"Nah, I hadn't noticed it."

"We'll have a medic take a look at you."

An officer came rushing in, "Sir, there's three more dead in the waxworks and a couple tied up in the basement. Looks like that's the last of them. And there's something you should see in the waxworks room"

"Very well. Where's the prisoners?"

"All secured in the entrance hall, sir."

"Good, good. Have them all transported to Inverness. Secure the grounds, allow no one in and no one out."

"Yes, sir."

"Did you get the Jacobite?" I asked.

The cop laughed. "Aye, that we did. Mad as a hatter. I suppose I should introduce myself. I am Chief Inspector Bainbridge special agent."

"I saw you in London."

"You did indeed. I wanted to meet you personally."

"How did you know I was on that particular plane?"

He smiled and began his strutting again. "I've been working on this case for fifteen years. It goes back as a legal enigma probably thirty years or so."

"And how did you know I was on that plane?"

"Mr. Spadafora informed me. Now would you like to follow this constable and leave the rest of the investigations to me?"

We followed the cop. I've never seen so many police in one place before, all wearing body armour and carrying really neat looking rifles. We were hustled outside where a medic looked at my injuries, about half a dozen pellets had entered the skin, nothing serious. "You'll have to go to Inverness hospital," he said.

"Sure, later."

We were hustled into a police car and whisked off into the distance. Well not a very great distance. The driver took us to Pitcalver, man! The place had been taken over by the fuzz. About two dozen cars, three trucks and a large semi. I don't think the village has ever seen a crowd of that magnitude in its entire existence.

My car still remained parked next to the Cuckoo inn. We stopped outside the Pools offices and were taken into the building. The place looked a hive of activity, just about every office area had been occupied, women and men scurrying hither-and-thither. We were taken to the private office at the end of the main aisle. What a shock, as I walked in Gran tuned to greet us.

"How did you get here, Gran?"

She hugged me then said: "I told you to stay away from Scotland, when will you learn to do as you are told, look at you."

The cop left us alone. I sat as my legs seemed no longer able to carry me. "How did you get here, Gran?"

She smiled and sat back on her chair. "I'm sorry, William, I haven't been quite honest with you." She sighed. "You see I arranged for you to take this last trip. I had a suspicion, we were close to solving this hideous mystery. The real clue was that Mr. Cameron."

"You mean you sat at home and solved it while Newf and I risked our lives for nothing?"

"Not for nothing, William. Your Mr. Critton, well he was a surprise. The London police have taken care of him."

"How did you solve it, Gran?"

"What you had reported and a clue from Dagwood."

"Well don't keep us in suspense, Gran."

"Mr. Spadafora has many contacts in the police world, you see. Well he knows DCI Bainbridge, they met on a case that Mr. Bainbridge was investigating, as a matter of fact it happened to be this very case, though it was several years ago."

"So?"

"Dagwood was never fired from the Donjon estate, it was a setup. The house and the woman had been taken several years ago."

"So why did he say he had been fired?"

"Very simple, William. We were the next target. The whole charade was a cleverly arranged plan to ensnare us. Cameron had set his sights on our millions."

"Wow! I still don't understand. How did you solve it and get all these cops to believe you?"

She chuckled for several seconds. "Dear, William, you were instrumental in the solution. I read your report, then you called me with information about your traffic accident. It all suddenly became clear. I reasoned, the McLeans known as the cuckoos operated in a subtle manor. They would somehow dispose of you, accidentally, then whilst I came to England to discover the reasons, mysteriously I would also disappear and be replaced."

At that moment the door opened and DCI Bainbridge came in. Strange man, doesn't look a bit like a cop. I think he gets his clothes from the Salvation Army. He sauntered over to the desk and sat, grinning at me and Gran in turn. "Anyone for tea?" he asked.

We all agreed. Bainbridge pressed a few buttons on his cell phone and said: "Execute plan 3-15." Then replaced the device in its pouch.

"Wha's plan 3-15?" Newf asked. "Is it the capture of the McLeans?"

"No, it's code to bring in the tea."

'Oh!"

A young man; even younger than me; came in carrying a tray loaded down with all the accruements of tea making. "On the desk, Evans," the chief said.

"So is this case over?" I asked.

Bainbridge smiled. "I'll be mother," he said and got up to pour the tea.

"Well is it?"

He smiled nonchalantly as he trickled the golden liquid into the cups. "Fortunately you are rather rash, in a hurry. A typical North American. You know Rome was not built in a day. Thanks to you Mr. Reyner Edward Cameron's empire came tumbling down."

"If you've known about this guy for so many years, how come you didn't arrest him?"

Bainbridge smiled. "Very simple, I needed proof, evidence I could use in court. Cameron and his cronies exercised patience, sometimes taking years to acquire one estate. Nothing left to chance, no evidence. With no bodies, no one complaining, no evidence, and no one really caring, where's you case?"

"I see. So how come you've broken the case now?"

You could see his pride glowing. "Fifteen years of work and you." He handed me a cup of tea. "I can't go into a house and punch-out the occupants, break and enter is a crime."

"So you're going to arrest us?"

He chuckled and took a tea to his desk. "No, no. You gentlemen have handed me the biggest case in years. Did you have a good look at the wax dummies?"

"No, why?"

"They're the remains of the McLean victims. Somehow they kill their prey then pickle them in wax. A most interesting way of both shipping a body and hiding it. Not able to see the wood for the trees, so to speak."

"I saw wax makin' fings at Donjon towers," Newf said.

"Yes, that's probably why they removed the house. Mrs. Cloey Macalister left Canada, not as a holidaymaker, but a waxworks display. You see, you did not respond exactly as Cameron had expected. Nonetheless his pragmatism allowed him to manipulate the scheme to accommodate slight disruptions."

"Slight disruptions?"

"Indeed, you should have died in Bristol, Mrs. Hubert would have come to collect your body and at that time probably be replaced by a cuckoo."

"Holy mackerel! But I screwed them up."

Bainbridge chuckled. "You certainly did."

"What happened to Ellen, where is she?"

"Ellen?"

"The girl that helped us. She used to run the inn."

"Oooh! Yes, I see. You mean Miss Meall McLean."

"Meall McLean? You must be mistaken. Her mane's Ellen, she helped us."

"No, Mr. Reyner, Meall McLean is one of the key organizers. She very cleverly acted as decoy and friend. Her only purpose is to keep the village clean and honest."

"But she helped us."

"No, she guided you within the bounds the McLeans desired."

"I told yah," Newf smirked. "Anyfin' that wobbles, you go blind and stupid."

"Alright thank you, Doctor Einstein."

* * * * *

Man was I ever gland to see home again. The heat of a Canadian summer, the blueness of the sky and the sweet smell of gasoline fumes. The new house felt almost as comforting as the old one. Back to the comfortable and peaceful regimen of normal daily life. If you'd ever had breakfast at Gran's place, you would know what I mean.

I sat at the table with Newf, as Gran served our good wholesome all Canadian breakfast. "Now this case is solved, Gran I think I'll retire from detective work altogether."

"Really, William? What will you do?"

"I'm not sure, Gran. When we were in London this guy there, beat the hell out of me."

"Moderate you language, please, William."

"Sorry, Gran. Anyhow, this guy beat me up and Newf had to sort him out. I think I'll take a course in Kung-fu or something."

Gran giggled. "Excellent thought, William. I'll see what I can find for you."

"And no more detective stuff, eh?"

"We'll see, William, we'll see. You do realize this case in not yet completed."

"What do you mean?"

"Eat your breakfast, dear." She sat and with that Cheshire cat grin on her face watched me.

"Gran, for heaven's sake. I hate it when you do this to me. What do you mean this case is not finished? All the bad guys are in jail or dead. The English cops are happy."

"They surely are, William, but you have to appear in court when the trial is held."

"Court?"

"Yes, aren't you interested in what happened to all the other people involved?"

"No, if they're dead, good, if they're in jail, also good. If any of them are running around I don't want to know about it."

"And you have no questions to ask?"

"Well, all the house-sitters, that you left living, have been arrested. Mr. Critton is apparently out on bail. He's been charged with attempted murder, and perverting the course of justice.

"What happened to Ellen, I mean Meall?"

"She along with the rest of her family are charged with more crimes than can be written on a single sheet of paper. I think what you have uncovered will keep the British courts busy for several years."

"Gran, I really don't want to know. I have finished with detective stuff. Newf and I are going to take up education, not police work."

Gran smiled that sickening know-it-all smile. "We have one, maybe two functions remaining in this affair, William."

"We don't; you do; not me."

She smiled again and removed an envelope from her pinafore pocket. "Perhaps you should read this, William."

I took it, extracted the letter and read it. My heart turned cold and I could feel my knees buckling. "You have to be kidding, Gran."

"No dear. We will comply."

"No we won't." The letter asked that Gran, Newf, and I visit Balgowan castle on Drumvanich Island. An invitation of none other than Malcolm Garston, chief of the clan. "No, no, no, I won't go. I've seen that place."

"Did they cause you any harm?'

"No, but they are God on that island."

"While you were cavorting about the British Isles creating mayhem, Mr. Spadafora and I were doing some investigating of our own. Dagwood admitted his part in the proceedings, consequently I contacted Malcolm Garston and asked for his side of the story. Though reluctant, he did confide in me."

"Yeah, you are somewhat persuasive."

"Together we can solve anything, William. I do wish you would reconsider your decision."

"Consider, no way. We're learning self-defence, and I'm joining a gun club to learn about weapons."

"Excellent, William. Though you have nothing to fear from the Garstons. I shall be going. I do wish you would come."

"I don't think you should go, Gran, these people are very dangerous."

Newf walked into the room. "Oo's dangerous?"

"The Garstons. Gran wants us to go back, she wants us to go to the Garston castle on Drumvanich Island."

"Oh! Great! That's a fantastic idea. I'll go. When?"

Gran smiled politely. "It's nice to know one of you has sense. The tickets are already purchased. Mr. Garston ordered them and sent them to me."

"How'd he know your address, Gran?"

"I gave it to him when I called him."

"Oh!"

"The tickets will be used. I'm sure you wouldn't like me to go alone, would you William?"

I sighed very loudly. "NO."

"Then you'll be accompanying North and I?"

"When?"

"October."

I shook my head in sad disgust. "Alright, It'll give me time to get a few lessons in."

It's amazing how time flies when you're not looking forward to something. Before I'd properly reintroduced myself to the Rolls, we were on the way to Pearson Airport. Gran, Newf, and I were the only passengers in the first class compartment of the airplane. The service seemed adequate and the flight smooth. We landed at Prestwick and caught another plane to Drumvanich Island.

The second plane turned out to be a very tiny little thing that only held four people, including the pilot. This flight was not so smooth, but we did get a splendid view of the highlands. The landing could have been a lot smoother. Though they say any landing you walk away from is a good landing. A car awaited our arrival. I have to admit the service was first class.

This time I don't think there was as much mist, or fog as last trip here. The castle looked as dank and dismal as it had before. What a dump, it made my heart pound with anticipation. Once inside that place we could disappear forever, and who would know?

"I think we are a little early," Gran said as the car stopped at the huge gate.

"Nay lassie," the driver said speaking for the first time.

The gigantean door swung open revealing a huge cobbled courtyard, surrounded by stone walls. As we drove in some guy closed the gate or door. The car stopped by some stone steps leading to an iron-riveted-wooden door. A geezer in a green kilt walked down the steps to greet us. His dress though striking looked old fashioned. He carried a knife in his sock and a short-sword by his side.

He opened the door and greeted Gran. "Mrs. Hubert, how nice it is to see you at long last. Welcome to Scotland." He had a very nice almost singsong accent, and perfectly clear.

Newf and I were almost ignored, he seemed taken, only by Gran. I half expected dingy corridors lit by flaming torches stuck in the dirty walls. A room the size of a small house presented itself at the top of the steps. Polished hardwood floors, clean painted walls with huge circles of antique rifles, splayed out like daisies. The furniture, far from being hand hewn looked new and expensive.

"Welcome," said the host. "I'm Malcolm Garston. Though my mother was a Campbell. Would you all please follow me into the great hall?"

Another room of megalithic proportions, just down a short hallway. The room had twenty or thirty tables, each seating eight to ten guests. It looked like the entire island had turned out for the event. We were led to the head table where seven people were already seated. Our host pulled out a chair for Gran, then indicated where Newf and I would sit.

"I'm sorry to rush you into a doo like this," he said. But my people have been waiting for almost an hour." He walked to a small stage or rostrum just beyond our table, a microphone had been set there. Malcolm cleared his throat, tapped the mic a couple of times. "My lairds, ladies and gentlemen, the moment we have all been waiting for has arrived. After almost a century of fear the feud with them MacLeans has concluded.

"I won't say that there hasn't been any skulduggery on our part, though I'm certain we did not break the law of the land. A knight in unusual form came to our rescue. Mrs. Zelda Hubert extended her arms and began the incredulous decline of that hideous family of cuckoos." He turned and smiled at Gran. "As chieftain of this clan I wish to confer two honours on our savoir, Mrs. Hubert."

The entire hall broke out in raucous applause. I've never seen anything like it. I wasn't sure whether to grab Gran's hand and run or hide under the table. The public reaction was so wild and spontaneous, I felt sure they were dangerous. Malcolm put his hands up in a crowd shushing fashion. After a few moments the yelling and cheering quieted down to just a murmur.

"My friends, you all know why we are here. I would. I would like to express my thanks to Mr. North East, and William Reyner, both of whom risked their lives to defeat that terrible family."

He continued singing our praise for best part of half an hour. I thought he would never stop. It was after all quite embarrassing. I didn't understand half what he was talking about. Then this second geezer got up and in a deep Scottish drawl continued the praise, I think. Malcolm came and sat with us.

"So what are the two honours?" I asked.

Malcolm smiled. "I canna tell yee that laddie, it must be kept a secret until the moment of presentation."

"Oh! I came here once before."

He slapped me on the back almost hard enough to regurgitate my lunch. "Aye, laddie. I gave you your money."

"Where did you get it?"

"I had a man following you. We thought you might be a new and dangerous part of the McLean Conspiracy. He followed you to that house, where they attacked you. Being only one person and on foot he could'na dee a thing. Thinking you'd been murdered, he called for assistance. Before help arrived they drove away, obviously taking you with them.

"My men broke into the house and found the truth of the matter. Your wallet was recovered. He took it and brought the news of your demise to us. Fearing reprisals we closed the castle."

"The man in the pub, near the harbour said you lot ruled this island and were not a very nice bunch to know."

Malcolm laughed. "The peasants always think that I charge rent, and taxes, to the maximum. Who loves the tax man?"

At very long and torturous last the proceedings returned to Malcolm. He stood up and approached the microphone, then beckoned Gran. "This is the auspicious moment," he said.

Gran walked to his side, and grinned like a Cheshire cat. "Thank you."

From a little shelf in the podium he took two rolls of paper. "Mrs. Hubert, I would firstly like to present you with an honorary membership to our clan. The Campbells." He handed her one of the scrolls. "Secondly, I would like to present you with the deeds to Cromlet castle."